Rebel Child

KATE EDEN

This is a work of fiction. Names, characters, places, and incidents are either the product of the author's imagination or are used fictitiously. Any resemblance to actual persons, places, or events is coincidental.

Rebel Child

Copyright 2013 by Jaye Wells

All rights reserved. This book or any parts thereof may not be reproduced in any form without permission. The scanning, uploading, and distribution of this book via the Internet or any other means without the permission of the publisher is illegal and punishable by law. Please respect this author's hard work and purchase only authorized electronic or print editions.

BOOKS BY KATE EDEN

THE MURDOCH VAMPIRES SERIES
The Hot Scot
Rebel Child

CHAPTER ONE

You kidnap one lousy mortal, and everyone freaks out.

That's what I was thinking as my "escorts"—four muscle-bound guards—led me into the office. My boots sunk into the thick Persian rug underfoot. Cocking my hip—both for effect and to take the weight off one of my feet for a blessed second—I thanked the goddess I'd worn my favorite boots.

Here's the thing: Most women can't pull off a red, stiletto-heeled boot.

But I am not most women.

Boots like those required a certain presence—an elusive combination of confidence and a devil-may-care attitude. Oh, and a high tolerance for pain.

The damned things pinched in awful places, and the pointy tips made my toes go numb. But I looked kick-ass, which counted for a lot. The confidence boost was necessary if I was going to get through the coming confrontation.

High Councilman Orpheus Coracino was the most powerful vampire in existence. As the head of the Brethren Sect, it was up to him to decide my punishment.

Oh, yeah, he also happened to be my father.

The room was as imposing as the man who had yet to

acknowledge my presence. To mortal eyes it would probably look like the office of any high-powered CEO with the exception of the lit display cases filled with wicked-looking ancient weaponry. Each piece once used by my dear, very old dad in battle.

My father dismissed the goons with a wave of his hand, not bothering to look up from the document he was reading. The guards released my arms and left the room, closing the doors behind them. I almost missed the support of their firm grips. Aching feet, stress, hunger, and the impending sunrise wreaked havoc on my stamina as I struggled to look unaffected. My hands shook anyway.

"What, no hug for the prodigal daughter?" I said into the silence, extending my arms for an embrace I knew would never come.

Orpheus slowly raised his piercing eyes to look at me. He said nothing, just stared at me with the familiar mixture of disappointment and distaste.

I dropped my arms, not quite sure what to say next. It had been ten years since our last meeting. Back then, daddy dearest issued an ultimatum: Clean up my act or else. Well, of course I ignored him. But now I was about to find out what "or else" really meant.

"Gabriella—" he began.

"Stop right there." I held up my index finger with its black lacquered nail. "The name is Raven, you know that."

"Young lady, your name is Gabriella. I named you myself."

His baritone vibrated with authority. It matched his form perfectly. If he'd stood, he would have towered over me. With two black holes for eyes and a jaw so hard and sharp it could cut through metal, the man was a prime example of a civilized predator.

He looked like a highly paid executive in a pinstriped suit instead of an alpha vampire. But the civilized veneer couldn't hide the ruthlessness in his eyes. No wonder he had been the leader of the Brethren Sect for more than one hundred years. Only a fool would dare challenge his authority.

Which made me the fool, I guess.

"You also know I renamed myself a century ago. If you expect a response, you will refer to me as Raven," I shot back. I was probably one of the only vampires in existence with enough bravado to talk back to him. However, egging my father on was sort of a hobby for me.

He ignored the name issue, no doubt considering it not worth his time.

"Would you like to take this opportunity to explain your actions?"

I shrugged. "What's there to explain?"

"You can start with trying to sabotage the most important development in vampire history and finish with kidnapping the mortal woman," he said.

"I am not a member of your precious sect. I don't owe you an explanation."

"You have no excuse for your actions, as usual. Nor do you exhibit one sign of remorse." His voice was maddeningly calm, in complete opposition to my defensive tone.

"Why would I show remorse for standing up for what I believe?" This was an old argument, and I was trying not to let it get my hackles up.

"You could have launched a formal complaint through the proper channels. Instead, you wreaked havoc, as usual."

"Again, what good would a formal complaint have done when I am not in good standing with the council?" I countered.

"Exactly." He steepled his fingers and pressed them lightly to his lips. "Which brings us back to the issue of why you are not in good standing."

Well, shit.

He reached behind the desk, and I heard the sound of a drawer opening and closing. He sat back up, and a large stack of folders thumped on the desktop.

"As you can see, your transgressions have been well documented." He flipped open the top folder and started shuffling through pages. "Here we have the report on the fire alarm you pulled during the council meeting, causing mass panic. Hmmm. And let's not forget the skunk blood incident of 1886." He paused to scowl at me when I snorted with laughter. "Then there's the time you replaced the beds of all the council members with coffins. Shall I go on?" he asked, looking up from the foot-tall pile with fake courtesy.

I bit back a smile. I was damned proud of everything he listed and more. A lot of work and preparation had gone into those feats. Everything he considered a stunt, I considered civil disobedience for a good cause. I hated everything to do with the council's goals to make us more like mortals.

Don't get me wrong. I didn't think everything the council did was bad, but give me a break. Vampires are gods. Mortals are our food. You don't see humans going around eating grass and mooing all the time. And why not? Because mortals understand they are superior to cows.

"Come on," I said. "Nothing you mentioned there was all that bad. No one was hurt. Besides, last time I checked, the council didn't ban freedom of speech or expression. Or is that next on your totalitarian agenda?"

"As the leader of the council, it is my goal to create a democratic life for all of my constituents. I even encourage debate on topics of import. However, your pranks have nothing to do with taking a stand and everything to do with getting attention."

My mouth dropped open. Of all the freakin' nerve! I forgot all about the throbbing in my feet and the hunger pains clenching my stomach as centuries-old resentments bubbled up in me like a volcano.

"You're wrong. You just can't stand the idea that your daughter hasn't toed the line of your administration."

"What I can't stand is the idea that my daughter turned out to be nothing more than a spoiled brat who has not one ounce of self-respect."

"What the hell does that mean?"

"Look at yourself. You're all tarted up like an extra from one of those horrible vampire movies." His eyes raked me with a distasteful glare.

"Excuse me? These clothes are the height of fashion!" No one, but no one, insulted my clothes. The black leather miniskirt and red corset were two of my favorite pieces. He obviously was stuck in the Dark Ages when it came to fashion.

"Where? The Best Little Whorehouse in Transylvania?"

I opened my mouth to rebut, but his words cut so deep I couldn't think of a response. My own father had just called me a whore. Nice.

I took a deep breath to calm the fire in my belly. "My fashion choices have nothing to do with why I am here."

"You're correct." He leaned back in his leather executive chair. "Your behavior is the issue at hand. If I recall, the last time you were in this room I warned you that further disobedience would not be tolerated."

"Disobedience?" I repeated, struggling to keep my voice level. "I am four hundred years old. I will not be treated like an ill-tempered child."

"Then perhaps you should stop acting like one," he said quietly, leaning forward with a clear warning in his cold eyes.

I bit my tongue, hating him for being right. And I was annoyed with myself for taking his bait.

He regarded my silence for a moment. "The council is recommending banishment," he said as if casually commenting on the weather.

My gasp sounded before I could stop myself. He took me completely off guard. My heartbeat kicked up about twenty notches.

"That's insane!" I said.

"Is it?" he asked, raising his eyebrows. "Time and again you have demonstrated your lack of respect for the council. We have threatened, we have cajoled, we have bribed. None of it has worked. You crossed over the line this time."

I stood in sullen silence. My anger and resentment felt like a poison vine in my belly.

"What were you thinking?" he continued. "The Murdoch family is one of the oldest and most respected among the Brethren." He shook his head with disgust. "I don't have to remind you how important Logan Murdoch's work is. The Lifeblood formula he's creating will make all of our lives better.

"And how is he rewarded? My own daughter tries to cast a spell to gain control of his mind. And if that isn't enough, you kidnapped the mortal woman who may be Logan's soul mate. It's unconscionable."

"Are you more upset by my actions or by how they make you look?" I asked, keeping my voice calm.

"Both." His clipped tone felt like a slap.

"And for that you are ready to throw me to the wolves and let the council use me as an example for all the other naughty vamps? You're going to sacrifice your own daughter?"

"Your actions are a threat to our entire way of life. You bring dangerous attention to all of us with your antics. We, the council, believe you must be rehabilitated by any means necessary."

"So you're going to ship me off to a remote area where you know I will have no source of food? Well, I guess death is the ultimate form of rehabilitation," I said with a bitter laugh.

"Don't be melodramatic. We would provide you with synthetic blood as sustenance. Logan is almost ready to release it to the public, despite your efforts to the contrary. You will be one of the first to use it."

I narrowed my eyes and leaned forward. "A little poetic justice, huh? I tried to stop his efforts to develop Lifeblood, so now I am doomed to depend on it for survival."

I laughed again, the sound hollow. "You know I won't do that. You might as well stake me now."

My words hung in the air for a second. I just knew I had him. He would have no choice but to come up with an alternate punishment.

He laughed instead.

"Don't be ridiculous. Your tantrums don't impress me," he said between chuckles.

If anyone could spontaneously combust, it would be me.

"You're an asshole!" I seethed. "I am sure you would love it if I was dead. Then you wouldn't have that inconvenience of being embarrassed by my every word and action."

"Grow up, Gabriella."

"Raven!" I knew I sounded like a fledgling, but I couldn't help myself. He had me cornered. Like a wild animal I struggled to think of a way, any way, to free myself from this trap of my own making.

"Calm down," he commanded, his voice hard with warning. "I am sure if you look at this rationally you will see it is best for everyone. You get two hundred years to think about what you've done—"

"Two hundred years? Fuck that!"

"Charming language," he admonished. "Yes, two hundred. You must pay for your crimes and have sufficient time to learn your lesson. At least for you, the banishment isn't permanent like it is for some of our more notorious criminals. In fact, it's not really banishment, so much as a period of exile."

Yeah, that made me feel tons better.

"Vampires are banished for murdering other vamps or mortals in cold blood. I kidnapped one measly person and didn't hurt a hair on her head!" I said, trying to make him see reason.

He continued as if I had not spoken. "Now, in addition to exile for the next two hundred years, you must also apologize to the Murdoch family. Since you will be leaving for Norway—"

"Norway? Norway! As in the 'Land of the Midnight Sun?'"

"Yes, that Norway. As I was saying, since you ship out tomorrow, there is no time for you to go back to Raleigh to make a formal apology to the whole Murdoch family. Thus, I have decided an apology to Callum is sufficient until such time as you return from your exile."

"And the hits keep on coming," I grumbled.

Not only was I going to the fucking frozen tundra—where I'd have to deal with two solid months of sunlight a year for two hundred freakin' years—but now I had to apologize to that arrogant asshole, Callum Murdoch, Logan's younger brother.

When the family busted in on my lair to rescue the chick I kidnapped, Callum had volunteered to take me into custody and deliver me home to dear old dad. I couldn't stand the guy. In addition to being the Brethren Golden Boy, Callum ran a company that produced all the products that helped vampires blend into mortal society.

"Do you have any questions?" my father asked.

"Were you born without a heart, or did it dissolve from lack of use?"

He ignored my comment as he pushed the intercom button. As he told Callum to come into the office, I tried to compose myself. Not exactly an easy feat since my entire world had collapsed.

The thought of apologizing to Callum made me want to puke. I never, ever begged anyone for anything, least of all forgiveness. Desperation was a novel and unwelcomed sensation.

The doors opened, and Callum strolled in as confident as you please. Seeing him with the bright light from the reception area framing him in a golden aura was overwhelming. I guess it had something to do with the fact he seemed so . . . capable, while I felt so trapped.

The thought of apologizing to that man made me dizzy and short of breath. I know it probably had more to do with my empty stomach than my pride, but it was there nonetheless.

Finally, I did something I have never done in my four hundred and eleven years on this earth.

I fainted.

CHAPTER TWO

When I came to, masculine voices talked above me.

"Leave her. She's just making a scene," my father said.

"With all respect, sir, I don't think she would have hit her head on the desk if she was faking it."

Well, that explained the throbbing ache on my forehead. I groaned, alerting them I was conscious. I had no idea how long I had been out.

"Are you okay?" Callum's voice sounded as if he spoke through a bullhorn. I couldn't see him since I had my eyes clamped tight against the throbbing, but I felt his hand on my forehead.

"Ouch," I said. The hand abruptly left my head, accompanied by a quick apology.

The pain started to recede then, and I doubted with my superfast healing ability that there'd be a bruise. I peeked open one eye and saw two male faces peering at me—one concerned, the other disapproving.

Some things never change.

"Are you quite done with your display?" my father said.

I ignored him and opened the other eye. Lying sprawled next to a desk wasn't my style. I struggled to sit up with as much pride as I could muster, which wasn't much.

"When was the last time you fed?" Callum asked as he reached to help me into the chair.

"Don't remember," I mumbled.

"Here, drink this," Callum said and handed me a glass filled with blood. Normally, I would have said no. Bagged blood was disgusting. But I could feel my fangs extending as soon as the rich iron scent hit me.

Pride be damned. I was in pain and starving. Desperate times called for desperate measures and all that. I lifted the glass and chugged it in one gulp, trying to ignore the taste of plastic commingled with the cold fluid.

I felt better almost instantly, though. I probably needed more, but I felt well enough that I couldn't justify consuming another ounce of that shit.

Wiping my mouth with the napkin Callum offered, I saw my father's mouth hanging open.

"Well, I'll be damned. I have been trying to get her to do that for decades."

"Let's not send out a press release yet," I said. "That was a one-time shot."

"Not to worry, you'll be drinking synthetic blood where you're going," Father Dearest shot back.

I flinched at the reminder of our conversation before my nosedive.

Callum's eyebrows shot together. "Where is she going?"

My father walked back to his chair, as if relieved to have the histrionics over with, and indicated Callum should take the chair next to mine.

"Actually, that is why I called you in. The council has decided on Gabriella's punishment."

Callum's eyes shifted toward me in surprise when he heard my real name. I gritted my teeth, knowing that correcting my father again would be a waste of breath. I ignored his curious look and examined my fingernails, idly wondering if manicures were available in Norway. He took the hint and looked back at my father.

"We are banishing her for two hundred years for her crimes against your family as well as her misdeeds in the past," said Father of the Year.

"We feel she needs some time to think about what she has done and accept the Brethren doctrine," he continued, ignoring Callum's shocked expression. "Furthermore, as your family's representative, she is required to offer a formal apology to you for her actions."

"Sir, forgive me, but don't you think that is a little extreme?"

My head swiveled toward him so fast I felt dizzy. Not that I didn't agree with him, but I couldn't help question his motives.

"Excuse me?" My father's outrage was clear. "Are you questioning the wisdom of the council?"

"Of course not, sir. Obviously she should learn a lesson, but it seems excessive given the circumstances."

"Are you forgetting everything she did to your family?"

"Of course not, but I don't think banishing her will make her more sympathetic to the Brethren way. I think she needs to be taught to understand our way of life."

"Um, hello? I am in the room." The night was shitty enough without being talked about like I wasn't there.

They ignored me as they continued to debate the best way to "rehabilitate" me.

"So, what would you suggest is the right way to change her?" Orpheus asked.

"Has anyone considered I don't want to change?" I asked. "Guys?"

"I think she needs to be immersed in the lifestyle. To take the products which allow us to live like mortals. Plus she need to be exposed to humans so she can learn they deserve our respect, not to be treated like food," Callum argued.

"Over my dead—" I began, only to be cut off by my father.

"And how exactly would you accomplish these lofty goals?"

"Let's see, first she would need to be monitored by someone familiar with the products who could make sure she actually used them. Second, she would need to be around mortals, perhaps in a volunteer capacity," Callum said. "Community service, maybe."

I started to rise to tell them where they could shove their community service when my father spoke again. I expected him to put Callum in his place for his presumption, but what he said instead caused me to drop in my seat in shock.

"An excellent idea. Thank you for volunteering."

"What?" Callum said.

"What?" I shouted.

If I hadn't been so horrified by what was happening, seeing Callum's mouth drop open like an idiot would have been comical.

"Yes, I think it's a wonderful plan. Gabriella will not only be forced to learn our ways, but she will also be making restitution directly to your family."

"Sir, I . . . I didn't mean . . ." Callum began.

"No way!" I said loudly over him.

"It makes perfect sense because your family is responsible for creating the products," Orpheus continued, ignoring our protests. "Not to mention you have a stake in seeing her rehabilitated."

"And you," he said, turning his dark gaze in my direction, "it is either this or the Land of the Midnight Sun. Take your pick. But be aware, whether you do it now or in two hundred years, you will be expected to embrace our ways before you are released into society again."

I opened my mouth to respond, but he cut me off again. "Oh, did I mention that the prison you'll live in has no running water?"

Shit. He had me, and we both knew it. Exile would be frozen hell on earth. But I wasn't convinced being under Callum's power would be much better. However, while there would be no escape from banishment, I might be able to fake my way through the rehabilitation plan.

Keeping one eye on Callum, I sorted through the pros and cons of each option. He shook his head ever so slightly with his eyes narrowed and his lips pursed. That decided me. If he was reluctant to go along with this, then it suited me perfectly.

"All right," I said with what I hoped was a resigned sigh. "I guess I have no choice."

"Gabriella," my father said, "if you think you can fake your way through this you're wrong. I will expect daily reports on your progress, and it will be me who makes the final judgment."

I tried not to flinch as he called me on my plan. Still, even with those rules, I figured this would be a piece of cake.

Callum cleared his throat. "Sir, are you sure this is the best idea?"

Orpheus smiled widely and said, "Absolutely."

I looked at Callum and sent him a look that clearly said, "serves you right for brownnosing."

"Fine. I'll do it. However, I insist on a time limit and a zero tolerance policy if she refuses to follow my rules."

"Just what do you mean by that?" I asked, offended.

He looked at me, a grin on his full lips. "It means, princess, the first time you throw a tantrum, it's off to Norway with you."

"Excellent," Orpheus said, clearly enjoying my suffering.

"But that's not fair!" I said, slapping a hand on the desk.

"How many times have I told you? Eternal life isn't fair."

Instead of responding, I glared at Callum, warning him with my eyes that he'd better watch himself. They might have me in a corner now, but once I passed their little tests, they would pay for every moment of humiliation.

"Gabriella, you are dismissed. The guards will take you to your rooms."

"Excuse me? I want to stay and hear about what you have planned."

"I'm afraid that's not possible. The brilliance of this plan is that you have no say in how you repay your debts."

I was furious and ready to hold my breath until he let me stay. But then I imagined myself standing on the tundra—freezing and alone. Not a blood donor or Starbucks in sight.

I clamped my mouth shut and nodded. Throwing tantrums this early might make them scrap this idea altogether. Best to keep them off guard.

"Can we at least decide on the time frame before I go?

Knowing how long I have to prove myself will help me muddle through."

My father's eyes narrowed. I smiled angelically.

"I suppose that's fair," Orpheus said slowly. "Callum?"

"One month," he said.

I could have kissed him. Given the alternative of two hundred years, one month would be a walk in the graveyard.

"No, I think she needs longer. After all, she has much to learn. How about six months?"

Callum sputtered for a moment. "Sir, with all due respect, I have a business to run, and we are scrambling as it is to get production of Lifeblood up and running."

I silently cheered his logic and quick thinking.

"Three months. Your family can pitch in if you need to attend to the business."

Callum's shoulders slumped. He knew he'd been beaten by a superior negotiator. My hope of getting away with a shorter sentence died a painful death. "Three it is," he said through clenched teeth.

"I suggest you go get some rest," my father said. "You have a busy three months ahead of you."

I nodded because I didn't trust my voice. Three months? I knew it wasn't that long for an immortal, but it still stunk.

"Before this is through you'll be thanking me for making you do this," Orpheus said.

I nodded again, this time to keep from gagging. My fists clenched in an effort to keep my cool. How dare he go all "tough love" on me?

I looked at Callum one last time. A muscle worked in his jaw as he watched me rise. Well, tough cookies. It served him right for opening his big mouth to begin with.

As I walked away, my father said, "I see a great future for you in the council, son."

That decided it. Starting tomorrow, Callum Murdoch was going to rue the day he ever met Raven Coracino.

CHAPTER THREE

The next night Callum and I boarded the Murdoch private jet to leave New York, home of the Brethren Sect's official headquarters. He had wanted an earlier start back to Raleigh, but I couldn't travel in the daytime.

Callum, like all members of the Brethren, took medication to deal with his sun allergies. Because I refused to take them on principle, going in the sun for even a few minutes would incapacitate me for days.

On the way to the airport, he kept muttering about my backward ways and swore he'd start me on the sun regimen the minute we touched down in North Carolina. I sat silently, but inside I was laughing. Not even a day into this debacle, and I was already annoying him. What can I say? It's a gift.

We boarded the plane and were greeted by the bubbly flight attendant. She introduced herself as Misty. She'd been with us on the flight up from Raleigh. I still hated her. She had one of those perky peroxide-enhanced hairdos and wore a lot of makeup in nauseating pastel colors.

"Mr. Murdoch, everything is ready for takeoff. Miss Coracino, it's a pleasure to have you back on board. Can I get you something?"

"A stake would be nice," I said.

Misty's perfect Cupid's bow turned into a frown. "Oh dear, I'm sorry. We don't have any steak. I could whip up some pasta, though," she said, her singsong voice raising the hairs on my neck.

I was proud of myself for not smacking her. "Just get me a whisky. No ice."

"Coming right up! Mr. Murdoch? Care for anything?"

"Just a bag of blood, if you don't mind," he said with a sigh, taking his seat.

"Of course I don't mind! It's my pleasure!" she enthused and practically skipped toward the galley.

I watched her go, shaking my head. "What do you feed her? Speed?"

"Misty is good at her job. That's no reason to mock her," Callum said, his deep voice disapproving.

Sighing, I walked over to the seat on the opposite side of the plane from Callum. Some people just didn't have a sense of humor.

I slid slowly into the buttery leather of the seat, both for effect and in deference to my corset. It tended to pinch if I wasn't careful. Not for the first time, I wished I'd thought to grab extra clothes when Callum took me into custody.

Plus, my feet were killing me again. One might think I would be immune to such annoyances—being a vampire and all—but no such luck. The shoes couldn't literally kill me, but right then I'd have shucked eternity for some Epsom salts and a tub of hot water.

I had to admit that some days being a vixen vampiress really wasn't all it was cracked up to be. Sometimes I really wanted to forget all about my bid for world domination and just lounge around my lair in sweats. But what kind of message would that send my minions?

Damned human minions, I thought, recalling the sniveling rats who had abandoned ship when the Murdoch family burst into my hideout to save that chick I kidnapped.

Freakin' mortals. Couldn't live with them, couldn't suck

them all dry. And while I was at it, I decided to curse the entire Murdoch clan.

Narrowing my eyes, I glared at Callum. He seemed to have forgotten my presence and was engrossed in a copy of *Forbes*.

I reached down and rubbed my feet through the leather of the boots, biting back a groan at the pleasure-pain sensation the move caused. Removing the cursed things wasn't an option since I'd only have to put them back on when we landed.

"I'll never get why you women wear those torture devices," Callum said, interrupting my moment of bliss. Obviously he hadn't forgotten about me.

If he wasn't careful, one of my boots was going to end up thrown at his head.

"What?" he asked, looking genuinely perplexed.

"A woman's shoes are her calling card to the world," I said patiently, as if explaining something to a child. "They send a message about her sense of self-worth."

"The only message those shoes send is that you're a masochist."

"I'm sorry. I am really not in the mood to get into a footwear debate with you," I responded, feeling weary and distracted. Normally I could have talked him into the ground about the philosophical state of our soles, but I was beyond exhausted.

"You're bitchy when you're nervous."

"I'm not nervous. I just find you tedious."

"Sweetheart, women have called me a lot of things in my life. Tedious is not one of them."

"I am sure 'insufferable' and 'idiot' are also on the list." Part of me enjoyed the verbal sparring because it kept my mind off what awaited me in Raleigh.

"That's big talk from a spoiled brat," he said, the edge to his words erasing the joking banter.

"Oh no, whatever shall I do? The Golden Boy called me a brat. I guess this means you aren't asking me to prom?"

He stared at me for a moment, his jaw working.

Misty returned, saving me from whatever response he'd

planned.

"Here's your drink, Miss Coracino! Captain says we're ready for takeoff. Please fasten your seat belt."

Misty stopped by Callum's place to drop off his bag of blood before heading to her seat at the rear of the plane. Seeing the dark red fluid reminded me that I had not eaten since last night's post-faint meal. The reminder caused my stomach to cramp. But I'd be damned if I lowered myself to ask for a bag. Instead, I sipped on the whisky, hoping its burn would distract me from my hunger.

The plane started up with a whir of engines followed by a jolt as it started moving down the runway. We quickly gained speed and suddenly my stomach dropped out from under me as we left terra firma.

My free hand gripped the armrest. It wasn't that I was scared of dying in a fiery crash or anything. But having been born in the seventeenth century, I sometimes still had problems adjusting to the advances of the modern age. I felt that if the goddess had intended for us to fly then she would have given us wings.

Another belt of whisky, with its smoky flavor, helped a little.

I couldn't wait until the fasten seat belt light went out. Nicotine was of the essence. In the rush to get to the plane, I hadn't had time to stop for a smoke break. Lighting up at my seat would probably just make Goody Two-shoes Murdoch give me a hard time about the smell. So, being the considerate person I am, I decided to head to the lavatory.

"Where are you going?" Callum asked as I got up from my seat.

"I need to use the little vampire's room. Or do I need your permission to pee, too?"

He didn't blush, but I could tell he was embarrassed for overreacting. Where else would I be going? It's not like I could escape at 20,000 feet.

"Just go," he said.

"Fine. I will."

"Fine."

"Whatever," I said in a lame attempt to get the last word. With that, I sauntered off to the head. I passed Misty on my way back. She smiled enthusiastically at me, although her eyes looked worried. "Is everything okay, Miss Coracino? The Captain hasn't turned off the seat belt sign yet."

"Sorry, Misty, but nature calls. You won't tell the captain on me will you?"

"Well, I suppose an exception can be made. Just try to hurry."

"Scout's honor. I won't even flush."

She opened her mouth and then shut it quickly. Her brows knit as if she were working out a complex calculus problem.

"Uh, that's okay. You can go ahead and flush."

Obviously, someone was a few chuckles short of a sense of humor. I patted her on the head and continued down the aisle to my destination.

I slammed the sliding door and clicked the lock, which engaged the light. The cramped space smelled like that awful blue toilet water. I scrunched my nose and tried to breathe through my mouth.

Then I gasped when I saw my reflection in the mirror. Fluorescent light did nothing for my complexion. As a creature of the night, I was already pretty pale. But seriously, I looked dead.

My usually luminous midnight black hair—the color achieved with a wonderful human invention called Miss Clairol—hung limply around my face. My black lipstick had faded away, leaving my lips looking chapped. Damned recycled airplane air. The only spot of color in my entire face was the brown of my eyes. I stuck my tongue out at the boring color. What I really needed was colored contacts—violet perhaps. Maybe I'd looked into that once I got myself out of this mess.

Remembering the source of my anxiety, I reached into my purse and grabbed my smokes. Stressful times called for some serious nicotine.

I plopped down the lid of the commode and sat gingerly on the edge. I lifted the cigarette to my lips, already anticipating the first drag as I clicked my silver monogrammed Zippo.

I watched the flame dance for a second before touching it to the tip of my Marlboro Red. Inhaling deeply, I prepared for the relaxation to begin.

Only it never came. Instead, a shrill alarm rang out.

The cigarette fell to the ground.

"Shit!" I squeaked, scrambling to grab it. The position caused my butt to bump the door. I grabbed the cig triumphantly, but before I could move, the door opened behind me. I flew backward and landed on my rear with a thump, smoking cigarette in hand.

"What the—" I yelled. But my tirade died on my lips when I saw the pair of faces looming over me.

"Miss Coracino!" Misty squeaked. "Are you all right?"

"What the hell are you're doing?" Callum yelled over the keening of the alarm.

I held up the cigarette and said, "Filing my taxes?"

"You idiot! Who smokes in an airplane bathroom?" he said and grabbed my cigarette with distaste and tossed it into the sink.

"Hey! That's mine!" I said as I scrambled to my knees.

"Did you not see the No Smoking sign?" He said, ignoring my outrage.

"Obviously I didn't," I lied. It was hanging clear as day next to the mirror. But I didn't think it was smart to say that I ignored it since he looked like he wanted to strangle me. "Besides, it's not like there's some federal regulation about smoking on a private jet. Is there?"

"No, but my regulations state absolutely no smoking anywhere on the jet. That stuff will kill you." Behind him, Misty nodded vigorously with a disapproving frown. It was refreshing to see an emotion besides perky on her face.

"In case it slipped your mind, we're *immortal*. I'd have to fall asleep in a bed with a lit cigarette for them to kill me."

Behind Callum, the door to the cockpit burst open, and the captain came rushing down the aisle toward us. "Mr. Murdoch, is everything all right?"

"Yes, our guest decided she couldn't wait until we landed for a cigarette."

Great, now I had three judgey faces glaring down at me. What was this? Glare at the gorgeous vampire day?

"Don't stare at me like that. Callum, your help leaves much to be desired."

Captain Hawk's face turned a mottled shade of red, and he took a menacing step toward me. Misty's lower lip trembled, and moisture made her blue eyes sparkle.

"Raven, Captain Hawk is hardly one of the *help*. He taught the Wright brothers a thing or two. And Misty is very good at . . . mixing drinks."

Misty's face crumpled. Captain Hawk looked like he was ready to throw me off the plane.

Callum opened a panel in the wall and punched in a code. The alarm abruptly shut off. All four of us sighed in relief.

"Will you get up already?" Callum said and grabbed my arm to lift me.

"Don't manhandle me, Callum Murdoch," I said, ripping away from his grasp.

"What are you gonna do, tell your daddy on me?" he challenged as he backed off.

As I struggled to gain my footing in the crowded corridor, I started to get angry. It was his fault I was on this stinking plane to begin with. It was his fault I didn't get to have my cigarette. It was his fault I was still wearing the same freakin' clothes I'd worn yesterday. And I am sure I could have thought of a dozen other things. So I did what any mature vampire female would do in my situation.

"Oh, real original, princess," Callum replied to my one-fingered salute. "You can put that finger away, because I wouldn't fuck you if my life depended on it."

I ignored him and cat-walked my way back to the front of the plane.

His glare burned into the back of my head, so I put a little extra sway in my hips just to show him I wasn't embarrassed about making an ass out of myself.

My motto had always been "Confidence should faked until it's felt." That approach had served me pretty well throughout my life. And I would probably be using it quite a bit over the next few months.

"You are going to sit in that seat until we land," Callum commanded as he stalked to his chair. "And once we land you are going to keep your mouth shut and do whatever I tell you."

"Excuse me?" I said, turning a glare on him that should have singed him.

"You heard me. Your father gave me complete control over you, and what I say goes. One phone call and your ass is on a plane to Norway."

I bit my tongue and swallowed my retort. I was going to have to watch myself if I wanted to get through this charade. The reminder that I was at his mercy caused resentment to eat at me like acid, but I kept my mouth shut. I turned toward the window instead, watching the tiny lights which dotted the landscape far below.

Captain Hawk stopped by Callum's seat on his way back to the cockpit after giving up on Misty. Apparently, all the excitement had been too much for the poor dear. She had locked herself in the galley and refused to come out.

"Mr. Murdoch, we are running a few minutes ahead of schedule. We should touch down at approximately eight p.m."

Shit, only an hour until we landed. I had lain awake last night trying to come up with a plan for my three-month punishment. However, beyond "annoy Callum as much as possible," I had no idea how I was going to play this.

The Murdoch family wasn't a group of weaklings. Take Kira Murdoch, the matriarch of the family. At seven hundred years old, she was one of the elders of the Brethren Sect. She wasn't on the council, but she held a lot of influence among the members. Fiercely protective of her family, she wouldn't be rolling out the red carpet for me, that was for sure. Plus, like most elder vamps, she had a fine-tuned bullshit detector. She'd know immediately if I was planning on faking my way through my lessons.

So where did that leave me? I was at the mercy of a powerful family who wouldn't hesitate to ship me off to an icy exile. Callum had already made it clear that he wouldn't tolerate any rebellion. I was starting to wonder if the Land of the Midnight Sun might have been a better option.

After being briefed by the captain, the cabin was silent for several minutes except for the sound of pages turning. If paper could sound angry, then Callum's magazine was furious. I peaked over my shoulder at him. His jaw was clenched so tightly I wondered if his teeth could withstand the force.

I decided it might be smart to extend an olive branch before we landed. After all, as much as I loathed the guy, three months was a long time to have him punishing me for smoking in the girls' room. So I swallowed my pride.

"Callum? Would you mind if I had a bag of blood before we landed?" I said, trying to sound meek.

His head snapped up and his eyes narrowed.

"Are you serious? Last night you acted like you'd rather drink mud."

"Look, I think we started off on a bad note. I have had some time to ponder my situation. I understand now that I have no choice but to change some of my habits," I said, hoping I wasn't laying it on too thick. "Besides, I'm starving. I figure if I want to eat for the next few months, I might as well get used to the taste, right?"

He stared at me for a moment before answering. I held my breath, hoping he wouldn't call "bullshit" and laugh at me. Yes, I was doing this to manipulate him. But also, I really was starving.

Just then, my stomach decided to growl. Loudly. That must have convinced him because the next thing I knew, he rose from his seat and went to the bar at the front of the cabin. The overhead lights caused the golden highlights in his brown hair to glisten. He bent down and opened the minifridge. The action caused his faded blue jeans to stretch taut over an amazing ass.

I shook my head. He didn't *have* an amazing ass; he *was* an ass, I reminded myself.

I had had a few run-ins with Callum over the years. Mostly I found him to be someone who got by more on charm than wit. He actually was considered quite a catch among the twittering single vamp chick population. I supposed I couldn't blame them. After all, he had it all—a distinguished ancestry, money, looks, and a tight ass—dammit, my eyes wouldn't behave for some reason.

He was a bit too white bread for my taste though. I liked my men with a little bit of an edge to them. They didn't have to be smart, but they had to be interesting.

Oh, I also preferred it if they didn't have me by the balls, metaphorically speaking.

"Would you like it heated?" he asked solicitously.

See what I mean? I had gone after his family and been nothing but a bitch too him for the last twenty-four hours, and he politely offers to warm my beverage. If I were him, I would have smacked me around a little and let me suffer. But this guy? Best manners. Sheesh.

I gulped at the thought of cold blood. But I had to soldier through this. Plus seeing the bag in his hand had my fangs already extending.

"Uh, no, that's fine," I said, extending my hand for the bag. I hoped he didn't notice the slight tremble caused by stress and hunger.

He walked over and handed me the bag. His hand grazed mine in the exchange, and his fingers felt furnace warm compared to my clammy ones. I looked at the bag suspiciously. Other than last night, which was an extreme case due to my fainting spell, I'd never had anything other than fresh blood.

Despite my hunger, I didn't know how any self-respecting vampire could tolerate drinking cold blood from a plastic bag. I'd normally rather drink from an anemic than ingest that sludge. But there was no helping that. If I wanted to stay strong, bagged blood was my only option.

"Cheers," I said with a shaky laugh and bit into the bag. Cold, metallic-tasting blood spurted into my mouth immediately. My gag reflex threatened to act up, but I focused on swallowing as fast as I could. My instinct for feeding took over quickly, and soon I could almost feel my cells greedily absorbing the nourishment.

He watched me the entire time. It felt . . . intimate, him watching me feed. Normally I fed alone, with the exception of whatever criminal I had chosen for my meal. The added element of drinking a form of blood I normally shunned added to my sense of vulnerability. I tried to avoid his eyes, but when I finished the first bag, he immediately was there with another. I looked up at him in surprise. How did he know I needed more?

His expression wasn't what I expected. Instead of mocking or smugness, I saw a touch of understanding in his gaze. I quickly looked down at the new bag and jabbed it on my teeth without thanking him. I was too hungry and too confused by everything going on to say anything.

I finished the second bag quickly and immediately felt energized. Callum held his hand out for the two limp bags, and I handed them over without meeting his eyes.

"That wasn't so bad, now, was it?" he said as he walked back to the bar to dispose of them.

Cold blood from a plastic bag tasted just as awful as it sounded. I was used to warm blood fresh from the vine, so to speak. But I supposed that the cold shitty stuff might not taste good, but it got the job done.

"I am sure I'll get used to it," I said diplomatically.

"When we get back, we'll get you started on Lifeblood. Logan has formulated it so it tastes almost as good as the real thing."

Whoop-di-freakin'-doo, I thought. Not only had I just drunk bagged blood, which I would have sworn two days ago would never touch my lips. But now I was about to take it one step further and drink faux blood. Oh, the humanity.

"Speaking of Logan, does he know about what's happening? With me, I mean?"

Callum sat in his seat with a thoughtful frown. "No, I haven't told him yet. I called Mother last night and filled her in, but we both thought it best to get you situated and see how things are going before we tell him."

"I guess he won't be too thrilled to see me again, huh?"

He snorted. "That's an understatement."

"So, what's the game plan?" I asked. I figured forewarned was forearmed.

"Honestly, I don't have everything worked out. Your father and I hashed out the big stuff, but he left the details up to me. I know the first step will be to get you on the sun allergy regimen—we call it Sun Shield. It takes about a week to take effect, so we need to get you started right away."

I frowned. I hadn't expected it to be so fast. I had lived an exclusively nocturnal life. The thought of stepping into the sun for the first time scared me.

"Don't worry, they're safe. Plus, Logan found a way to include the formula into Lifeblood, so after a couple days you won't even have to think about taking pills."

"Okay," I said, tamping down my unease. "What else?"

He smiled a smile that put me immediately on edge. "I think that's all I'll tell you for now. The less you know, the less you can plan."

With that, the tenuous truce was shattered.

"Asshole," I said, abandoning all efforts to make nice.

"Bitch," he said, returning my glare.

"Mr. Murdoch? We're making our descent into Raleigh. Please fasten your seat belts," said Captain Hawk over the loud speaker.

Callum and I ignored the announcement and continued to shoot daggers at each other.

Fasten our seat belts, indeed. It was definitely going to be a bumpy ride.

CHAPTER FOUR

The car was tomb-silent as we left the airport. I didn't ask where we were going, and he didn't offer up the information. Which was fine by me. I was exhausted and frustrated. My priority was finding a dark room in which to pass out for about four days.

Eventually, Callum turned his red Ferrari into the heart of Raleigh's Hayes Barton neighborhood. Home to some of Raleigh's oldest and most distinguished families, the area was a hodgepodge of everything from stone manors to brick colonials. The air filtering into my open window reeked of old money.

The neighborhood was quiet, with only a few cars passing under the stately old pine trees and oaks lining the narrow roads. After a few minutes, Callum turned into a driveway bordered on either side by a tall privacy hedge. The heavily treed lot combined with the large yard prevented a clear view of the house.

As we curved along the driveway, the house appeared—a glowing white apparition among the dark backdrop of vegetation and nighttime shadows. Two stories tall with white brick and black shutters, the house was a prime example of

Federal architecture. But beyond the structural beauty, there was something . . . an aura about the house. If houses could have old souls, this one did.

I knew immediately this was not Callum's house. The distinguished design and exquisite landscaping seemed too dignified for him. Instead, I pictured him in a trendy loft in the heart of the city's social scene, all concrete and steel. Cold cash and hard business.

No, someone else owned this house. I sensed a shift in the power emanating from the house, like a low hum in my head, and realized it wasn't the house giving off vibes, but a vampire. A very old one.

Kira Murdoch.

I wanted to ask Callum if I was right, but knew I'd find out soon enough. Besides, I wasn't speaking to him. The fact he wasn't speaking to me had no bearing on my decision.

He pulled the car to a stop on the circular drive, the wheels crunching on the grey gravel. Without a word, he got out and headed to the black front door, leaving me to follow.

He used the polished brass knocker and waited, still ignoring my presence. That was fine with me. If I was right, and this was Kira's house, I was about to walk right into the lion's den. A protective lioness who wouldn't be too friendly to the hyena who recently threatened her cubs.

After a few moments, the door swung open, and sure enough there was Kira in the flesh. She smiled at Callum and pulled him in for a hug. Over his shoulder, she glanced at me. Her smile vanished. She squeezed Callum tighter for a brief second, closing her eyes as if to absorb every bit of sensation out of the embrace.

"Mother," Callum complained.

"Sorry dear, I've missed you," she said with an overly bright smile as she pulled back from the hug.

"I was only gone for twenty-four hours," Callum said with amusement.

She paused and said quite seriously, "Any amount of time away from one's child can be painful, Callum. You'll understand when you have fledglings of your own."

Callum muttered something under his breath that sounded suspiciously like "subtle hint."

I stood to the side during their interchange, feeling awkward. Watching her reveal her love for her son so openly made me shift uncomfortably. I told myself it was the damned boots again, but deep down I knew I was embarrassed to witness such honesty of emotion. The concept of expressing real emotion in front of others was completely foreign to me—unless it was anger. That I had no problem expressing in public.

"Well, come on in. I had Hannah prepare a snack," Kira said to her son. Both ignored me as if they expected me to follow without hesitation.

I hadn't really expected a warm welcome, but I figured I'd at least be acknowledged. I tamped down my frustration, though, knowing an attitude wouldn't help me get through this. The meeting would probably set the tone for the next three months. Besides, I was outnumbered.

I followed the pair through the foyer and into a parlor to the left. While mother and son chatted, I took in the surroundings. As expected, the tastefully decorated house looked like a spread out of one of those interior decorating magazines. I chuckled to myself, imagining a publication called *Homes and Gardens of the Damned* with this house on the cover.

The walls of the sitting room were creamy beige. In fact, most of the room's furnishing were variations of the color. A crystal vase overflowing with scarlet roses stood as a focal point on the mantel. The scent of the flowers gently sweetened the air. For all it's expensive adornments, the room was welcoming. More welcoming than the expression on the hostess's face as she turned to me.

"Raven, please be seated," she said, motioning to a pair of Queen Anne chairs. She and Callum sat across from me on the sofa. Between us sat a glass-topped coffee table with elaborate scrollwork for legs.

A young woman entered the room at that moment with a tray bearing a tea service and finger sandwiches. Her almost white blonde hair and light blue eyes gave her the appearance of innocence, yet I felt old energy emanating from her. The contrast was odd, but I dismissed her quickly. Servants weren't worth my time. I studied my fingernails as she set the tray on the coffee table and looked toward Kira for permission to serve.

"Would you care for refreshment?" Kira asked, looking at me reluctantly.

"No thanks," I said. I made myself as comfortable as possible in the chair as blondie poured tea for Callum and his mom. The silent woman left the room after Kira dismissed her with a nod. When she reached the door, her eyes cut to me. She saw me catch her but didn't flinch. She just turned slowly and walked out. What was up with servants these days? They had no respect anymore.

Kira sat back toward the cushions, looking relaxed as she took her first sip of tea. Callum cradled his own cup in his large palm and glared at me, adding to my discomfort. Only an idiot would miss the tension hanging in the air like a black fog, permeating each nook of the room.

"Now," she said after taking another sip. "Callum has filled me in on his meeting with your father. I must say, if it were up to me, you would already be on a transport plane to Norway."

She paused and looked to me for a reaction. She frowned when she saw none.

"However, Orpheus is the leader of our sect, and I will concede to his wishes. For the present. But, young lady, I must make this very clear. Are you listening?"

I nodded. My aggravation was rising, but decided to see how this all played out.

"Good because I am only going to warn you once. You so much as look at one of my children or any member of our staff the wrong way and I will forget my allegiance to your father and take matters into my own hands. You are lucky you were allowed to walk out of that rat hole you held poor Sydney in without a severe limp."

"Mother—" Callum tried to interrupt.

"I am not finished," she said, waving him off with her hand.

"Furthermore, I will not tolerate tantrums or balking. Our job is to transform you into a solid citizen of the vampire community, and you will do as we say without question. Is that understood?"

I hesitated, struggling to suppress the dozen retorts fighting to get out. How dare she speak to me this way? As a "Pure Blood," a genetically pure vampire born and bred, I outclassed her. Kira was turned by her husband, which made her a "Halfie," as all turned vamps were called. Granted she was a lot older and more respected in the Brethren Sect.

Despite all that, I believed each of her threats. One call to my father and this woman could get my threatened exile bumped up by a few hundred years. In addition, if I pissed her off enough, she would find far worse ways to make me pay for my sins.

I swallowed my pride, doubting it would be the last time in the near future.

"I understand. And let me say, I fully appreciate the gravity of my situation. I know I am at your mercy," I said.

A cough that sounded suspiciously like the word "bullshit" sounded to Kira's right. I glared at Callum, who smiled angelically back.

"That's enough, Callum," Kira snapped. "Raven may have a history of outrageous stunts, but she is no dummy. She knows she has no choice but to concede. To do otherwise would be most imprudent."

Actually, she was right. Before this meeting, I had thought I could bluff my way through this charade. But now I understood that even if I could fool Callum, Kira's eagle eyes would be watching my every move.

"Now that that's settled, we need to discuss how to deal with Logan," she said. "I'm afraid the situation has become a little more complicated since we last spoke."

Callum cut her off. "Perhaps we should wait until later to discuss this," he said, glancing at me meaningfully.

"Nonsense. Raven needs to understand what's going on if she is expected to understand our way of life."

Callum sighed. "Okay, so what's the problem?"

"Sydney," Kira responded.

"Shit, what happened?"

"It seems your brother declared himself to her last night after we rescued her."

Two sets of eyes cut to me. I tried not to flinch guiltily. Here's the deal: Sydney was a curator for the Raleigh Museum of Fine Art. A few weeks earlier, Logan had showed up at the museum to claim a portrait of himself in the museum's possession. Some villagers stole the painting from him a couple of centuries ago, and somehow it ended up at the museum.

Instead of admitting he was a vampire, Logan told Sydney that he was the descendant of the man in the painting. Unfortunately for him, he didn't have any hard evidence of that fact. So Sydney had to go through the Murdoch archives to verify his claim. In the course of working together, Logan and Sydney took a shine to each other.

"His sense of timing always did suck," Callum observed.

"Sydney threw a fit. She accused him of asking her to give up everything while he made no sacrifices. I talked to the poor dear this morning."

"Mother, you didn't," Callum said, sounding exasperated. "Logan will be furious if he finds out you meddled."

"I couldn't be expected to sit idly by. Those two children are so in love with each other yet so scared of love it's ridiculous," Kira said.

She shook her head and continued. "I told Syd just because two people are soul mates doesn't mean they don't have any issues. My dear Angus and I argued all the time."

Callum patted her hand as Kira looked off in the distance for a moment as if recalling a bittersweet memory of her long-dead husband. Then she shook herself and refocused on the conversation.

"Anyway, I have confidence they'll work it all out soon. In fact, I believe Sydney may be over there right now begging him to take her back," she said with a smile.

I started to ask what made Sydney change her mind, but

then I realized I had no interest in getting wrapped up in family drama. Luckily, Callum was curious too and asked so I didn't have to. "Mother, what did you do?"

"Me?" Kira asked innocently. "Really nothing other than talk to Syd and help her finally admit she loved him. I also helped her understand that being turned didn't mean she couldn't have a life. The rest was up to them to work out."

Callum looked unconvinced. "What does that have to do with Raven's rehabilitation?"

Kira sighed impatiently, as if the connection should be obvious. "If I'm right, and I normally am about these things, Logan and Sydney will soon be getting married. I don't think after what happened he'll be too happy about his future wife's kidnapper hanging around."

We all fell silent at that point. Callum and Kira obviously were pondering what to do about this new development. I was trying to figure out how to stay out of Logan and Sydney's way for the next three months.

"We can't very well hide Raven's presence for the next three months," Callum said, running his fingers through his thick hair.

"We have a few days while the two love birds figure themselves out, I guess. Let's just see what happens and decide on a course of action later," Kira said.

Callum nodded absently, seeming to be lost in his own thoughts. I didn't bother hiding my yawn. It couldn't be helped. I was tired, and this conversation was boring the crap out of me.

"Now, is there anything you need tonight to help get Raven settled?" Kira asked.

Callum shifted in his seat. "Actually, I was kind of hoping she could stay here."

Kira laughed. "Nice try."

"Mother, I live in a one-bedroom condo in the middle of downtown Raleigh. There is no way she can stay with me."

Kira considered this for a moment. "I see your point. Okay, fine. You can stay here."

He frowned. "Raven will stay here, you mean."

"No," she said slowly. "You and Raven will stay here. You didn't really think you could just drop her off here and expect me to handle her rehabilitation, did you?"

A faint blush rushed up his cheeks. I was really enjoying this. Despite the fact they were discussing me like I wasn't there, I loved watching his mother make Callum squirm.

"Of course not. But there's no reason for me to sleep here too. I'll just come by every evening after work and give her lessons."

Kira snorted and speared her son with a look that I was glad wasn't aimed at me. "You listen to me, young man. You will move your things here and work from here if necessary. If there is business you cannot handle from here, either Hannah or I will pitch in. But I will not allow you to dump her off on me to deal with for the next three months. She is your responsibility."

I tried not to laugh, really I did. But a chuckle escaped anyway. That was a mistake.

Kira's blue gaze turned on me then. "If I were you, I would wipe that grin off my face right now. If you think that you will be able to coast through your time here, you're wrong. Tomorrow morning, Callum and I will sit down and devise a plan for your training. I can promise you that your debt to this family will be paid in full by the time you leave here."

Callum smirked at me as I sat there like a kid in the principal's office.

"Now that that's settled, Callum, why don't you run to your apartment and get your things. I'll have Hannah show Raven to her room."

Callum stood and started for the door, but I interrupted him.

"Excuse me, I know I am just a lowly prisoner here, but when is someone going to go get my stuff?"

Kira's mouth opened in surprise. "Oh dear. It didn't occur to me that you didn't have anything with you. Callum, you'll go to Raven's place and get her stuff on your way back, won't you?"

"Can't she just borrow something for tonight? I have no desire to go all the way there and try to figure out what she needs. Knowing her, she'll bitch that the shoes I pick don't match the outfits or some nonsense," he said, looking as if he'd rather handle a snake than my clothes.

"I refuse to wear someone else's clothes. And I am ready to burn this outfit after wearing it for two days straight. If I have to, I'd rather walk around naked for three months."

Honestly, why didn't anyone think about my feelings here?

Callum looked me up and down quickly, and I swear I saw a flash of interest in his eyes. But I decided it must have been a trick of light. No way was a guy who obviously hated me and everything I stood for interested in seeing me strut around in my birthday suit.

"No need to get melodramatic," Kira said. "Callum, why don't you take Raven with you? That way she can get exactly what she needs."

Now, this idea I liked. Not only would I be able to get some fresh clothes and my other necessities, but I could also check on my lair and see if the minions were around. The poor souls were probably twisting in the wind without my inspirational leadership.

That's what I got for recruiting mortal teenagers to run my errands and do my dirty work. I seriously needed to consider trading the pimple brigade in for a badass gang of rogue vamps. But right now, what I needed more was a clean pair of panties.

"That would be great, thank you," I said sincerely to Kira. Callum glared at me from behind her.

Once in the car, we switched back to silent mode. I wasn't mad anymore. I was simply too worn out to make small talk with my captor. Although, I had to admit the meeting with Kira had gone much better than I'd anticipated. Sure, she'd threatened me, but that was to be expected. It didn't sound so far like they had any nefarious payback plans for me.

Feeling a little better about my plight, I settled back into the soft leather seat of Callum's car. My captivity would be tough, but I'd made it through rougher patches. I could handle rearranging my sleep habits and drinking synthetic blood for a little while. Besides, no one said I had to maintain the Brethren lifestyle once my three months were over. I figured I'd take some time off from my underground activities to get the council's attention off of me. Then I could go back to my old ways, being more careful to stay under the radar.

"What are you scheming over there?" Callum asked, breaking into the silence.

I looked at him, feeling affronted by his suspicions and chagrined that he could read me so well.

"Nothing," I promised. "Just wondering what I'll do with my time after you rehabilitate me."

"Yeah right," he said.

"What? I have every faith that I'll pass your tests."

"I wouldn't be so sure about that. Your father was pretty confident you wouldn't last three days," he said.

I snorted. "Yeah, Dad never did give me much credit."

Callum glanced at me, his expression incredulous. "Can you blame him?"

"What's that supposed to mean?" I said, affronted.

"It's no secret you have done everything in your power to undermine his vision for the Brethren. Although, I have to admit, I used to kind of grudgingly respect the way you stood up to your old man."

"Used to?" I asked.

"Before you attacked my family," he said, his tone hard.

"Callum, it was not an attack on your family specifically. I have no grudge with you guys. It's the synthetic blood I was against."

"You kidnapped the woman my brother loves! It doesn't get much more personal than that."

"It wasn't personal!" I yelled back. Taking a deep breath, I tried to regroup.

Sitting in silence, I wondered how to approach this with him. How could I defend my actions to someone who didn't understand my philosophies?

"It must be nice. Sitting there all smug knowing that you're in the majority. All you Brethren types are alike. Thinking you know the right way to do things. Believing that anyone who differs from you is automatically wrong," I said.

"So it's better to fight a losing battle in a war no one believes in but you? Raven, your ideals are so outdated they're laughable."

I clenched my fists. "Laugh at me all you want, but at least I am not a sheep following the herd. I am an independent thinker, unlike some vampires I know."

"I am an independent thinker," he said defensively.

"Oh, really? Is that why you're still under Mommy's thumb? Is that why you run your family's company instead of branching out and making your own mark on the world, out from your brother's shadow?"

He lurched the wheel to the right and slammed on the brakes, stopping on the shoulder. Then he turned to me, his eyes blazing in the darkness of the car.

"Let's get something straight. You do not know me, and you do not know my family. It doesn't surprise me that someone with no understanding of family or duty would believe I resent my station. But you're wrong. Just because you're miserable doesn't mean everyone else is."

My mouth dropped open. No one ever spoke to me that way.

"I'm not miserable."

"Bullshit. You've got more baggage than the carousel at JFK Airport."

"I do not!"

"Frankly, you don't need to be banished. You don't need rehabilitation. What you really need is a damned shrink!" he said, banging his hand on the steering wheel for emphasis.

I wanted to scratch his eyes out. I wanted to slam out of the car and run as fast and far away as possible. But I sat there stunned, unable to move or fight back.

My silence must have thrown him off guard because he took a deep breath and ran his fingers through his hair.

After a moment of tense silence, he threw the car in gear

and spun back onto the road, spitting gravel with his rear wheels.

It wasn't true, I told myself. He was just trying to tear me down so I'd be more compliant.

"I'm sorry I said that," he said quietly after a few moments.

"No, you're not," I whispered.

He glanced over at me, a frown marring his golden features. "Really. I know this has to be tough on you too. But don't you see? Don't you understand how your actions have led you here?"

I refused to reply. To go from accusing me of mental instability to trying to counsel me? Fuck that.

"Don't try to play therapist with me, you schmuck. You just told me I don't know you. Well, you know what? You don't know me either. And frankly, I'm not interested in hearing your opinions or advice."

"Unfortunately, listening to both my opinions and advice are part of the deal. So get used to it. If you can't take it, there's a nice resort in Norway waiting for you."

"I really hate you, you know that?" I said, crossing my arms.

His jaw clenched as he stepped on the gas. "Yeah, well, the feeling's mutual, sweetheart."

CHAPTER FIVE

Two days later at the butt crack of dawn, someone knocked on my door. I rolled over and covered my head with a pillow.

"Time to wake up, sunshine," Callum's voice came through the door.

He probably couldn't hear my groan, muffled as it was by the bedding, but it wouldn't have stopped him if he had.

The door clicked open, and a few moments later he ruthlessly ripped the pillows from my grasp. I squeezed my eyes shut tighter as light blasted through my eyelids.

"What are you trying to do, kill me?" I yelled and pulled the covers over my head.

"You've been on Sun Shield for two days. Indirect sunlight won't actually hurt you. Your eyes are just sensitive."

"Sensitive?" I said, my voice muffled by the down comforter and sheets. "I feel like my eyeballs were dipped in acid."

"Come on. It's not that bad. I brought you some sunglasses to wear around the house. That should help you adjust," he said.

It was hard to tell from under my protective bedding, but he sounded both amused and annoyed.

"What time is it?" I asked, knowing I wouldn't like the

answer.

"Seven a.m.," he replied patiently. "Get up. You need to reset your internal clock."

"Reset this," I mumbled.

"Excuse me? I didn't quite catch that," he said.

"Never mind. Just give me the sunglasses," I said, sticking one hand out from under the covers. I felt cool plastic hit my hand and pulled it back under. Sunglasses in place, I slowly lowered the sheets.

"Open your eyes," he said, laughter in his voice.

"They are," I lied.

"Bullshit. Open them."

Slowly opening my left lid, I prepared for a blast of pain. Surprisingly, though, it wasn't too bad. The glasses had super dark lenses, and the frames wrapped around my temples, preventing any errant rays from attacking my poor corneas. My right eye opened, and Callum came into view.

"See, what did I tell you? Not so bad, huh?"

"It's almost bearable," I said, squinting. The shades were drawn, but the room still seemed unnaturally bright, even with the aid of the sunglasses. He was right, though. It wasn't as bad as I thought it would be.

"Now, if you're done complaining, it's time to get moving. Mother's waiting for us in her study. You've been asleep for almost twenty-four hours as it is. It's time to go over the details of your punishment."

"Couldn't this have waited until a more civilized hour? I'm exhausted."

"That's the sleeping pills talking," he said, referring to meds I took yesterday morning at his insistence. "They're quite strong because we wanted your body to adjust to the new schedule. Since you haven't fed in more than a day, the fatigue is also to blame. A couple bags of blood and a shower and you'll be good as new."

His mention of blood made me aware of another pain besides the one lingering in my eyes. My stomach cramped, and my temples pounded. I doubted I had enough energy to even get out of bed.

"Here, drink this. It will help," he said, placing a pint of blood in my hand. Even through the plastic, I could smell the rich iron scent. Greedily, I stabbed my fangs into the bag.

Gulping down the cold type B, I thought about how clever Callum was. Every time I had fed over the last few days, I was so starved I didn't care that I was throwing out my principles in favor of nourishment. Like a person trapped in the dessert, I didn't care where the liquid came from as long as I got enough of it down my throat to stop the pain.

After sucking down the last drop, I licked my lips, feeling stronger. I handed the bag back to Callum and mumbled my thanks. I caught him staring at me with an odd look on his face.

"What?" I asked, feeling embarrassed for some reason.

"You have a little bit next to your mouth," he said, sounding amused.

I stuck my tongue out and tried to lick away the errant droplets.

"Better?"

"The right side," he said, his voice no longer amused. His expression seemed very serious as he focused on my mouth. Intrigued, I slowly licked around my lips, making sure to take my time. His eyes flared for a second and then narrowed as if he had figured out my game.

"Did I get it all?" I asked innocently.

His jaw clenched. "Yeah. Get dressed and meet me downstairs. And be quick about it. We don't have all day."

He turned and stalked out the door. I watched him go, wondering if the light was playing tricks on me or if I had really just witnessed Callum Murdoch with a hard-on.

With a smile on my face, I got out of bed and went into the attached bathroom. When I saw myself in the mirror, a bark of laughter echoed in the tiled space.

A small red smear marred the pale skin to the right of my lips.

#

Having my clothes back added a little spring to my step an

hour later as I descended the staircase. I took extra care with my appearance this morning. The knowledge I turned him on was a weapon I planned on using to my advantage. I had no choice about following his dictates about adopting a Brethren lifestyle, but that didn't mean I couldn't have a little fun driving him nuts.

Back to my clothes. Thanks to the trip back to my lair two nights earlier, I had my full wardrobe safely ensconced in the walk-in closet in my room. Today I chose a pair of buttery black leather pants and a tight black tank top. Simple yet sexy, the outfit showed off my curves and left little to the imagination.

Despite the necessity of wearing the shades all day, I applied smoky makeup. My eyes were tearing up even with the sunglasses due to the light filtering in through the foyer windows. Thank goddess the house faced west. If it had faced east, I'd probably have been struck blind. Nevertheless, I was glad the large lenses disguised any signs of raccoon eyes. Plus they went really well with the Goth-chic look I was going for.

The best part of my ensemble was the shoes. The black leather boots with the hand-tooled red flames—which matched my lipstick perfectly—shooting across the toes and up the sides were my shit-kickingest pair of footwear. They even sounded cool as they thudded on the foyer's marble floor.

I guess the sound announced my arrival because I had barely taken three steps off the stairs when Callum strode into the foyer looking like a thundercloud.

"An hour? What part of 'hurry up' didn't you understand?"

"Why, Callum, I don't know what you mean." I motioned to my bare earlobes. "See? I didn't even have time to properly accessorize."

He crossed his arms and opened his mouth as if preparing for a lengthy lecture. His mother's entrance saved me from dying of boredom.

"Raven, don't you look . . . awake this morning," she said, obviously trying to hide her shock at my fashion choices.

I nodded my thanks, keeping one eye on Callum. A vein had appeared over his right eyebrow. I didn't take that as a good sign.

"I was just about to tell Gabriella that we have been waiting for her to make an appearance," he said calmly.

Asshole. He knew I hated that name and was trying to bait me. So, I ignored him, knowing it would piss him off.

"Kira, I am so sorry to keep you waiting. I am afraid the sunlight is affecting my energy levels."

"That's to be expected. In a couple of days, you'll be right as rain. Now, let's adjourn to the study to discuss our plans for you. Shall we?" She motioned to the hall off the foyer.

I followed her down the hall, still ignoring Callum. He had no choice but to follow, and I could feel his eyes burning into my back.

I had just sat in one of the chairs facing the delicate antique table Kira used as a desk when the doorbell rang. Callum's head snapped up, and he looked at Kira. She rushed to the window to look out at the driveway.

"Logan and Syd," she said, quickly closing the drapes to look at Callum.

"What are we going to do?" Callum asked. "If he finds her here, he'll freak."

"Raven, please go upstairs. We'll continue this discussion later," Kira said calmly.

I nodded and rose. Callum looked at me sharply. "Whatever you do, don't come down until one of us gets you."

"Believe me, Logan Murdoch is the last man I want to see right now. Other than you, that is," I said and walked out of the room.

The doorbell rang again as I entered the foyer. Hannah was almost at the door when she saw me.

"I think they want you to wait until I'm out of sight to get that." She merely nodded and waited patiently as I climbed the stairs. Once I reached the landing, I walked a couple of feet down the hall and then stopped to listen in. I felt no guilt about eavesdropping. I wanted to know everything going on so there would be no surprises later.

The front door squeaked open after a third ring. Logan's

voice sounded excited as he asked Hannah where his mother was.

Kira and Callum had obviously decided to greet the lovebirds themselves because soon the foyer was filled with happy exclamations.

"Sydney, dear, we are so happy to have you as part of our family," Kira said. "How are you coping with the transformation?"

"I'm doing okay. Logan has been so great, explaining everything and helping me through the worst of it. I feel great now, though," Sydney replied.

I almost gagged as she gushed some more about her soon-to-be husband.

"So when is the big day?" Callum asked.

"Well, I tried to convince Sydney to elope—a" Logan said but was cut off by protests from his mother.

"Nonsense. We haven't had a wedding in this family in at least a century!"

"Mother, I know. Besides, Sydney already put her foot down."

"I did not. I simply pointed out that every woman dreams of her wedding day, and I am no different."

"You deserve to have the fairy tale," Callum said. "Even though my brother resembles Rumpelstiltskin more than Prince Charming."

The group chuckled, eliciting an eye roll from me. These vampires were far too happy. Why, they were a disgrace to our species.

"Anyway, we decided to get married in March. Spring in Raleigh is so beautiful," Sydney continued.

Silence filled the foyer for a moment. I cocked my head and scooted closer to the landing, wondering what had caused the silence.

"Only three months from now? That's not much time to plan a wedding," Kira said hesitantly after a few moments.

"We don't want to wait too long. Besides, it won't be very large, we'll just invite close family and friends," Logan said.

"Why the rush? After all, you two will have an eternity together. Why not take six months?" Callum asked, sounding a little stressed.

The room fell silent again, and even I, up on the balcony, could feel tension floating in the air. Obviously, Kira and Callum wanted me out of their hair before they had to deal with the wedding too. But Logan and Sydney didn't know that. I crept a little closer to the balcony overlooking the foyer, careful to keep back a bit.

"Is there a reason why you're pushing us to take more time?" Logan demanded.

"Darling, no, of course not. It's just everything has happened so fast. Poor Sydney just got turned. Why not take some time before you add the stress of planning a wedding on yourselves?" Kira sandbagged.

"Actually, I feel great. Besides, it shouldn't be too much work for us. Jorge and Geraldine have decided to start a wedding planning company, and they're going to handle all the details," Sydney said.

I stifled an outraged gasp. Geraldine? As in my former minion? That turncoat! Forgetting that I was supposed to stay out of sight, I got even closer to the railing.

"Geraldine and Jorge?" Callum said, chuckling. "With those two in charge, you're begging for drama."

"I think they'll do a lovely job," Sydney said defensively. "Besides, Jorge knows all about you guys. I mean us."

"You told Jorge?" Callum asked, sounding alarmed.

"Relax, bro. Jorge figured it out on his own. He's fine with it," Logan said.

Sydney laughed. "I couldn't believe it when he asked me. But he said it explains a lot, especially why all of you guys are so hot."

"Well, dear, I am sure they will do a fine job. But I still think this is all rather hasty," Kira said.

"Mother, it's already settled," Logan said, his tone making it clear there would be no more discussion. "Now, tell me how things went with Raven."

This was going to be good. I couldn't resist peeking over the railing to catch Callum's face and hear how he was going to handle this one.

Only I was so intent on Callum that I didn't notice my sunglasses were slipping until it was too late.

Everything happened at once. My glasses fell straight into the foyer with a thunk. Right at Logan's feet. I stood stunned for a moment. Then sunlight attacked my eyeballs like ice picks. I screamed and collapsed on the floor, clawing at my eyes. So much for inconspicuous.

Before I knew it, four pairs of feet flew up the staircase, and I was surrounded.

"Here, take the sunglasses, but for God's sake stop that yelling!" Callum said, shoving the glasses back on my face.

My howls turned into whimpers as my eyes went from being on fire to merely throbbing. Fortunately, the pain receded quickly. Unfortunately, my ears were also working well. Someone was shouting.

"What the hell is she doing here?" Logan demanded.

"Dear, we can explain," Kira said, holding her hand up.

"Logan, calm down and I'll tell you," Callum said at the same time.

"Someone better start talking," Logan demanded. "I can't believe this! Were you even going to tell me she was here?"

He resembled Mt. Vesuvius right before it erupted. His cheeks were flushed and his blue eyes flashed. He had Sydney pushed behind his back. Her expression was a combination of concern and annoyance at his behavior.

"Logan, calm down and let them explain," she said, laying a hand on his arm.

He abruptly stopped yelling and took a deep breath. "Fine. Now, I want you to tell me why the bitch who kidnapped my future wife is in this house." His voice was calm, but any idiot would recognize the menace underlying the words.

Callum cleared his throat. "We were going to tell you, but we wanted to wait until another time. Not right after you announced your engagement. See, Raven is the reason we were pushing you to hold off on the wedding. She's going to be here for a while."

Logan narrowed his eyes. "What? Why? And how long is 'a while'?"

"Three months. Wait!" Callum said, trying to hold off a new outburst from his brother. "Before you freak again, let me explain. Orpheus decided that since we were the victims of her recent stunts, we should decide her punishment."

I almost spoke up to correct him, because we both knew he was glossing over a lot. But Callum must have sensed my thoughts because he shot me a deadly look that promised severe repercussions if I said anything. One look at Logan's enraged face and my mouth clamped shut again. Totally against my nature, I continued to sit there on the floor, not wanting to draw any more attention to myself.

"We get to decide her punishment? Fine. Go tie her up, and I'll get a whip," Logan said.

I gasped, drawing his eyes to me. He wasn't joking.

"Now, son, there's no need for violence. Listen to your brother. There's more."

"Yes," Callum said. "Orpheus wants us to rehabilitate Raven, to get her to understand the Brethren philosophy so she won't be a threat to anyone any longer."

Logan snorted. "That's bullshit. What kind of idiot thinks that will work?"

Callum's color rose. I stifled a grin since the rehabilitation plan had been Callum's idea to begin with.

"Actually, I think the idea has some merit. She can pay her debts to us and learn that there's a better way of life," Callum said, indignation clear in his tone.

"So, she's here for three months and has to do whatever we say?" Sydney asked. She sounded far more reasonable than Logan. I didn't believe for a moment that she liked me or anything, but the fact I had done nothing to harm her when I kidnapped her probably had something to do with it. Logan was just being an overprotective asshole, in my humble opinion.

"Yes, she also has to live like us, meaning Sun Shield therapy and no more human meals. I thought we'd also get her started on Lifeblood as soon as possible," Callum said.

"Over my dead body," he said. "She doesn't deserve it after everything she did."

"But, son, don't you see? It's the perfect form of justice. She has to depend on Lifeblood for survival or she doesn't eat."

Logan seemed to think this over for a moment. I was starting to get bored, and my ass hurt from sitting on the floor. Plus, it pissed me off that they were talking about me like I wasn't there. As I rose, Logan's gaze shot to me.

"Look, I know you don't want me here, but guess what," I said, cocking a hip. "I like it even less than you do. So quit your bitching and deal. I'll be out of your hair in three months."

He took a menacing step toward me, but I refused to back down. Logan Murdoch might have a few inches on me, but I wasn't intimidated. No lab rat was going to make Raven Coracino back down.

Fortunately for Logan, his mother grabbed his arm before he could do anything stupid. "Son, there will be no fighting in my house. She's right. We must accept the will of the council and make the best of this. Look on the bright side."

Logan's head swiveled to look at is mother in disbelief. "What the hell is the bright side of this?"

Callum smiled wickedly. "She has to do anything we tell her."

#

After Callum's not-so-subtle threat, I excused myself from the group. If I had to listen to one more second of their bullshit, I was going to scream.

Since I was already upstairs, I went straight to my room. Once there, I collapsed on my bed facedown.

Sometimes it was tough to maintain my tough-chick persona. Sure, I talked a good game and usually even believed my own bullshit. But the truth was sometimes being misunderstood sucked. If they weren't talking about all the ways I needed to change, they were attacking my beliefs. It was frustrating as hell to constantly be put on the defensive, which was why I tried to attack first.

The result was that I had to keep everyone at arm's length. That wasn't so bad usually since most people pissed me off. Yet, every now and then I felt . . . I don't know. Lonely, I guessed.

I know it's silly since I had a group of minions who practically worshipped me. But in reality, I only really had one true friend in the world, Miranda. She and I had not spoken since the shit hit the fan, and I missed her.

Making a mental note to get in touch with her soon, I sat up. A tear splashed on my cheek. It shocked me since I wasn't even aware I was crying until then. I swiped at my cheeks, telling myself it was anger—not self pity—making me cry.

Crying was for weaklings. Kick-ass vampire chicks didn't boo-hoo just because people didn't like them.

Yet, the tears still fell, and the feeling in my gut wasn't white-hot fury. It was more of the misty grey fog of melancholy.

Grabbing a pillow, I hugged it to me, burying my face in its softness. Even though I struggled to keep my emotions together, they got the better of me.

What the hell, I thought. Might as well get it out now since no one would ever know.

My quiet tears quickly turned into gasping sobs as I thought about my life. My father hated me; Callum and his family hated me; everyone thought I was some misguided misfit, and for the next three months I'd have to endure goddess knew what kind of tortures. And if I failed, it was two hundred years of solitary confinement in a frozen wasteland.

Thankful for the pillow, I allowed myself to really let it all out. The cotton pillowcase was soggy under my face, but I didn't care.

Suddenly, I heard a click. My head jerked up. It was hard to see through my swollen, tear-soaked eyes. Wiping them quickly with the back of my hands, I looked around. Not seeing the source, I jumped up, thinking it sounded suspiciously like a door closing.

Moving fast, I went to the door and eased it open. Just

down the hall, I saw a foot clad in a very cute pair of brown boots disappear around the corner.

Sydney.

Well, shit, I thought, closing the door. Letting myself get all weak and cry was bad enough, but Sydney seeing the display was mortifying.

I only hoped she wouldn't run and report what she'd seen to everyone else. Cringing, I imagined them all laughing at me.

All feelings of sadness evaporated at the thought. That was it, I thought. No one would ever see me be that frail again.

From that moment on, I was going to be Raven, ice queen and all-around bitch.

CHAPTER SIX

"**B**ullshit!" I yelled, coming out of my chair.

Callum laughed. "If I recall correctly, we discussed community service as part of your rehabilitation."

We were sitting in Kira's study. Logan and Sydney had left an hour before, promising to come back the next day. Now, I was finally learning the rest of the Raven Rehabilitation Program. And I didn't like what I was hearing.

"But . . . but . . . can't I just hand out magazines at a hospital or something? Like one of those, what do you call them . . . candy strippers?"

Kira chuckled. "I think you mean candy stripers."

"Whatever."

"Look, in order for you to pay your debt and learn your lesson, you can't do something easy. It has to be uncomfortable for it to mean something," Callum explained.

"A blood bank, though? Are you crazy?"

"It makes sense. You'll be doing something to benefit mortals as well as learning to overcome your weakness for fresh blood," he said. "Besides, we are shorthanded right now in one of the Murdoch Biotech blood banks. The timing is perfect."

"Aren't you afraid I'll go crazy and eat some of the blood

donors?"

"First of all, we'll make sure you feed well before you go to the clinic, and second, you'll be watched very closely. Besides, you won't actually be drawing blood. You'll be handing out cookies and juice."

"I am a goddamned vampire! I do not hand out cookies and juice to mortals!"

"You do now," Callum said quietly.

I clenched my fists to resist knocking the smug look off his face.

"Raven, I know you don't like it, but I'm afraid we're quite determined on this. Or perhaps you would like to call your father and tell him you're ready for your extended vacation?"

I sat back down, feeling impotent. The emotion didn't sit well with me, but what choice did I have? Handing out refreshments to humans was much better than a two-hundred-year isolation.

The phone rang, interrupting my brooding.

Kira answered, and her eyes shot to me. I knew immediately who was on the other end.

"Callum, it's for you," she said. Her words surprised me; I was expecting to be called to the phone for a lecture. At Callum's questioning look, she mouthed, "Orpheus."

He looked at me briefly and went to take the phone. After listening for a few moments, he said, "Yes, sir. We were just discussing the terms of her punishment."

I tried not to squirm, wishing I could hear both sides of the conversation.

"Actually, she may want to speak with you about our plan for community service," Callum said and raised his eyebrows. I couldn't tell if he was issuing a challenge or calling my bluff.

We stared at each other for a moment. I battled with myself. Part of me wanted to throw in the towel and avoid all the humiliation, but the other part of me said "screw that."

I shook my head at Callum, signaling my decision to stick it out. My choice wasn't as noble as I'd like to believe. In all honesty, the thought of admitting defeat to my father made me feel physically ill. I would just have to suck it up and see this through. It pissed me off that my father would win no matter what I did—gloat if I gave up, take credit if I succeeded. But at least if I passed these tests, I could throw it in his face the next time he tried to call me a quitter.

"Actually, sir, she says she is fine with our plan. I must have been mistaken," Callum said into the phone, but he kept his gaze on mine. Perhaps that was a tinge of approval I saw in his eyes, but it could just have easily been a trick of the light.

"Yes, sir, I'll tell her. Are you sure you don't wish to speak with— Okay, then. Good-bye."

A few moments passed after he returned the receiver to its cradle. My impatience got the better of me. I couldn't stand the suspense.

"Well?" I demanded.

Callum frowned. "He said to give Mother his regards and to congratulate Logan and Sydney on their engagement."

I shouldn't have felt anything. But I did. When would I learn that my father didn't give two shits about me?

"How did he know about Logan and Sydney?" Kira asked.

I laughed, hearing my own bitterness echo in the sound. "Believe me, you can't hide anything from him."

Callum and Kira exchanged a look, but I wasn't feeling a compulsion to interpret it. I was too busy feeling sorry for myself.

"So!" Kira said, breaking into the silence. "Raven, I am pleased you decided to give the community service a try."

"Uh-huh," I mumbled.

"Yes, well," Callum said, looking at his watch. "I need to get into the office for a few hours."

"That's fine, dear. I thought Raven and I could spend some time discussing the history of the Brethren this afternoon."

I snorted. "Are you forgetting who my father is? I could recite the Brethren code before I could walk."

"Yes, but perhaps hearing it from another perspective might be helpful. Your father might have focused too much on the philosophy and not enough on the practical aspects behind the creation of the sect."

"Whatever," I said, knowing I had no choice. Kira could lecture me about the migratory patterns of lemmings, and I'd still have to listen.

Callum headed for the door. Just before he disappeared he said, "I forgot to mention—the blood bank gig begins tonight."

#

Sweat beaded my brow as the phlebotomist set aside a vial filled with bright red blood fresh from the source. With shaky hands I accidentally threw the cookie at the donor—a plump, middle-aged grandma type. She looked startled as the cookie bounced off her forehead. It landed on her lap while she stared at me in shock.

"Sorry, it's my first night," I explained lamely.

"Oh, that's all right, honey," she said as she munched on the cookie. "You'll get used to it. The first time I donated I almost fainted. Isn't that right, Alvin?" She asked the twenty-something brunette who was applying a bandage to her arm.

Alvin laughed. "That's right, Mrs. Jones. But now you're a pro." He looked at me, his smile dimming somewhat.

Alvin obviously wasn't as forgiving as Mrs. Jones about tossing my cookie, so to speak.

"Mrs. Jones comes in every month to donate."

The grey-haired woman, who smelled of roses and sugar cookies, beamed proudly. "I sure do. Happy to help. After all, my darling Frank never would have survived his double bypass a couple of years ago if some other generous soul hadn't donated their blood. So I figure it's just my little way of doing my part."

"That's nice," I said absently, eyeing the tray next to her—my mouth watering and my fangs threatening to extend. Luckily, Callum had insisted I down three bags of blood before dropping me off at the clinic, or I'd be doing blood shooters right in front of Mrs. Jones.

The sound of a throat clearing broke my trance, and I drug my eyes away from the vials of blood and looked at Callum. He stood about ten feet away leaning against the white wall with his arms crossed. He shook his head and mouthed, "Don't even think it."

I stuck my tongue out at him and turned back to Mrs. Jones, who was chattering at Alvin about her grandchildren.

"Well, enjoy the cookie. Here's your sticker."

This time I managed not to throw it at her. Instead I gently handed her a red heart that identified her as a donor.

"Thank you, honey. And good luck."

I mumbled my thanks and scurried over to the credenza next to Callum. Needlessly, I refilled my tray of cookies. I'd only handed out—okay thrown—one so far.

Callum chuckled.

"Smooth," he said. I ignored him in favor of artfully arranging the cookies. Less than fifteen minutes into it and I'd already made an ass out of myself. Since it was my first night, though, I only had a two-hour shift.

"So you're not talking to me now?" Callum tried to bait me again.

I stopped my arranging and speared him with a glare. "Don't you have anything better to do right now?"

"No. Playing babysitter to a spoiled bitch is my idea of a fun time," he retorted.

I snorted. "My heart bleeds for you. Need I remind you that this was all your idea? I wouldn't need babysitting if you hadn't insisted I do this in the first place."

"Don't worry. From now on Hannah or Alaric will be chaperoning you. I just wanted to be sure we could trust you in this environment."

I focused on the tray again, not wanting to admit I wasn't sure I could be trusted. "I have to admit, owning a blood bank is a smart move on your part. Easy access."

He shrugged. "It started out that way, but only about fifty percent of our donations go for . . . personal use," he said looking around to make sure we weren't overheard.

We were the only two vamps in the room. When he saw no one was listening, he continued in a hushed tone. "Now that we have Lifeblood, though, we'll give all of the blood to hospitals or charitable organizations like the Red Cross."

I rolled my eyes. "You really are a do-gooder aren't you?"

"Don't you have some cookies to hand out?"

I turned my back on him and returned to the area where the blood was drawn. Mrs. Jones had already left, leaving a young-looking guy and girl as the only donors. They occupied two of the room's four stations.

Each station held a recliner and a rolling tray for the person taking the blood. That night, Alvin was the only technician on hand.

To the mortals I guessed the room probably smelled of rubbing alcohol. But to me the scent of blood overpowered everything. It was so distracting I almost missed my name being called at first. But since the voice sounded like nails screeching down a chalkboard, I heard it loud and clear.

Nancy Simkins.

Nancy was in charge of the clinic. She was also in charge of me, a fact she made very clear when we were introduced.

In her sixties, she had a perfect silver helmet for hair and wore too many pearls. She also reeked of White Shoulders perfume. I didn't think we were going to become best friends.

"Gabriella?" she said again, louder this time. I could have killed Callum when he introduced me to her with that blasted name. But it would have been a pain in the ass to correct him and then explain to Nancy why she needed to call me Raven.

I stopped before I reached the teenagers and turned, pasting a smile to my face. I didn't want to give Callum any more enjoyment by showing how pissed off I was.

"Yes, Nancy?" I asked sweetly as I made my way to her desk, which stood next to the front door.

"How are you doing?" she asked.

I didn't for a minute think she was asking out of concern. She had a glint in her eye that indicated she hadn't called me over just to shoot the shit.

"Oh, I'm fine," I said casually. "I've only been on shift for fifteen minutes, though."

She nodded and wiped an invisible speck of dirt from her

pristine blotter.

"I notice you aren't wearing your apron," she said.

The words were casual, but we both knew it wasn't a random observation.

"Yeah, about that, I was hoping you were kidding. It's not like handing out cookies is all that messy." Plus, the damn thing was butt ugly.

"Gabriella," she said, looking me in the eye. "I know you are new here, so some leeway can be given for your ignorance. But every volunteer wears an apron."

"You're not wearing one," I said before I could stop myself.

Her eyes narrowed, and her nostrils flared. "Young lady, I am the director of this clinic. If you don't want to wear the apron, you can find another place to work off your community service."

Yeah, that was the other thing. Callum told Nancy I was working off court-ordered community service hours. I didn't necessarily care about what this lady thought of me, but I knew he was trying to make this ordeal as difficult as possible for me. So not only did I have to adjust to being around blood and not indulging, I also had to deal with people thinking I was a petty criminal. I chose to ignore the fact that kidnapping a mortal was a felony in the mortal world. Whatever, it didn't really matter, because I knew Callum was just trying to make this difficult so I'd quit and he could happily get back to his life.

"Fine," I said, thrusting my hand out for the apron.

Nancy smiled and handed it over. I probably imagined that it burned my hand, but it sure felt that way. It could also have been that the pink monstrosity was the most embarrassing garment I had ever been forced to wear. Made of bubble-gum-colored cotton, it had white ruffles along the edges and embroidered darker pink hearts all over it. The damned thing looked like Cupid had puked all over it.

"See, that is much better," Nancy said, her smile bordering on malicious. "Now, run along and give those kids some cookies. After they leave it should be pretty quiet, so we can go over the paperwork procedure."

"Great," I said without feeling and turned back toward the room. That was my first mistake. My second mistake was glancing at Callum.

I can only imagine what I looked like to him—a Goth goddess in Betty Crocker couture. But the knee slapping seemed a bit much.

"Bite me," I said to him as I passed. He wiped the tears from his eyes and took a breath. He looked like he had calmed enough to respond, but then he just started laughing all over again. I didn't have time to pay him back for that. I had cookies to deliver.

The sound of Callum's chuckles echoed behind me as I approached the remaining donors. The girl needed a fashion lesson. The baggy jeans and baby blue T-shirt did nothing to hide her chunky frame. She wasn't fat, but she definitely wasn't skinny either.

Serious but pretty blue eyes peered from behind blue-framed glasses. Her mousy brown hair was pulled back in a ponytail. She was a combination of tomboy and nerd. She already had a bandage on her arm.

Her companion looked a couple years older, twenty maybe. Alvin had just finished up with him when I arrived. A navy T-shirt stretched over his broad athletic shoulders. Fashionably shaggy brown hair fell around his face.

I'm not into younger men—and definitely not mortals—but this kid was a hottie. He had heartbreaker written all over him.

First I approached the girl, who regarded me curiously. I'm pretty sure the apron was to blame for the smile she tried to hide. Holding up the tray, I asked her if she wanted a cookie.

"Yeah, thanks," she said quietly and took one. She seemed so earnest for someone so young. I wondered what brought her here.

"Hey, sis, maybe you should have some juice or something instead," the heartbreaker said.

The girl looked at her brother guiltily and then glanced at me. With pink cheeks, she put the cookie back.

"Sorry," she whispered. "Is there any juice?"

Her eyes never left the cookie as she spoke.

I watched the whole thing with my mouth hanging open. This girl was not fat. She just looked as if she hadn't grown out of her baby chub yet. How dare her brother embarrass her like that? I wanted to throw a cookie at him, but this time it wouldn't be an accident.

"Are you sure?" I asked. "One cookie won't kill you."

She looked unsure for a second. Just when I thought she was going to go for it and eat the cookie, her brother jumped in again.

"Jenn, think about how proud mom will be after her surgery if you've lost some weight."

I felt my eyes widen as I looked at him. Despite his handsome features, he suddenly looked very ugly to me.

Jenn's chin wobbled. "Just juice, please."

"Fine," I said, my tone clipped. It took everything I had not to stand up for this girl. But then I reminded myself that these were mortals. If that girl wanted to let her brother bully her, then what business of it was mine?

Despite my resolve to stay out of it, my temper continued to grow as I marched to the minifridge next to the credenza for some juice.

"Calm down," Callum said as I slammed the door to the fridge. I poured a glass of orange juice before I glanced at him.

"He's an asshole," I whispered.

"Yeah, he is," he said, glancing at the kids. "But do you really want to end up exiled because you lost your temper? Imagine what your father would say if he found out you couldn't last one night."

I took a deep breath and nodded. He was right. Losing my temper wouldn't do any good. I had to be crafty instead.

I poured another glass of juice, smiled at Callum—who looked suspicious—and strolled back to the teens.

The girl smiled shyly at me when I handed her the little plastic cup of orange juice. I returned her smile with a confident one of my own.

Alvin had just finished up with Jenn's brother. I offered him the other glass on my tray.

"No, thanks, I'll have a cookie," he said with a cocky grin.

Gritting my teeth, I moved closer to the recliner he was on. His eyes ran over my body, giving me the creeps. What I wouldn't give to get this kid in a dark alley and scare the shit out of him with my fangs.

"So what's your name?" he asked.

"It's Ra-Gabriella," I said.

"What time you get off?" he said as he took the cookie from my hand. I leaned in as if to whisper to him and tipped the tray.

"Shit!" he yelled, lurching upright. Bull's-eye! The little creep now spotted a huge wet spot on the crotch of his khaki shorts.

"Oh no," I said in feigned concern. "I'm so sorry. Here, let me help you."

Setting the tray on the table next to the bed, I grabbed a few napkins. I'm ashamed to admit that in my haste to help the poor dear that I "accidentally" punched him in the balls.

Whoops.

"Argh!" he yelled, curling up in the fetal position with his hands covering his tender bits.

"Oh my! Did I hurt you? I'm so clumsy."

"Bitch," he said in a high-pitched pant.

I bit back a smile and glanced over at Jenn. Her eyes were wide in shock. I winked at her, and her lips twitched.

"Gabriella! What is going on here?" Nancy's voice broke in over the sounds of Romeo's moans. "Are you all right, son?"

I opened my mouth to make up an excuse, but Jenn beat me to it.

"My brother accidentally knocked her tray. It's not her fault." Jenn's normally timid voice suddenly sounded a lot more confident.

"Is that true?" Nancy asked me.

I shrugged. "Yeah."

"Then why is he currently writhing in pain?" Nancy asked suspiciously.

"When he knocked the tray," Callum cut in from behind me, "the glass fell and hit him in the ba—I mean between the legs."

I spun around to stare at Callum. My mouth hung open in shock as I tried to process the fact he had just defended me.

"Well, Mr. Murdoch, if you say so, I'm sure that's what happened," Nancy said hesitantly.

"He's right. My brother was just being careless," Jenn chimed in again.

I must have hit the kid harder than I thought because the entire time the rest of us talked, he groaned. Although, after a few minutes he did manage to vomit in the wastebasket.

A real shame.

As I continued to stare at Callum, I vaguely heard Nancy tell me to get back to work. He returned my gaze, a small smile playing on his lips.

"Thanks," I said when I'd finally recovered from my shock.

He glanced at the boy, who was cupping himself while his sister wiped his face with a napkin, a smile hovering on her lips.

"He deserved it." I regarded him for a moment, confused about what just happened. Callum wasn't supposed to be cool. I shook myself and decided it must have just been a fluke.

A throat cleared behind me, Jenn was trying to catch my attention. I had almost forgotten about her. I drug my gaze from Callum's and turned to the girl.

"Thanks," I said, appreciating her defense with Nancy.

"Thank you," she said. She cast a distasteful glance at her brother.

"Don't let him push you around so much," I said, unable to help myself. "You gotta keep men in line, or they'll walk all over you."

"I wish I had as much confidence as you do," she said.

"Hah, that's funny. Sometimes I feel like I don't know what the hell—I mean heck—I'm doing. But the key is to act confident even if you don't feel it. Good shoes help too."

"Shoes?" she asked, her brows knit together.

"Never mind, you have time before you're ready for advanced footwear. Just stand up for yourself."

"I know. It's just hard. Everyone in my family is crazy. Do you know why we're here? My mom is getting a face-lift. She insisted we donate blood in case she needs a transfusion."

She laughed, a musical sound that made me smile.

"You've got a good head on your shoulders. Keep your sense of humor, and you'll do fine."

"Thanks again. Well, I guess I better get him home." She motioned to her brother, who was lying very still with his eyes closed.

"Do you need any help?" Callum asked.

"If you don't mind," Jenn said.

Callum roughly dragged her brother up, eliciting a moan from the kid. As the trio left the clinic, I noticed Jenn had a little spring in her step.

For some reason, I felt pretty great. Who would have thought this volunteer gig would turn out to be kind of fun? Sure, I hated helping people. But I figured if I ran into any more mortals like Jenn, maybe I could handle it for a few months.

A few moments later Callum returned from the parking lot. Nancy was on the phone, and Alvin had disappeared into the break room. Callum and I were alone in the clinic. I busied myself cleaning up the rest of the mess from the spill as he walked to me.

When he reached my side, I glanced up at him. For some reason he was smiling at me.

"What do you want?" I demanded.

"What you did was pretty cool," he said.

"Getting punched in the nuts is cool to you? I'd be happy help any time."

He shifted his stance and moved back a little bit. Men were funny that way when it came to their balls.

"You know what I mean," he said. "Maybe there's hope for you after all, Gabby."

I threw down the juice-soaked napkin and turned on him. "What did you just call me?"

"Gab-by," he enunciated.

I got in his face. "Say it one more time, and you're losing your tongue."

"Why, Gabby? I think Gabby is much better than Raven. Don't you think, Gabby?" He backed away chuckling as I advanced on him. It was strange. I was annoyed that he continued to torture me with that name—Gabby? Gag me. But something about his infectious smile, complete with dimples, and my residual good feelings after helping Jenn broke through my normal tough exterior. Suddenly I was laughing, too.

I grabbed a cookie off the tray and shoved it in his mouth. "There! Maybe that'll shut you up." He chuckled around a mouthful of cookie, sputtering crumbs everywhere.

"Gabriella, get back to work! Mr. Murdoch, I know you own this blood bank, but please keep it down."

Callum's arms stopped midreach, and we both turned guiltily toward Nancy.

Callum met my eyes, but we both quickly looked away. He wiped the crumbs from his face and apologized to Nancy.

"That's fine, Mr. Murdoch," Nancy cooed.

She turned to me, her smile replaced with a frown.

"Gabriella, we should go over that paperwork since it is quiet right now."

My cheeks were burning, so I didn't look at Callum before I walked away. What the hell had I been thinking? I had been flirting—flirting!—with Callum Murdoch.

Sure, he had a great ass, and his face was somewhat (really) nice to look at. And sometimes he was kind of funny. But mostly he was annoying. I also couldn't forget the fact that he was my jailer. Flirting with him was not an option unless I was using my feminine wiles to get something I wanted.

I was going to have to be careful with him, that was for sure. I glanced over my shoulder at him as Nancy droned on and on about forms. He was talking on his cell phone. He paused midsentence when he saw me looking at him. Our eyes held for a split second, and then he looked quickly away and continued talking.

Thank goodness he wasn't my type. Because I had a feeling that Callum had some potent wiles of his own.

CHAPTER SEVEN

For the next three days, things weren't so bad. Callum or Kira woke me up. I bitched at them. Then I dressed and went through my Brethren lessons (snore). In the evenings I worked at the blood bank.

Callum assured me that I wouldn't be there every night for the next three months. He just wanted to immerse me in it for a while so I got used to it—or so he claimed. I suspected he was testing me. Making me be around blood and deal with humans until I cracked. But I was pretty proud of myself so far. Other than the couple of slips that first night, I was really getting into the rhythm of the place. Sure, the readily available blood distracted me—that place was like Willy Wonka's factory for vampires. But it didn't totally suck.

Alvin actually proved to have a decent sense of humor for a mortal. Nancy was another story, but luckily she left me alone most of the time. I would never admit this to Callum, but on my second night I "suggested" that she give me some space. Amazing how easy it is to manipulate mortals' minds sometimes. I knew Callum would consider that cheating, which is why I did it when he was out of the room.

Anyway, things weren't exactly what I would call exciting,

but it wasn't too bad. I was even getting used to the taste of bagged blood. Callum told me that he was still trying to get Lifeblood from Logan, who apparently was still acting like a big baby. It's not like I was looking forward to depending on Lifeblood, but I didn't get Logan's deal. I mean, get over it already. Geez.

My body must have begun to adjust to my new sleeping schedule, too, because on the seventh day of my ordeal, I didn't wake up feeling as bitchy as normal. I was far from perky, but no one was in danger of being maimed for talking to me before my coffee, either.

That is, until Callum announced our day's agenda over breakfast.

"Well, Gabby," he said, using the nickname he'd taken to using since my first night at the blood bank, "we have a full day today."

I regarded him over the rim of my huge coffee mug and then took another gulp. Fortified with half a cup so far, my guard didn't go up at his enthusiastic tone. Stupid me.

"It's been a full week since you began on the Sun Shield therapy. Which means we're going outside today."

He barely got the word "today" out before I spewed coffee all over the table.

"The hell!" I yelled as Callum swiped his napkin over his face and shirt. Kira laughed aloud from her dry end of the table. I found nothing funny about the situation. Although, if the situation were different, Callum's expression—a combo of shock and disgust—would have been knee-slapping hilarious.

"First of all, gross," he said as he regarded his coffee-sprinkled eggs. As he looked up at me, a drop of brown liquid fell from his hair and onto his nose. He grimaced and wiped his face again.

"Second, I don't know why you're so shocked. I warned you about this when you started the therapy."

I set my mug down with a thunk. "Yeah, but you could have at least warned me so I could prepare myself."

He shrugged and pushed away his plate. "Prepare? It's not

hard. You just open the front door and walk outside."

I sputtered at his casual dismissal. Kira stepped in before I blew a gasket though.

"Callum, dear, you are forgetting that Raven has never been in the sun."

"Yeah," I said, imbuing the word with indignation.

"I understand that, but it's not like you can ease into something like this. You either go outside when the sun's up, or you don't," Callum said to both of us.

"I vote for don't," I said.

He rolled his eyes. "You don't get a vote."

"I thought democracy was the Brethren way?" I retorted sarcastically.

"It is. But Callum's way trumps the Brethren way when it comes to your rehabilitation," he said.

"How about I show you a little of my way right now, you ass?"

He laughed, "Please. What are you going to do?"

I stood up to show him exactly what I could do, but Kira intervened.

"Sit down, young lady. Callum, stop egging her on."

Plopping back in my seat, I settled for glaring at Callum. He smirked back, making my blood boil. In truth, I wasn't so much angry with him as scared. Not of Callum. Of the sun. Kira was right; I had never been out in the sun. Ever. My whole life it had been a glowing orb of evil to be avoided at all costs. Now they expected me to just forget centuries of ingrained thinking and take a stroll outside.

"Raven, I know you probably have some trepidation about going outside today. However, I can assure you that the Sun Shield is quite effective," Kira said.

I nodded, unconvinced but knowing I had no choice.

"Trust us. It'll be fine," Callum said.

Fifteen minutes later we stood in front of the French doors which opened onto Kira's garden in the back of the house.

"I understand the sunglasses and the hat," Callum said as he tried to ease my grip on his arm. "I even get the turtleneck. But don't you think the rain poncho and gloves are a bit much?"

In my terror I didn't even try to think of a snappy comeback. I might look ridiculous, but all I could think of was protecting every inch of my body from the sun's rays.

"Hey," Callum said, dipping his head to see under the brim of my huge straw hat. "Relax."

"Easy for you to say," I mumbled, not meeting his eyes as I gazed out the windows at the glaring light beyond. Despite Callum's words, my hands trembled, and my heart beat a staccato rhythm. I knew thousands of vampires took Sun Shield and went outside during daylight without any ill effects. But my primitive brain wasn't listening to logic.

"I promise you'll be fine. A little hot maybe with all the clothes . . ." he joked. I frowned at him, letting him know I was in no mood for humor.

"Sorry. Look, I wouldn't let you go out there if I thought there was the slightest chance you'd be harmed, okay?" he said, his deep voice taking on a soothing tone.

"Right. How do I know the pills you've been giving me are really Sun Shield? Maybe this is your way of getting rid of me," I said, my voice sounding a little frantic.

"Now you're just talking crazy. I've never seen you this nervous. Where's the tough-talking bitch vamp I know and loathe?"

His words caused my quivering to stop in its tracks. Damn, he was right. I was a kick-ass chick. Kick-ass chicks didn't quiver in fear when faced with a challenge.

Taking a deep breath, I snapped my spine into line and gritted my teeth. The sun was nothing but a star. Stars weren't scary. They could even be pretty, I told myself.

I lowered my sunglasses and met Callum's challenging gaze with one of my own.

"Let's do this."

I pushed the shades back into place and grabbed the handle. Without waiting for Callum to follow, I pulled the door open with a flourish and marched outside.

It's just a star, it's just a star. I chanted this mantra as my boots clicked down the flagstone steps and onto the grass. Or at least I thought I was stepping on grass. I wasn't sure. My eyes were closed.

I stopped when I realized that tripping in front of Callum would totally ruin the brave front I was putting on for him. I heard a shuffle next to me.

"Gabby?" Callum asked.

"Yeah?" I said.

"Are your eyes open?"

"Of course they're open. Why do you ask?"

A slight snickering sound came from my right. "Because you just trampled my mother's chrysanthemums."

My eyes shot open, and I jumped back, embarrassed. Lifting my heel, I saw clumps of dirt and bruised bright orange petals clinging to my boots.

"Shit."

Callum laughed Aloud then.

"Shut up, Callum Murdoch," I said, putting my hands on my hips.

He laughed harder then. I went to punch his arm, but he was too quick. He walked farther into the garden, which, except for a few splashes of orange or red, was pretty sparse due to the cold weather.

I started to follow him but stopped suddenly. My mouth dropped open as I took in the scene around me. My embarrassment over my mistake had completely distracted me from the fact I was standing outside—at ten o'clock in the *morning*.

A slight breeze blew the tree leaves, creating a kaleidoscope of fall color. The sun-dappled grass was a blanket of emeralds under my feet. Scanning the garden, dazzling orange, yellow, and red fall flowers caught my eye. I had never seen such vivid hues in my life—until I looked up.

Squinting, I scanned the sky—a deep, cool blue sky punctuated with a few fluffy white clouds. I had seen paintings of scenes like this, but they didn't do the reality justice. A painting didn't let a person feel the cool breeze, smell the sharp tang of mowed grass or the smoky smell of fallen leaves. Even the Impressionists couldn't do justice to the vibrant reality of sunlit flowers.

I chanced a glance at the sun, careful not to stare for too long. Instead of being a ball of deadly flame, it appeared more benign—a glowing halo of warmth. My eyes started to leak a little bit. What could I say? Nothing I had seen in my entire life was as beautiful as that sun-washed garden.

I took a deep breath of the intoxicating air, which seemed to smell fresher in the daylight than it did at night. The air at night seemed more seductive somehow—dark and musky. I didn't know which I preferred, but right then the crisp, clean scent was a novelty I wasn't ready to give up.

Someone laughed aloud. I realized with a start it was me. I laughed again and spun around, throwing my arms in the air. I ripped off my hat and shucked my poncho. I rushed over to a small bed of bright yellow flowers and inhaled their scent, which was both spicy and earthy. Heaven. I picked up a crimson leaf from the ground and watched the light play across its surface as I spun the stem in my fingers. I sniffed and smiled, drunk off the aroma of sun and smoke.

I took another deep breath as I scanned the garden once again, looking for more visual treasures. That's when I saw Callum—I had forgotten about him altogether. His dark blond hair was ablaze with golden highlights, and his eyes sparked with green fire. His smirk was gone, replaced by a serious expression I couldn't name.

We stood staring at each other for a few moments, a palpable tension zinging in the space between us. Even though it was October, the day was fairly warm despite the breeze. A bead of sweat dripping between my breasts. Despite having rid myself of the poncho, I decided the sudden heat in my body was a result of my attire. But part of me felt very aware of him physically. As if with his eyes alone he had raised my body temperature.

Remembering the girlish delight I exhibited in the last few minutes, my cheeks burned along with the rest of me. I wanted to be angry with him for witnessing my abandon. Angry at him for being right about the sun being harmless to me now. Angry at him for being so damned infuriating and attractive.

But as he moved toward me, I didn't feel angry. I felt nervous—unsure of myself and exposed. He stood before me for a moment, staring at me with a bemused expression—as if trying to figure out a complex problem. He took one hand and slowly peeled the glove from my fingers.

"I don't think you need these anymore," he said quietly, taking the other hand and removing that glove as well. I stood docile as a lamb, too confused to know how to respond. It was as if he hypnotized me.

I swallowed hard. "Thanks," I said, breathless.

A beat of silence, then, "You should smile more often," he said, still holding my left hand.

The corners of my mouth twitched in a self-conscious facsimile of a smile. Realizing I was acting like an innocent schoolgirl, I pulled my hand from his gentle grasp and stepped back, breaking the spell.

"I'll smile the day I get to leave this place," I said with a flick of my hair.

Disappointment flashed on his face. For some reason I felt guilty for being such a bitch when he'd just complimented me. But Callum wasn't allowed to be nice to me. It made me nervous.

He sighed, seeming resigned that we were reconvening our linguistic sparring. "I told you it wouldn't be so bad," he said motioning to the scene behind him.

"Yeah, it's okay, I guess," I said. "But seriously, I don't see what is so great about being allowed in the daylight."

"For one thing, it allows more flexibility. I couldn't run my business if I was stuck in the house all day."

"So it all comes down to pandering to mortals?"

"Where did you get that from? I help mortals, yes, but they don't rule me."

"Whatever," I said flippantly and wandered away. I could almost hear his teeth grinding behind me. Good, I thought.

This kind of interaction with Callum was more like it. Keep him pissed, and he'd stop looking at me in that way of his that made my insides feel funny.

"So, how long have you been taking Sun Shield?" I asked.

His footsteps shuffled through the grass a few steps behind me. "About twenty years. I have to give you credit. You handled your first time a lot better than I did."

I spun around. "What? You told me it was no big deal!"

He held a hand up, trying to stall my newest tirade. "What was I supposed to say? 'I nearly pissed myself the first time I did this, but don't worry I'm sure you'll be fine?'"

A giggle escaped from me before I could stop it. "You were that scared? What a baby."

"I'll have you know that I was one of the test subjects for Sun Shield. Unlike you, I didn't have the word of anyone else to go by. I had to just trust Logan and hope for the best. So, yeah, I was pretty nervous."

"Wow, I don't think I'd trust anyone enough to take that risk."

"Now why doesn't that surprise me?" he said. "I guess we just had different families. Logan and I have always been pretty close."

The last thing I wanted to talk about was about just how different our families were, so I just nodded.

"So, admit it. It's pretty cool isn't it?" he asked. When I turned and raised my eyebrows in question, he said, "This." He motioned around us.

I hesitated, but considering he already saw my true reaction, it was useless to pretend I wasn't enjoying myself. "Actually, it's pretty spectacular. It's like I entered a different world."

"I know what you mean," he said. "And this is a great time to discover the daylight too. Fall in Raleigh is amazing."

"I didn't even think about that. At night, the seasons change too, but I have no idea what spring really looks like or snow. Or a sunset or sunrise for that matter," I said, getting excited.

"As long as you keep taking the Sun Shield you can see all those things and more."

We continued to stroll through the garden in companionable silence—each wrapped in our own thoughts. I didn't want to tell him that once I left this place, I wouldn't be continuing my treatments. In all honesty, part of me felt depressed at the thought of not being able to experience the world in the daytime anymore.

I stopped and turned to him. "Listen, I . . . never mind," I said quickly and started walking again. He stilled me with a hand on my arm.

"What?" he asked, turning me back around.

I couldn't meet his eyes. As annoying as he could be, I admitted to myself that without Callum I probably never would have known what I was missing.

"I just wanted to thank you for making me come out here today," I said, fiddling with the leaf I had picked up earlier.

I glanced at him when he didn't say anything. I didn't know what to expect, but a blinding smile wasn't it.

"What?" I demanded.

"Give me a moment. I can't believe you actually thanked me for something."

I playfully hit his chest, not able to stop my own smile from forming.

He caught my hand and pulled me closer to him. We both stopped, suspended as we tried to decide what would happen next. Finally, Callum must have decided because without warning, his head swooped down and he placed a quick, firm kiss on my lips.

He pulled back quickly, the whole thing lasting less than three seconds. My mouth fell open as my mind scrambled to figure out what the hell was going on. My mouth tingled where his lips had branded them. Callum looked equally shocked, as if he couldn't believe what he had done.

Quite suddenly, having his lips on mine again was the most important thing in the world to me—more important than breathing. I grabbed the back of his head and roughly pulled him toward me. Our lips crashed into each other hard and fast. As often happens when I feel extreme emotion, my fangs extended. They bumped into his fangs as we angled for better position. Soon our tongues tangled as we figured out a rhythm. I don't know what came over me but I wanted to consume this man. From the way he was grabbing my ass, I figured Callum wanted to do some consuming of his own.

I rubbed my pelvis against his, feeling the diamond-hard erection there. One of his hands left my ass, and he reached up under my turtleneck. I moaned as he took one of my breasts in his hot palm. He rang in response.

Wait a second, I thought. He rang again. With a disgusted sigh, he pulled back, jerked his cell phone off his waist, and glanced at the caller ID.

"Hold that thought," he demanded with a growl, his fangs flashing and his breathing fast.

Shocked, I tried to catch my own breath. I didn't know whether to be insulted or relieved. Then I heard him speak into the phone.

"High Councilman Orpheus, how are you?"

Gone was my confusion. Gone was my lust. In their place, a bright crimson haze of fury rose up. Too distracted with kissing my father's ass, Callum didn't see my fist flying through the air. But he sure as hell felt it.

CHAPTER EIGHT

"Ooof, hey!" Callum yelled at my back as I stalked toward the house.

I had to clench my fists to keep from going back for another wallop. Throwing open the door, I turned for one last look at the bastard's face.

His mouth hung open in shock even as he continued to hold the cell phone to his ear.

"Sorry, sir. Yes, everything is fine," he said finally, staring at me with a bewildered look.

To me he mouthed, "Wait."

Tossing my hair over my shoulder, I marched into the house, slamming the door behind me.

Like I was going to wait for him to stop sucking up to my father. The nerve of that guy!

First, he makes me go out into the sun despite my vigorous protests. Sure, I enjoyed it, but that's not the point. Then he had the nerve to kiss me. Okay, so I'd enjoyed that too, but again, not the point. And after all that, he stopped midsmooch to take a call from my freaking father. That I definitely did not enjoy.

Stomping upstairs to my room, I thought about what had

just happened. Perhaps I was looking at it all wrong.

Instead of being angry with Callum for taking that call, I should be thanking him. Things were getting pretty hot and heavy—which frankly surprised the crap out of me. Who would have thought Callum would turn out to be a world-class kisser?

Anyway, hot and heavy was definitely not something I was prepared for, especially with a man who annoyed me hourly. Besides, I knew from the beginning Callum was only doing this to look good to my father. Somewhere along the way, I guess in between him showing he had a sense of humor and being entranced by the sun, I forgot he only saw me as a project. A means to an end. I didn't know how he thought seducing me would help him with my father, but that had to be it.

I entered my room and flopped down on the cushy down comforter. My anger had burned off somewhat and was replaced by a curious lethargy. Surely, it was just the result of being in the sun too long. No way was I depressed about Callum. It's not like I actually liked the guy.

One thing was for sure. No way was I going to let him work his mojo on me again. My lips and various other parts of my anatomy were off limits from now on. Even if he wasn't a bastard who was trying to use me to impress my father, he was totally not my type. His way of life was in complete opposition to everything I stood for. Sure, the last week of living his way of life hadn't been too bad, but the minute I was free I would go back to my old ways—for the most part.

And Callum's look was all wrong for me too. He was clean cut and professional—I preferred my men with more of an edge. Except, my mind whispered, the last few guys I'd been involved with got boring after a while. It was like "Okay dude, I get it. You're sooo dangerous."

I reminded myself that none of that mattered anyway. From now on, I was going to put the kibosh on any familiarity with Mr. Murdoch. My focus would be getting through the next couple of months without getting any more involved in his life, or the lives of his family, than necessary.

For that matter, I wasn't going to waste my time here lying

around thinking. I needed to get busy on making a plan for after my punishment was up. After pulling myself up from my comfy cocoon, I sat at the small writing desk in the corner of the room.

My first order of business would be writing a note to my minions letting them know I was still alive. My poor minions, I thought. They must be adrift without me.

For a few moments, the only sound in the room was the scribbling of the pen. When I was done, two pages were filled with instructions. Just because I couldn't be there didn't mean they couldn't continue our work in my absence.

Most of the items on the list were mundane, like finding a new lair. But I also instructed them to get to work on a contingency plan in case I needed to go underground. The only way that would happen was if things got really screwed up, and my father made good on his threat of exile. I didn't plan to fail, but a good leader always had a Plan B.

It felt good to work on something productive. But the satisfaction was short-lived when I realized I had no way to get the letter to my minions. When Callum or Kira weren't with me, Hannah was around. They never let me out of the house on my own. My initial wave of excitement dulled as I realized the list was probably a waste of time. I crumpled up the paper and put it under my pillow. I would have put it in the trash, but I didn't want to risk someone finding it when they emptied the basket.

Just when I was about to plop on the bed again in frustration, the doorbell's chime echoed through the house. I went to my window to see who it was.

Sydney was standing on the front porch with a handsome man who was not Logan. The man's dark hair and olive skin contrasted nicely with his pink dress shirt. I wondered who he was until I saw a third person approach the porch carrying a large portfolio. My eyes narrowed when I recognized her— Geraldine Stern, my former minion.

What was she doing here?

That's when I remembered what Sydney had said the other day about Geraldine and Syd's former assistant, Jorge, handling the wedding.

I closed the curtain when the front door opened. The sounds of greetings filtered through the house from the foyer. I briefly debated staying in my room versus making an appearance. Chances were good that if I went down there I'd run into Callum, which, after what had happened in the garden, I wasn't thrilled about. On the other hand, I was curious about how Geraldine would react if she saw me.

She had been one of my star minions. Her work had been impeccable, and she had actually been the mastermind behind Sydney's kidnapping. However, we'd had a falling out when she demanded I turn her into a vampire. She had actually thought I was serious when I promised her just that when she came to work for me. But I was quick to remind her that as a lowly mortal she didn't deserve to become immortal like me. She left in a huff and went straight to Logan to rat me out—the turncoat. She even had the nerve to come with the Murdoch family to "rescue" Sydney and then lecture me about my behavior.

Given her new role as wedding planner for Sydney and Logan, they had obviously forgiven Geraldine for her indiscretions. But I hadn't forgotten. So I decided to go down there and stir up some shit.

When I got downstairs, the sound of laughter and excited conversation came from Kira's study. Apparently, everyone was chattering about the impending nuptials. I glanced into the rooms attached the foyer and was relieved not to see Callum.

Just when I was about to head to the study, I heard a gasp from the vicinity of the front door. The guy I assumed was Jorge stood frozen by the door holding a box overflowing with fabric in one muscled arm. His mouth hung open in shock.

"Yes?" I asked impatiently, anxious to confront Geraldine.

"Oh, honey, no, no, no," he said, finally recovering from his shock enough to walk toward me.

"Excuse me?"

"You're Raven, right? Sydney told me you'd be here. Anyway, that look is all wrong for you. The Goth look is so

1990s. Besides, with your coloring you're definitely a 'summer.'"

"Hey!" I said, swatting his hand away from my hair and backing away. "What the hell are you talking about?"

"All that black you're wearing is washing you out. Your coloring screams 'summer,' meaning you should opt for soft tones, like pink or aqua."

"First off, crazy much? Second, I wouldn't be caught dead in pink. And third, who the hell are you?"

"Let's just say I'm the man who's going to turn you from fashion foolish into fashion fabulous." He snapped his fingers in some bizarre Z pattern in the air. The gesture made him look like some kind of effeminate Zorro.

Before I could figure out what the hell was going on, Sydney walked in.

"Jorge? What's taking you so long?"

When she noticed me, she said, "Oh, Raven. Sorry, I thought Jorge might be talking to Callum out here. We couldn't find him earlier."

"I saw him drive off when I went to the car to grab the box of fabrics," Jorge said.

"Dammit, he knew we were coming over, too. Oh well, we can go over this with Kira and she can fill him in later. Now, what were you two talking about?"

I shook my head because I'd be damned if I had any clue what he'd been gushing about. Jorge, on the other hand, hopped up and down in his excitement to tell her.

"Raven's getting a makeover!" he exclaimed.

My mouth dropped open. I didn't recall any mention of a makeover in his ramblings, and I sure as hell hadn't agreed to get one.

"Now just a damned minute—" I started, but he cut me off.

"First order of business will be getting rid of that awful black hair. What do you use to get it that color? Rub your head inside a chimney? Anyway, that has to go. Then we need to get rid of every piece of black clothing she owns. She looks like a corpse," he babbled.

"Hold on—" I started to protest the insults he was hurling

at my carefully crafted look, but he took off again. I looked at Sydney for support, but she just shrugged and smiled indulgently at the lunatic.

"And the makeup? Way too severe for your features. Besides, smoky eye makeup is for evening only. And you definitely need the works: waxing, facial, manicure, and I would bet my collection of In Style magazines that your feet are in desperate need of a pedi."

Suddenly a piercing whistle interrupted Jorge's recitation of my fashion foibles. We all turned to see Geraldine removing her fingers from her mouth. Kira stood next to her, chuckling.

"What is going on out here?" Geraldine asked. "Jorge, the last time I saw you this excited was the shoe sale at Saks."

"Geraldine! We have a new project." He paused dramatically. "Raven's getting a makeover!" He actually sang the words as if merely speaking them couldn't express his joy at the prospect.

Geraldine's mouth dropped open as she pointed at me.

"That Raven?" she asked, infusing the words with incredulity.

"Now hold on," I said, holding my hands up to stop the insanity. "No one is making me over."

"Oh, come on! It'll be fun," Jorge said, sounding like I just ruined his special dream.

"Actually, it might not be a bad idea," Kira said, hesitantly. "I've been meaning to talk to you about your appearance."

Okay, now I was starting to get offended. I looked at Sydney, who nodded reluctantly. Geraldine stood to the side, looking uncomfortable.

"But I look great," I said defensively. "I'll have you know this skirt is Donna Karen."

"Honey, that may be Donna Karan, but on you it looks like a reject from Elvira's closet."

I gasped, outraged by his continued slander.

"Okay, that's it. I'm not going to stand here and let you insult me. And you," I said, turning on Geraldine to vent my frustration. "How dare you stand there and look smug."

She pointed a finger at her chest. "Me? I'm not smug."

"Like you all aren't enjoying this. It's bad enough I am forced to work in a fucking blood bank and undergo hours of Brethren brainwashing every day. But I draw the line at a makeover. I will not let you people turn me into some kind of Stepford Vampire!"

I wanted to run from the room and go kick something in private, but the pitying looks on their faces stopped me.

"Raven, I know this must be hard for you," Geraldine said quietly. "But you have to know this is all for your own good."

"Don't give me that crap! A week ago you kidnapped Sydney in the hopes I would turn you into someone like me."

Geraldine flashed an apologetic look at Sydney, who smiled back.

"We've forgiven Geraldine for what she did because she has made an honest effort to make up for it. We understand that her actions were misguided and that she never meant to really harm anyone," Sydney said.

"Can you all please give us a moment?" Geraldine asked.

The other three nodded and quietly left the room. Kira shot me a warning look on her way out.

When we were alone, Geraldine turned and met my gaze straight on.

"I know you're here under duress," she said, her expression somber, "but if you know what's good for you, you'll take advantage of this opportunity."

"You're pathetic," I said. "Do you know why I approached you about becoming a minion? Because I could smell the desperation on you."

She closed her eyes as my attack hit home. When she opened them again, I saw a strength I had never noticed before.

"I was foolish. But I actually have you to thank for helping me see the error of my ways."

"Me?" I scoffed.

"Yes, you. If you hadn't refused to turn me, I never would have realized how stupid I was. And I wouldn't have had this second chance at making things right." She laughed a little and shook her head. "So, thank you for being such a bitch."

I put my hands on my hips and regarded her. Her words left me feeling uncomfortable and a little itchy. Where did she get off thanking me for anything?

"You've been listening to Tony Robbins, haven't you?" I asked, trying to defuse my discomfort with sarcasm.

She just shook her head at me. "I hope that one day you'll find what you're looking for."

With that, she turned and left the room, leaving me stunned.

Before I could recover fully, Jorge and Sydney returned.

"So, did you change your mind?" Jorge asked hopefully.

I thought about it for a moment. A makeover sounded like hell on earth.

"You're not going to shut up until I say yes are you?"

Shaking his head, he smiled.

Sighing, I nodded. "Okay, then."

It's not that I had some change of heart or anything, but there was one benefit to letting him change my appearance.

We'd have to leave the house. That meant I'd maybe have a chance to contact the minions in some way. Remembering the letter I'd planned on discarding, my plan fell into place.

"Really?" he squealed. "I have so much work to do! I'll call and make the spa appointments right now. If we're lucky they can fit you in this afternoon."

He spun on his heel and grabbed his cell phone off his waist. Before he made it out of the room, he was already talking to someone. It wouldn't surprise me if he had the number of a spa on speed dial.

Syd turned to me with raised eyebrows. "What made you change your mind?"

I shrugged. "Dunno. Guess I figured it was time to change my approach."

"Huh," she said. "I hope you're ready for this."

"I've never been more ready," I said, thinking of my plan. "If you'll excuse me, I have some things I need to get from my room."

She nodded, looking at me with a speculative gleam in her

eyes. Instead of trying to interpret the look, I turned and ran up the stairs.

Reaching my room, I went straight to the bed and grabbed the letter I had placed there earlier. I smoothed it out and stuck it in my pocket.

By the end of the day, I might regret letting Jorge change my look, but at least I might be able to take some action. Contacting the minions wouldn't get me out of this mess. But I would feel a hell of a lot better with a contingency plan.

I only hoped Jorge had been joking about wearing pink.

CHAPTER NINE

See, the thing was, even with all my preternatural powers, nothing could have prepared me for the agony that is bikini waxing.

It was all I could do not to punch the chick for smiling as she ripped the cloth from my inner thigh. Of course, I was too busy screaming to hit her.

"Oh come on, sissy. It's not that bad," Jorge said from behind the room divider. "You're lucky it's not a Brazilian. Those really sting."

I wasn't about to ask how he knew so much about waxing of the groin region. Some things a person just didn't need to know. Besides, Tammy the Destroyer was slathering on a fresh coat of liquid hot magma to my other thigh.

"Yow!"

"It helps if you don't tense up," Tammy said helpfully.

"You try to remain relaxed when someone's pouring hot wax on your undercarriage."

"I do it myself all the time," she said with a superior smile.

Like that was something to brag about.

"Anyway, you're done," she continued. "Would you like for me to do your mustache too?"

"I do not have a mustache," I said, my hand flying to my upper lip. Bitch. She said that just to be nasty. She's lucky I was on a bottle diet now. Otherwise, she'd be dinner.

Tammy left the room, and I carefully maneuvered myself into a sitting position. The idea of putting my clothes back on wasn't appealing, but with Jorge in the room, I saw no other options.

After slowly pulling my clothes back on, I had to sit down for a minute.

"You okay in there?" Jorge asked.

"I think she ripped my skin off," I said, trying to catch my breath.

"Are you decent?"

"Yeah."

He came around the folding screen and looked me over.

"Oooh, the eyebrow wax did wonders for you," he said. "Really opened up your face."

My eyes narrowed when his gaze went lower.

"Don't even think about it, buddy," I warned. "I still don't see why I had to get a bikini wax anyway."

"You never know when you're going to have visitors at the Chapel of Love," he said with a wink.

"Believe me, no one's going to be praying at this altar anytime soon," I said, hoisting myself off the stool with a wince.

My thoughts briefly flicked to an image of a certain annoying man with a major case of cell phone interruptus, but I ruthlessly pushed them aside. If I was going to endure genital torture for any man, it certainly wouldn't be Callum.

"So what's next?" I asked. Due to the aforementioned vampy powers, the pain was already subsiding—not completely gone, but somewhat bearable.

"Let's see," he said pursing his lips in thought. "You've had your facial, your waxing, and your salt scrub. Next we do hair and makeup."

"Great," I said.

We walked—actually he walked, and I limped—to the door.

In addition to my various beauty treatments, we'd already scoured the shopping mall for new clothes, shoes, and accessories. If I'd thought I was a professional shopper, I'd learned I was an amateur compared to Jorge.

He dragged me through stores like a general leading an attack, tossing garments at me until my arms overflowed. A shocking amount of pastel pieces filled the dressing room I entered at Jorge's command. Ignoring all my protests, he made me model each piece. He then proceeded to critique everything with the eyes of connoisseur.

Though I would never admit this to him, he was right about everything. I had been wearing black for so long I had no idea that soft pink made my cheeks rosy, or that robin's egg blue complimented my brown eyes. Granted, the colors didn't jive with my carefully cultivated kick-ass persona, but I didn't look half-dead anymore.

Even though the day hadn't been total hell as I'd been expecting—painful waxing notwithstanding—I knew I was about to have a fight on my hands over the hair.

Three hours later, Jorge and Mimi, the colorist, were high-fiving each other. I sat stunned in my chair, staring at the stranger in the mirror. Gone was the seriously badass chick I knew and loved. In her place sat a bright-eyed, rosy-cheeked beauty I didn't recognize.

"Oh. My. God." Jorge touched the soft waves Mimi had created by adding layers to my hair. "You look gorgeous!"

I smiled weakly, still in shock. Granted, mocha brown wasn't too drastic a change from black. But the new hair combined with the new makeup was too much. I was wearing pink lip gloss for fuck's sake.

"Mimi, you're a genius," Jorge said, giving her a kiss on the cheek.

"All she really needed was to tone down the black. It was too severe for her features. The makeup is softer too, which makes her appear more approachable."

Approachable? Vampires weren't approachable. At least not this one, I thought. What they really meant was that I looked vulnerable. Weak.

"I hate it," I said. Their excited chatter died instantly, leaving the room in shocked silence.

"What do you mean? You look amazing," Mimi said, her eyebrows furrowing in confusion.

I merely shook my head as I felt my eyes begin to sting. What had I let them do to me? I despised weakness. Yet there I sat looking like a sorority girl—bright eyes, shiny hair, glowing skin. It was disgusting.

"Raven, what's wrong?" Jorge asked, his voice deepening with concern as he laid a hand on my arm.

"Everything's wrong! Don't you see? This," I said, motioning to the mirror, "it's not me. That's not me."

Jorge's laugh sounded strained, "But it is you. Your hair and makeup don't make who you are. You're still you."

But he was wrong. How could I still be me if I didn't feel like me anymore?

"I think you need to give it some time. It must be a shock," Jorge said. "I think if you give it a chance, you'll like it."

I shook my head. They'd never understand.

Since the minute I'd arrived in Raleigh, everyone had been trying to change me. I thought I had resisted their attempts pretty well until then.

Looking at myself, I realized how much I relied on my appearance as a shield. It kept everyone at arm's length, just how I liked it. The hair and clothes I wore before were almost like a costume I wore to play the role of Raven.

But the woman staring back at me—the one with the overbright eyes and the trembling lips—she was Gabby.

"Let's give her a few moments," Mimi whispered.

"No," I said. "I just need some fresh air."

By "fresh air" I of course meant I needed a smoke. They nodded and quietly watched me leave the room.

The place seemed deserted as I walked down the hall toward the small courtyard where spa guests relaxed between treatments. A glance at my watch explained it. Seven o'clock. Thus far, the makeover from hell totaled about eight hours.

We'd literally closed down the place. The whole ordeal had wiped me out emotionally and physically. I needed to be alone for a few minutes.

As I passed the empty treatment rooms, I took a deep breath. The chemical smell of hair dye in the salon had given way to the relaxing scent of candles and the fruity tang of body scrubs. The saccharine sounds of an Enya CD wafted through the hall.

But I knew I'd never fully relax until I had taken control of my life. Having a Plan B would ease my mind. As I passed the spa office, a thought occurred to me. Through the dark doorway, I saw a computer monitor glowing. After looking around quickly to ensure no one saw me, I ducked into the office and closed the door.

After jiggling the mouse to turn off the screensaver, I saw what I was looking for: Internet access. With a few clicks, I was on my Web-based mail system, quickly typing a message to my minions. This was working out perfectly, I thought as adrenaline surged through me. Even though I didn't know when I could access my account again, I could at least give them Kira's address and my schedule so they could find me.

I hit the Send button and leaned back in the desk chair, relieved. By morning each of my minions would know where to find me.

I didn't let myself think about the fact that my father would most likely hunt me down. Instead, I thought about how great it would feel to be back with my people again. People who adored me and didn't try to change me. People who didn't judge my every action and find it lacking.

But I couldn't afford to dally in the office any longer, so I got up and slowly opened the door. After peering down the hallway to make sure the coast was clear, I strolled back to the salon. I didn't need the numbing nicotine or privacy of the courtyard anymore. I had a backup plan.

#

"C'mon, just go down there."

"No."

"Raven, you're being a big baby," Jorge said.

"I look like a baby in all this pastel shit!"

"You're chicken," he challenged.

Here was the thing. I had hung out with Jorge all day. Despite his insistence that I was a moron in the fashion department, he was pretty cool. But no one called me "chicken."

"Take that back," I demanded.

He smiled and crossed his arms. "Bawk bawk!"

I ground my teeth against the attack of pride welling up in my stomach. Nothing he could say would make me go downstairs. I didn't want to see Callum, and I certainly didn't want to go out with him. I wanted to ring Jorge's neck for this asinine plan. Seemed he thought it was a shame for me to waste my "fabulous new look" by sitting around the house tonight. So he convinced Callum to take me out on the town. As if.

"First of all, I am not some pathetic person who needs my fairy gay mother to find dates for me," I said, ticking off the reasons on my fingers. "Second, Callum Murdoch is the last man I'd choose to hang out with right now. I haven't seen him since he ki—" I abruptly closed my mouth as I realized what I'd almost said.

"When he what?" Jorge's eyes narrowed, and I swear his ears perked up.

"Nothing," I said, trying to sound nonchalant.

"Hmm. Kicked you?" he asked, being purposefully obtuse.

"Yeah, right," I scoffed. The day that man kicked me was the day he lost a leg.

He laughed. "So Callum kissed you, huh? Girl, you have to give me details!"

"No, I don't. Besides, I barely even remember it."

"Right, that's why you're hiding out up here," he taunted.

"I am not hiding! I merely find him boring," I said, examining my nails.

Jorge just stared at me. As the silence stretched out, I started to get fidgety. *I am not nervous about seeing him*, I told myself. Jorge's eyebrow raised in challenge.

"I hate you," I said as I marched to the door.

His laughter followed me out the door. "Don't do anything I wouldn't do!"

As I walked down the stairs, the butterflies began. I nervously patted the pink peasant skirt that swirled around my ankles with every step. The silver bangles on my right wrist jangled as I smoothed my hair.

I had to get a grip. What did I care what Callum thought about my new look?

As I reached the ground floor, I heard voices coming from the sitting room to my right. Instantly my ears picked up Callum's deep voice.

". . . only doing this because I feel bad about ducking out of the wedding meeting today."

I stopped in my tracks as my hackles rose. So he was just doing this for Syd, was he? Well, great. I had two choices. I could turn around and go back upstairs, thereby letting him off the hook. Or I could march in there and make this the worst night of his life.

It took me a nanosecond to decide.

"Oh, Raven! Don't you look lovely!" Kira said when she saw me stride into the room. I didn't spare her a look as I made a beeline for my date.

Callum turned from the bar. When he saw me bearing down on him, his mouth fell open, and he froze, drink halfway to his lips.

I walked right up to him and grabbed his drink. After downing the burning whisky, I slammed the tumbler down. Callum didn't move a millimeter.

"What are you staring at?" I demanded.

His mouth opened and closed like a guppy's a few times.

"Well? Spit it out. I don't have all night."

He continued to stare; only this time his eyes scanned my whole body. When his eyes rose again, he swallowed hard.

"I'll be damned," he whispered, a slow smile spreading across his face.

I grasped onto my indignation, even though his words made

me feel a little flutter of warmth.

We continued to stand there until Kira cleared her throat.

"It's truly remarkable," she said, breaking the tension. "Jorge's a miracle worker."

I snapped out of my trance and drug my gaze away from his admiring eyes. It was time to clear some things up.

"All right, look. I know it's new and everything. But do you guys mind? It's not like I was toothless and warty before."

"Oh, dear." Kira brought her hand to her mouth. "I'm sorry. We didn't mean to insinuate that you were ugly before. But you have to admit your look was a tad . . . rough."

My cheeks burned. Had I really looked that bad?

"Mother, that's enough. Raven's right. It's not that you looked bad before. But the all-black thing was a little standoffish. But now. Now, you're . . . pretty."

The burning in my cheeks increased, only now it was due to embarrassment rather than anger. No one had ever called me pretty. Kick-ass? Check. Sexy? Check. But pretty? Never.

"Look, can we go already?" I said to cover my reaction to his compliment.

A slow smile spread across his face. Gone was the guy who sounded like he would rather get a sharp stake in his heart than go out with me.

"Absolutely."

CHAPTER TEN

"Stop staring at me, and keep your eyes on the road," I demanded twenty minutes later.

His gaze swiveled back to the road. "Sorry, I just can't get over it. Has anyone ever told you that you look like Angelina Jolie?"

I snorted. "Yeah, I get that all the time."

"I mean it. You look really good," he said, meeting my eyes.

There went that damned blush again.

"By the way," he said, looking at the road again. "I'm sorry about today."

Now, I could have approached this two ways. One, I could have ripped into him and made him beg for forgiveness. Or, two, I could have played dumb and let him dig himself into a deeper hole—before I made him beg for forgiveness.

"Oh? For making me mad at breakfast? Don't worry about it," I said, staring out the window.

"No. Not that," he said hesitantly.

"Then you must mean for making me go out into the sun even though it terrified me. Think nothing of it," I said with a wave of the hand.

"Thanks, but that wasn't what I meant either," he said, his

tone impatient.

"Well then, Callum, I have absolutely no idea what you think you need to apologize for."

"Cut the shit, Raven. You know damned well what I mean."

I turned to him then, ready for the kill. "You mean for kissing me?"

He stopped the car at a red light and turned toward me. His eyes almost glowed in the darkness of the car. "No, that I most definitely am not sorry about."

His words gave me pause. I could feel the tables turning on me as I sat there, and I didn't like it one bit. I opened my mouth to put him in his place, but he cut me off.

"If I am sorry for anything, it's that I didn't keep kissing you instead of answering that phone."

My mouth dropped open. "What? Of all the nerve! You're apologizing for not kissing me more?"

"Damn straight, sweetheart."

"You're going to need a larger car. This one isn't big enough to hold both your ego and your fat head!"

The light turned green. He punched the accelerator, a smug smile on his lips.

"Protest all you want, but I figured you out. At first I thought you hit me because I took the call from your father. But the more I thought about it, the more I realized you were pissed because I stopped kissing you."

I sputtered, unable to form coherent words powerful enough to tell him he was the biggest idiot on the planet.

"Act indignant all you want. But you're forgetting something—I was there. That was my ass you were grabbing. You want me."

"Stop. The. Fucking. Car."

He laughed. "Nope."

"Callum, I swear to the goddess, if you don't stop this car . . ."

"You'll what?" he challenged.

"I'll, I'll . . . I don't know what, but it will involve pain and your balls."

He laughed again. "As intimidating as that is, I'm afraid you'll have to spare my balls. We're here."

That's when I became aware of my surroundings again. He pulled up to the valet stand in front of a three-story Victorian house. Before I could argue with him anymore, a valet guy pulled open my door and offered me a hand.

"Stuff it," I said, getting out on my own. The bewildered kid stepped back immediately.

"Uh, welcome to Empire, ma'am," he muttered and scurried back to the stand.

Callum, in the meantime, had walked around the car. He tried to take my arm, but I yanked it back.

"Try it again, and you'll pull back a bloody stump," I growled.

He chuckled and held out a hand, indicating I should precede him up the wide steps to the front porch of the house.

"Where the hell are we anyway?" I threw over my shoulder as he followed me.

"You'll see," he said.

I stomped across the wide planked porch to a pair of French doors. Before I reached the threshold, a man in a tuxedo opened them for us.

"Welcome back to Empire Grille, Mr. Murdoch."

"Thanks, Phillip. Is our table ready?"

"Of course, sir. Ma'am, if you'll follow me?"

Phillip led us through a dimly lit entryway. I didn't really know what to expect, but I was shocked when we entered the next room. What must have been a parlor when the house was a residence had been turned into a lovely dining room. Chandeliers glowed overhead, making the crystal and silver on the tables sparkle. In the corner sat another man in a tux playing a violin. Well-dressed patrons chatted and laughed over glasses of wine. The aromas of juicy steaks and spicy pasta dishes wafted through the room. My mouth started watering instantly.

I expected Phillip to lead us to one of the tables in that room, but he continued on to a narrow staircase. As Phillip started up, I glanced at Callum. He nodded and touched my back, indicating I should follow. I jerked away from his touch, but I could still feel the heat from his fingers on my back. Instead of focusing on that, I concentrated on climbing the steps without tripping.

At the top, Phillip indicated I should precede him through a doorway to another room. The private room was, in a word, gorgeous.

My eyes narrowed as he sat us at the small table next to a large window. A few blocks down, the state capitol glowed, surrounded by oak trees. Candles on the windowsill and on the marble mantel, as well as the blazing fire in the fireplace, were the room's only light. It was a setting designed for privacy. Or seduction.

Callum chatted with Phillip as I quietly seethed. When Jorge said we were going out, I figured we'd go grab a beer somewhere. I had no idea Callum was going to take me to what was probably one of the nicest restaurants in the city. I gazed down at my outfit. The peasant skirt and white blouse seemed too casual for this place. I hated that flash of insecurity.

After Callum ordered a bottle of wine, Phillip left, discreetly closing the door behind him.

I didn't waste anytime. "You're an ass!"

He merely chuckled. "I thought we'd already established that."

"How dare you insinuate that the only reason I was angry today was because you interrupted that pathetic kiss. Because seriously, Callum? I was relieved when the phone rang."

"Oh, really? Then why did you punch me?"

"Because you kissed me!"

He placed his elbows on the table and leaned in. "Correct me if I'm wrong, but I don't recall you protesting during the kiss."

"I was just trying to figure out where I wanted to punch you," I said lamely.

"Uh-huh."

"Don't 'uh-huh' me! You had no right to kiss me."

He leaned back and regarded me for a moment. Then he

said, "You're right."

Well, color me surprised.

"Huh?"

"Look, I was as surprised as you were when it happened. It's not like I went outside planning on kissing you. In fact, most of the time I'm thinking about throttling you."

I ignored the last part because frankly I felt the same way about him.

"So why'd you do it?"

"Honestly? I guess I kind of got carried away in the moment. There you were so excited and happy. It was refreshing," he shrugged. "Anyway, it was a mistake."

I shoved down the disappointment I felt at his admission. In its place confusion stepped in.

"Wait, so what was all that bullshit in the car about me begging for it?"

He ran a hand through is hair. "I don't do apologies well. And when you started acting like you didn't even remember what happened, it bruised my ego. I figured the easiest way to deal with it without making either of us more uncomfortable was to piss you off."

I sat back in my chair, chewing over what he said. While I didn't like his methods, I kind of understood his reasoning in a weird way.

"So, you agree the kiss shouldn't have happened?"

He nodded. "I think we should just chalk it up to a mistake and move on. It's not like we're actually attracted to each other, right?" He laughed as if he'd just told the funniest joke ever.

I laughed too, but it was forced. It wasn't that I was attracted to him. But part of me wanted him to be attracted to me.

"Of course we're not attracted to each other. I mean I barely want to be in the same room as you most of the time."

"Right," he said with a strained laugh. "So we just forget it ever happened and focus on getting through the next few months without killing each other."

I nodded, wondering where the wine was. For some reason I

was parched. My prayers were answered when the waiter hurried in with a bottle after a brief knock. As he poured the pinot noir he rambled on about the specials.

I watched Callum out of the corner of my eye. For an ass, he looked kind of good. The grey pinstriped suit emphasized his broad shoulders, and his crisp white dress shirt contrasted nicely with his tanned skin. Then I reminded myself that everyone looked good in candlelight. Of course, my warped mind decided at that moment to wonder if he thought I looked good too. Stupid mind.

I grabbed my wine glass and took a sip as the waiter left. The oaky aroma and smooth taste were like heaven.

"That's nice," I said with a sigh as the wine warmed my insides, helping me relax.

"Listen," Callum said, twirling the stem of his glass in his long fingers. "I've been thinking about this whole project. I know it's only been a week, but you're doing pretty well."

"Yeah," I said with a grimace. I didn't want to be "doing well." Doing well meant I was changing.

"What?" he asked, looking confused by my sullen response.

"Nothing," I said, reaching for a piece of the bread the waiter left. I tore off a piece and shoved it into my mouth.

"I have to admit I didn't think you'd last the week. Hell, I didn't think you'd last two days," he chuckled, apparently completely unaware of my rising agitation.

"But you've done well. I mean you still have a long way to go, but . . ." He shrugged and took another sip of wine.

"Is that what you told my father?" I asked before I could stop myself.

He nodded. "Yeah. I told him that, all things considered, you were coming along nicely. He didn't— Never mind."

"He didn't what?" I demanded, even though I could already guess what my father had said. "On second thought, don't bother. I can tell you what he said. He didn't believe you, did he? Then he reminded you of all my faults and told you I probably wouldn't last another week. Am I right?"

Callum winced. He opened his mouth to speak, but I cut

him off.

"Don't worry about it. My father has never been my biggest fan," I said, taking another slice of bread and tearing it into crumbs.

"What's the deal with you two anyway?" he asked, looking genuinely interested.

"I don't want to bore you with the details."

"C'mon," he goaded.

"We just see things differently is all," I said with a shrug. "He's all gung ho on pushing the Brethren doctrine of democracy and living in harmony with the hairless apes. And I think everything he says is bullshit."

"So you don't see any redeeming value in trying to get along with mortals?"

"It's not the getting along with them I object to. It's the trying to become them I have a problem with."

He laughed. "We're not trying to become mortal."

"Really, Callum? What separates you from an average guy besides the fact you need blood to supplement your diet?"

"Well, there is the small issue of immortality."

"What kind of treat is that? Have you seen these people? They live in a freakin' rat race. And you want to do that for eternity?"

"I still don't get what you have against them."

Before I could answer, the waiter came back to take our orders. I had forgotten to look at the menu he'd left earlier. However, Callum insisted on ordering for both of us. Normally I would have taken him to task for going all alpha male on me, but when he ordered two rare steaks, I decided to let it slide.

The waiter left. "You were saying?" Callum prodded.

"Actually I wasn't. This whole conversation is boring. It's not like I'm going to change your mind."

"It only seems fair that you give your side. After all, you've had the Brethren philosophy shoved down your throat all week. Why not take this chance to explain your theories to me?"

I took a deep breath. For so long, people had been preaching to me about how I should think. I wasn't used to someone actually asking me what I thought.

"What year were you born?" I asked. He looked surprised but didn't question my reason for asking.

"In 1698."

"Hah, you're just a baby."

"How old are you?"

"Four hundred and eleven."

"You're the only female I've ever met who brags about being older than someone else," he chuckled.

"Whatev. Okay, so you were born where? Scotland?"

"Yes, near Inverness."

"Oooh, ever see Nessy?" I asked.

"Be serious," he said.

"What?"

"The Loch Ness monster is a legend."

"Uh, hello? So are vampires."

"Hmm. I never thought of it that way. Well, no, I've never seen her," he said. "And what does all this have to do with you telling me your theories?"

"It has everything to do with it! My father is a logical man. He sees things in black and white. Me? I believe in shades of grey. I don't think science and rational thinking can explain everything. You think our kind is the result of a genetic mutation, right?"

He nodded. "Logan is actually working on proving that theory. But, yes, we believe we're basically genetic cousins to humans."

"See, you all believe it, but there's no proof. So who's to say my theory that we were placed here by the goddess for a special purpose is wrong?"

He refilled my wine glass as he mulled that over. "For one thing, we have proof that genetic mutations exist. And frankly, your theory requires a lot more faith in the unseen than ours does."

"And what is wrong with faith?" I asked, leaning forward. I was surprised to find I was actually enjoying the debate.

He snorted. "Faith is what has kept humans busy killing

each other for centuries. It's an excuse people use to justify all sorts of horrible behavior."

"That's true," I said, rolling the stem of my glass between my palms. "But an awful lot of horror has been committed in the name of science, too."

He nodded. "Agreed. So what is your specific theory?"

"I believe that the goddess Diana put us here—" I began, only to be interrupted by the waiter returning with a large tray.

The savory scent of grilled steaks and the earthy aroma of baked potatoes filled the room. My mouth watered. I'd slugged down a couple of bags of blood when I got home from the spa, but I hadn't eaten real food since breakfast.

The waiter left after distributing the food. We busied ourselves with loading our potatoes and chatting about how good everything looked for a few moments.

The meat was so tender I almost didn't need a knife. I moaned when the flavor burst on my tongue.

I looked up to see if Callum liked his food only to catch him staring at me with his fork frozen halfway to his mouth.

"What?" I asked.

"Nothing," he said quickly and stuffed his first bite into his mouth.

After chewing for a moment, he said, "You were about to tell me about the goddess."

I had been so busy enjoying the meal that I forgot all about our conversation.

"Oh, right. How familiar are you with mythology, the goddess Diana in particular?"

Nodding, he said, "Goddess of the hunt."

"Yes, in Italy, there are witches, called the *strege*. According to their beliefs, they were created by Aradia, daughter of the goddess Diana, to help combat the forces of Lucifer."

Callum's eyes started to glaze over, so I got to the point.

"What if we were created by Diana as well? What if there is some divine plan for us?"

He perked up then. "What do you mean?"

"I mean what if we aren't here as some freak product of

nature? What if someone or something created us for a higher purpose?"

"I was around a long time before the Brethren Sect was created. I remember the chaos that existed. The superstition. The violence. My own father was a victim of those who wanted vampires to keep to themselves," he said, tension clear in the set of his jaw.

"I don't know if we have a purpose anymore than a mortal can know for sure what his purpose is. But what I do know is things are much more peaceful now that we have come together under the laws of the sect."

"So you'd prefer to just accept that things are easier this way than question whether things are right?"

"Who are you or anyone else to say what is right?"

"Ah, but my father is perfectly content deciding what is right for everyone, though. Do you honestly think anyone on that council would dare question him? Who do you think wrote those laws?"

"Okay, for the sake of argument, let's agree that your father is dictating the laws . . ."

"He is," I interrupted.

"Okay, so what does all of this have to do with you trying to stop the advances we've made in recent years?"

"You mean like the protests against Lifeblood and Sun Shield?" I asked.

He nodded impatiently.

"They're totally against everything I stand for," I explained. "They make us forget what separates us from humans."

"But I still don't get how they go against what you stand for. All you have said is that we were created by Diana for some purpose. If you don't know that purpose, how can you be sure our advancements are wrong?"

I looked at him for a moment, totally unsure how to respond. No one had ever asked me that before, and frankly it threw me for a loop.

"Because," I said, stalling as my brain scrambled to come up with a good reason.

Callum laughed. "Because? That's compelling."

"What do you want me to say? They just are."

"I find it funny that you've been fighting against everything my family and your father have been working for without any evidence it goes against some master plan."

"Callum, that's the difference between us. You want logical explanations for everything. Me? I believe in faith."

"I have faith that you're wrong. Does that count?"

I gritted my teeth. We had actually been having a decent time, and I didn't want to spoil the relaxing mood by starting another fight.

"I guess we're going to have to agree to disagree," I said finally.

He blinked. "No arguments?"

"Nope," I said casually, finishing off my wine.

"Huh. You surprise me, Gabby," he said with a grin.

Okay, that had to stop.

"Don't call me that."

"But why? It's your name. I heard your father say it."

"Look, I stopped going by my birth name a century ago. Only my father calls me Gabriella, and no one calls me Gabby."

"Why did you change your name?"

"When my father took over the Brethren Council, he kept trying to get me to buy into the bullshit he was selling the members of the sect. Changing my name was an act of protest."

"But why 'Raven'? It's a little cliché don't you think?"

"But that's exactly why I chose it. When I changed my name, I became a crusader for preserving the old ways. I needed a name that reflected that."

"Interesting. So you're saying that the whole Gothic persona was an act?"

I sighed impatiently. "No, Callum, it's not an act. It was more like I took things to an extreme. It is still me, but exaggerated to make a point."

"You mean it was still you."

"What?"

"You said, 'it is,' but you don't look like the stereotypical vampire you see in movies anymore."

I clenched my teeth at the reminder of the makeover from hell.

"Let's make one thing perfectly clear, shall we?" I asked.

He nodded.

"You can change how I look and what I eat, but I'm still me. I won't let you or anyone take away who I am. Got it?"

He fell silent for a moment. I think I threw him off. It was a good feeling.

"Who are you?" he asked quietly.

I blinked, not quite understanding his question.

"I'm me," I said with a shrug.

"But who are you? You spout all this BS about your beliefs, but from what I've seen you have built your entire life around rebelling against your father."

"That's not true," I said. His words pissed me off. Everyone thought they had me all figured out. But they didn't. I had layers. Like an onion.

"Tell me one thing you've done in the last decade that was somehow not related to your father," Callum challenged.

I thought about that for a moment. Surely there was something I'd done just for me. When nothing came to mind, I squirmed in my seat. Callum was wrong, but I'd be damned if I could think of anything to prove it. I couldn't let him know that, though.

"Screw you. I don't have to explain myself to you."

"A little defensive aren't we?"

I wanted to smack that smug smile from his face.

"I'm just sick to death of everyone thinking they know what's best for me," I said. "Isn't it enough that I'm here, and I'm going through this ridiculous twelve-step program?"

"It's enough if you're serious about it. But frankly, sometimes I wonder if you understand how serious your situation is. Do you want to be exiled?"

I leaned forward and looked into his eyes. "Callum, I would rather stake myself than live for two hundred years in isolation. If you or anyone else think I don't understand what will happen if I don't pass this test, you're wrong. Dead wrong."

He nodded as if satisfied with my response. I tamped down the voice in my head that reminded me of my email that afternoon. The council would put me on its most wanted list if I ran away. If they caught me, I wouldn't be exiled. I'd be banished. Forever.

I knew that, and yet as I looked at the man across from me I felt fear. Not fear of banishment, but fear that he might know me better than I wanted to admit.

"Like I said, you're doing pretty well," Callum said, breaking into my thoughts. "Just don't screw it up."

I laughed. "Thanks for the vote of confidence."

"You're welcome," he said, showing his dimples.

Uncomfortable with the warm feeling his smile caused, I looked down and realized that I had polished off the steak in record time. Callum's plate was clean too. The waiter returned, and Callum took care of the check.

"Thanks for the meal. It was delicious," I said.

"No problem."

An awkward silence ensued. I wasn't really ready to go home, but I didn't want to ask him if we could go somewhere else. After all, he was just doing this as a favor. He was probably anxious to be rid of me.

"So, you want to continue our conversation in the bar?"

I blinked. That was the last thing I expected him to say.

"Sure, I guess," I said, not wanting to convey my relief.

We didn't say much as we left the room and headed back downstairs to the bar area. But I was feeling pretty relaxed after the meal and the wine. Until I saw Logan and Sydney sitting not ten feet away.

"Shit," I mumbled under my breath.

Callum didn't hear me because he was too busy calling out to his brother. Logan smiled when he saw Callum, but it faded into a frown when he saw me.

I fell back behind Callum as he led the way to the table where they sat.

"Hey, bro. Syd," he said, leaning down to give his future

sister-in-law a hug.

"Callum, what are you doing here?" Sydney asked. She hadn't seen me yet.

Callum reached behind him and pulled me forward. "Raven and I were having dinner."

Syd's mouth fell open when she saw me.

"Raven! Oh my gosh, I almost didn't recognize you. You look amazing!"

"Thanks," I mumbled, embarrassed that her exclamation had several other diners looking at me. I had almost forgotten about the makeover. I wasn't thrilled by the reminder.

"I thought after a day being subjected to Jorge she needed to get out of the house tonight," Callum said.

I looked at him in shock. He could have easily told them Jorge talked him into taking me out.

"What are you two up to?" Callum asked, not noticing my look.

"Nothing special. Just finished dinner," Sydney said.

I noticed that the pair seemed like complete opposites. Where Sydney was friendly and talkative, Logan sat there with a scowl, saying nothing.

"We're headed to the bar. Care to join us?" Callum asked.

"Actually . . ." Logan began, only to be cut off by his fiancée.

"We'd love to," Syd said with a big smile.

I wasn't much on feminine intuition, but something told me Sydney was trying to play peacemaker. Logan was still mad at Callum for his part in bringing me back here. She probably thought getting them to relax over a couple of drinks might ease the tension.

I just wanted to leave. The last thing I needed was to have Mr. Grumpy Pants scowling at me all night.

"Great, shall we?" Callum said, putting a hand on my back to guide me toward the bar. I hesitated, trying to think of a way to get out of this. I glanced up at Callum, and he gave me a look that clearly stated I had no choice in the matter.

Reluctantly I started moving. Sydney fell in next to me,

chattering away with questions about the makeover.

Girl talk. Gag.

Behind us, Callum tried to make chitchat with his brother only to receive monosyllabic responses.

I was officially on the double date from hell.

CHAPTER ELEVEN

The bar sat toward the back of the house. Lined with bookcases, it obviously had served as a library when it was still a residence. The bar itself was made of rich mahogany with shiny brass accents. French doors opened onto a patio, which was currently empty due to the chilly autumn weather.

We chose a table toward the back, away from the few other patrons. Across the room, a cheerful fire crackled. The room smelled of wood smoke and scotch.

Logan held out Sydney's chair. She smiled at her fiancé, her teeth flashing white in the dim room. Callum tried to pull out my chair too, but my scowl made him back off. I was in no mood for fake gallantry. I wanted a drink and a cigarette.

While we waited for a waiter, I grabbed a smoke from my purse. I was about to light up when Logan decided to comment.

"That's a disgusting habit."

I paused, my unlit lighter poised before the cigarette in my lips. Deliberately, I flicked it to life and took my time inhaling my first drag. Then I blew the smoke in his direction.

He coughed and swatted the smoke away from his face. "Do you mind?"

"No, I don't mind at all."

"I see that despite your new look, you're still a bitch in sheep's clothing."

Leaning forward, I pointed my cigarette at him. "And don't you forget it, asshole."

He started to lean forward, menace clear in his movements, but Sydney put a hand on his arm to stop him.

"So, Raven, tell us how your work is going at the blood bank," Sydney said, trying to play peacemaker again.

I took another drag and exhaled before answering. Where was the waiter anyway?

"It's okay, I guess. They've got free cookies."

Syd chuckled, but Logan continued to look as if he'd like to ram the cigarette down my throat. Callum signaled for the waiter.

"She's doing pretty well," Callum said.

Before I could react to his public support, the guy arrived to take our orders.

Syd asked for a white wine spritzer. The men ordered scotches, neat. I ordered a shot of tequila.

No one commented at my choice of beverage, but Syd raised her eyebrows. Callum chuckled. Logan's scowl deepened.

"Logan, how's the Lifeblood roll out coming along?" Callum asked.

"It's fine," Logan responded.

Syd shifted uneasily in her seat, clearly wanting to start the healing between the brothers.

"Callum, don't listen to him. It's going great," she said, smiling at her betrothed. "He even altered the formula for me so it tastes like chocolate milk instead of blood."

"What?" I asked, nearly choking on my last drag.

"Oh, it's silly, I know. But it's not like it's easy to get used to the idea of drinking blood, or at least something that tastes like blood."

I guessed she had a point. Since I was raised with the stuff, it was natural to me. But I guess a mortal might have trouble with it.

"When do I get a case?" Callum asked.

"As long as *she's* here, you won't," Logan said, crossing his arms.

"Logan, be reasonable," Callum said, frowning.

"Reasonable? Explain to me how it's reasonable to expect me to give it to her when she did everything in her power to ruin Lifeblood?"

I was just about sick of people talking about me like I wasn't there. Unfortunately, the waiter arrived, preventing me from laying into Logan.

As I plotted my response, I licked my hand, poured the salt, and tossed back the shot. Then I slammed the glass on the table and sucked on the lime. My companions watched me quietly, obviously aware of my growing agitation.

I slowly wiped my mouth with the back of my hand. Then I focused on Logan's face, making sure he was paying attention.

"I'll tell you what. You can take Lifeblood and stick it up your ass."

Sydney gasped, and Callum was dead silent as he waited to see what Logan would do. I sat back and took another drag.

Logan took a sip of his scotch and regarded me over the glass. The tension at our table was palpable. The mortals in the bar continued with their laughter and conversation, unaware that a group of vampires sat in their midst.

"Nice display," Logan finally said. "But you and I both know that you're going to end up exiled. Why not quit now?"

"Logan!" Sydney said. "That's enough."

Logan looked at Sydney, the muscle in his jaw working. "It's true. The charade is ridiculous. I'm not wasting Lifeblood on her."

"Logan, you're being an asshole," Callum said, stealing the words out of my mouth. "None of us have a choice in this. It's the dictate of the council. Whether she fails or not, we have to do everything we can to rehabilitate her."

Their words stung. It seemed everyone was just waiting for me to fail.

And hadn't I sent an email to my minions that very day just in case I quit, thus fulfilling their expectations?

My pride took over. I wanted nothing more at that moment than to prove them wrong. Sure, it would mean many more weeks of pain-in-the-ass tasks and dealing with shit I didn't think I deserved.

"You know what? I don't need Lifeblood to succeed. I can continue living off the bagged blood."

Callum cleared his throat and wouldn't look at me. He was hiding something. I looked at Syd and Logan for a clue, but they looked as confused as I felt.

"Callum?" I said.

"What?" he said nonchalantly, still not looking at me.

"You'd better spill whatever you're hiding over there," I said. "You don't want me to make a scene."

He sighed and met my eyes. "Fine. I didn't want to tell you this, but your father decided that you had to use Lifeblood exclusively, or he'd consider your rehabilitation failed. That's why I've been pushing Logan to give us a few cases."

I laughed humorlessly. "He knew Logan wouldn't want me to have it, right?"

Callum nodded, his eyes sympathetic. "I'm sorry."

"So, dear old dad wants me to fail, too, huh?"

"Raven," Sydney said, her voice sympathetic.

"No, it's fine. Whatever."

Syd nudged Logan. They stared at each other for a few moments. I could tell they were mentally talking, or arguing if the glares were any indication. Finally Logan let out a long-suffering sigh.

"Fine," he said almost petulantly. "I'll send over a few cases tomorrow. But I still think it's a waste."

Callum nodded. "Thanks, man."

Logan nodded back, and the two men shared a look. Obviously, the tension between them was lifting.

Syd leaned over and kissed Logan on the cheek. He smiled at her adoringly. He was totally whipped.

"Well that's fan-fucking-tastic," I said.

I knew I sounded like a bitch, but I didn't know how to feel. I was confused that Callum seemed so earnest about getting the

Lifeblood for me when he knew not getting it would mean I'd be out of his hair. Then there was the prospect of taking Lifeblood. I was still opposed to its very existence. Plus the freaking stuff was to blame for me being in this bind to begin with.

On the other hand, I still felt like I wanted to prove everyone wrong. And I figured if drinking Lifeblood would help me accomplish that, I could deal. It couldn't be worse than cold bagged blood. Don't get me wrong, I wasn't planning on turning into the poster girl for the Brethren lifestyle. I felt confident I could get through the next few months and still resume my subversive activities on the sly.

The lovebirds continued to make eyes at each other, and Callum ordered another round of drinks. They all ignored me, which was fine. I wanted to sulk anyway.

Today had been a crazy day. First, I went outside during daylight for the first time in my entire life. Second, there was the stupid kiss. Next, I had to undergo the makeover from hell. Then, I decided to throw my principals out the window in order to prove to my father and everyone else that I could become an upstanding member of polite vampire society. That I was actually going to commit myself to changing.

The others started to talk about bullshit I had no interest in. I ignored them and sipped on my second shot of tequila.

". . . flowers?" Sydney said.

The table went silent. I looked up to see what was happening and saw that all three of them were looking at me.

"What?"

Syd laughed. "I asked you which flowers you'd pick for your wedding. Logan says red roses, but I think white are more elegant."

I stared at her in confusion, wondering why the fuck she thought I had any opinion at all. Marriage was a mortal institution. Besides, I couldn't imagine any guy I'd want to shackle myself to for eternity. But she looked like she really wanted me to back her up, so I threw her a bone.

"White, I guess," I mumbled.

"Ha! See?" she said to Logan.

"Darling, if you want white, we'll have white. All that matters is that we get married."

As Syd proceeded to reward Logan with a kiss, I looked at Callum. He rolled his eyes, and I had to bite my lip to keep from laughing. I was glad I wasn't the only one who wished those two would get a room.

"Thanks, Raven," Syd said when she was done slobbering all over Logan. "It's hard making the wedding plans without any help."

"What about Jorge and Geraldine?" Callum asked.

"They're wonderful, but it's not the same as having girlfriends around who would get excited about helping me pick out a dress and all the other details."

Her words took me aback. Syd seemed like the kind of chick who'd have a ton of girlfriends around. But then I realized that even if she had any, they couldn't really be too involved in planning a vampire wedding. I didn't feel bad for her or anything, but I could understand how hard it must be to adjust to her new life and plan a wedding by herself.

"That's too bad," I said, trying to be polite.

"I don't suppose you'd . . . Never mind." Syd said.

Suddenly I was regretting being polite. I knew where she was going with that, and I didn't like it one bit.

"I'd what?" I asked against my better judgment.

"Well, I have an appointment to try on dresses next week, and Jorge and Geraldine are busy. I just thought maybe you could come along and keep me company."

She sounded so hopeful it pulled at my conscience. But then Logan spoke up.

"Syd, darling, do you think that's a good idea?"

It's not like I wanted to go, but his implication brought my hackles up.

"Why not?" I asked, offended.

"Correct me if I'm wrong, but didn't you kidnap her just a week ago?"

Well, he had me there. While, at the time, I thought

kidnapping Sydney was the right thing to do. Now I was having some second thoughts. I had to admit now it wasn't my most brilliant plan. It wasn't just that I had been caught and was now paying the price for that decision. Part of me was coming to realize that there might have been a better, and less harmful, way to protest Lifeblood.

"Logan, I told you. She didn't hurt me."

Logan shook his head and looked at his fiancée as if she was crazy. I had to admit I was wondering about her sanity, too. Why was she all of the sudden pretending we were friends?

"Syd, the kidnapping notwithstanding, do you really think she would be the best choice of companion?" he asked.

"Hey!" I said.

"Logan, that was rude. I'm sure she'd be very helpful."

"Fine," he said. Then he turned to me. "I'm warning you, if she shows up at our wedding in anything black, I'll find you."

"Hmmm. Black might be interesting," Syd said, a twinkle in her eye. "So, Raven, you'll do it?"

I gulped and looked at Callum for help. He just shrugged and nodded his approval. I couldn't very well say no after getting all defensive with Logan.

"I guess," I said lamely.

"Oh, it will be so fun," she said, really getting excited. "We can make a girls' day out of it."

"Great," I said, knowing I had gotten myself into something I'd probably regret.

I had no idea what a "girls' day" involved. Something told me a lot of giggling and gossiping about boys was involved.

Ugh.

One of these days I needed to learn to keep my big mouth shut.

#

An hour later Callum and I were on our way back to Kira's house. We'd said good-bye to the lovebirds at the valet stand after another drink. Syd promised to call me in a couple of days to set up our wedding dress outing. Before we got in the car, Logan agreed to send over a couple of cases of Lifeblood the next morning.

When we finally were in the car, I yawned. It had been an exhausting day. While being in the sun didn't scare me anymore, my body still wasn't adjusted to the new schedule. I was ready for bed.

"That was really nice of you," Callum said as we sped through downtown Raleigh.

"What?" I asked, playing dumb.

He shot me a look. "You know what. I know Syd really appreciates you agreeing to help her."

"I only did it to get away from my duties for a few hours. Don't read some altruistic reason into it."

"Either way, it's still nice. Maybe there is some hope for you after all," he joked.

"Don't count on it."

He shifted gears and seemed to lose himself in his own thoughts. I contented myself with watching the scenery pass for a few moments, enjoying the silence. I actually had a nice time tonight. After being cooped up in the house most of the week, when I wasn't working at the blood bank, it was nice to be out.

"Tonight was fun," Callum said, breaking into my thoughts as if he'd been reading them.

I rolled my head to the left, looking at him with heavy eyes.

"Yeah," I said.

"In case I forgot to mention it, you really do look great."

"Thanks. I'm not sure if I'll keep it though. It's not really me," I said.

He pulled into Kira's driveway before answering. After he stopped, he turned off the car and turned to me.

"I think it's more you than you're willing to admit."

"What's that supposed to mean?" I asked, feeling my defenses automatically go up despite my fatigue.

"You don't fool me, Gabby. You might act like you don't give a shit, but I've seen behind that exterior. I think if you gave people a chance you might actually find they're more receptive to the real you."

I sighed, not wanting to get into another argument.

"Callum, this is the real me. And the sooner you accept that, the easier this will all be. I know the Boy Scout in you wants to believe that I have redeeming qualities. But you're wrong. Dead wrong."

He stared at me hard for a moment, the muscle in his jaw clenched.

"What happened to you?"

I looked away. "Nothing. I'm just a bitch. Deal with it."

I reached for the door handle, but he grabbed my arm.

"Look, I know you don't trust me. You have no reason to. But I'm not your enemy."

I laughed. "Yeah. Thanks. All right, I'm going to bed. Thanks for dinner."

With that I opened the door and stalked to the house.

Trust him? Right. Given the ass kissing I'd witnessed earlier when my father called, I'm sure Callum would just love for me to spill my guts so he could run to my father and report.

Before I could reach the door, he caught up with me. He took my arm and swung me around. I was about to lay into him when I saw the look in his eyes.

"Just so we're clear. Kissing you today was a bad idea. You are the most frustrating woman I have ever met—"

"Dude, we've already covered this."

"Will you stop interrupting for one second?" He shoved a hand through his hair. "But I want you to know something. The only reason I answered that call was because if I hadn't I wouldn't have stopped kissing you."

My mouth fell open. "What?"

"Don't play dumb with me. You know as well as I do we would have ended up in bed if that phone hadn't rung."

I didn't say anything, because he was right.

"And as much as we both try to deny it, there's an attraction here. You drive me insane, but I still want you."

His words sent a shock of heat all the way to my interesting parts. He wanted me? I guess I already knew that, but having him say it acted like an aphrodisiac. Suddenly, despite my protestations, I wanted to throw him down and ravage him on his mother's front lawn.

"So what are you gonna do about it?" I asked, the huskiness in my voice surprising me.

He leaned down a bit so our faces were level. I licked my lips in anticipation. Millimeter by millimeter he moved in. Just when I was sure his lips could capture mine, he veered to the right.

"Nothing," he whispered in my ear.

I started to push him away, but he grabbed my hands and held them to his chest.

"Stop," he commanded as I struggled to get away from him.

I looked into his eyes and saw that he wasn't teasing me. He was dead serious.

"You know we can't act on it. If word got back to your father . . . Well, let's just say you're not the only one who'd be headed to Norway."

"Please. My father wouldn't care. He already thinks I'm a slut. Let's prove him right," I said, reaching down to cup his groin. It jumped in response, and his heat burned my palm.

He swallowed hard and took a deep breath. Then he reached down and moved my hand with what seemed like great reluctance.

"You're not a slut. And I won't treat you like one. Maybe when this is all over we can act on this . . . chemistry. For now, we need to focus on your training."

That time, I really did push him away. He obliged by falling back a step or two. I watched him for a moment. His chest heaved and a mighty erection strained against his grey slacks.

Suddenly I felt so full of anger and embarrassment I didn't know what to do with myself.

"I wish I'd never met you," I said, my voice low and hard.

He frowned. "That's your sexual frustration talking. But if you think about it, you'll see I'm right."

His words were so like the ones my father spoke the last time I saw him that all the lust and anger drained from me. Callum was just another man who thought he knew what was best for me. Someone else who didn't trust me to make my own choices in life.

I'd had enough.

"Go to hell," I said, turning on my heel and marching into the house.

Just before I slammed the door behind me, he said, "I'm already there."

CHAPTER TWELVE

After a night spent tossing and turning, replaying my conversation with Callum, I decided I needed to avoid him for a while. He made me crazy. I decided I'd ask for more hours at the blood bank and try to spend more time with Kira. With any luck I could have a few days without his annoying presence.

Before I could put this plan into action, fate stepped in. When I showed up for breakfast, Kira was alone. She sat at the head of the table reading the newspaper.

"Good morning," she said, looking up as I took my seat.

"Hi," I responded, grabbing the coffee carafe.

"How was your night out last night?" she asked.

I thought about it a moment. Let's see, I argued with Logan, agreed to help Syd, and had a fight with Callum.

"The restaurant was nice," I said politely.

"Yes, it's one of my favorites," she said.

Idle chitchat was obviously over because she flipped the page and became engrossed in a story. I was happy I didn't have to make small talk anymore. Grabbing the platter of food, I loaded my plate with eggs and bacon.

The only sounds in the room for a while were the sounds of silverware clinking on my plate and the tick of the grandfather clock in the hallway. As I ate, I wondered where Callum was. I shrugged mentally and reminded myself that I was avoiding him. If he had to go into the office or something, it suited me just fine. Yep, I didn't care one bit.

"So where's Callum?" I asked.

Kira looked up from her paper. "He said he had an early meeting. He left an hour ago."

"Oh."

"Did you want him for something?" she asked.

"No," I said quickly.

I most definitely did not *want* him.

"You sounded disappointed," she said.

I did? Shit.

"I'm not disappointed," I said quickly. "Just surprised he isn't here to ruin my meal as usual."

"Hmm," she said, a small smile on her face.

What did she mean by that?

I avoided her eyes and refilled my coffee. What the hell was I thinking asking in the first place? I should be ecstatic that he wouldn't be around all day to annoy me. Isn't that what I wanted? A Callum-free day.

"How are things between you two?"

I almost spit out my coffee.

"What do you mean?"

She smiled again. I knew it was silly, but I got the feeling she could read my thoughts. Vampires couldn't usually read each other's minds. However, Kira definitely was giving off an all-knowing vibe.

"Oh, nothing," she said, her voice light. "Just wondering if you're getting along. Since you have to spend so much time together."

"Kira, cut the shit. You know damned well we can't stand each other," I said.

I expected her to act offended for cussing in her presence, but she surprised me by laughing.

"Dear girl, are you forgetting how old I am? I recognize sexual tension when I see it."

My jaw dropped. It was that obvious?

"Oh, my. I've shocked you haven't I?"

"A little," I said, recovering slightly.

She shrugged. "Understand, I'm not going to pretend that I approve of your actions in the past. And the jury's still out about how successful your rehabilitation will be. However, I've seen Callum around you."

"What do you mean?" I asked slowly, wondering where she was going with this.

"Let me ask you a question," she said. "Do you honestly think you could both get a rise out of each other like you do if there wasn't some interest there? I mean if you honestly hated each other, you wouldn't bother to bicker."

I thought about what she said for a moment. Of course I knew there was an attraction. Callum admitted his last night. And I had basically admitted mine by acting like an idiot when he refused to act on it. So the attraction wasn't in question. No, what bothered me was that other people were seeing it.

"Kira, I don't know why you brought this up, but let's drop it. Nothing is going to happen."

"I brought it up because I know you're dealing with a lot right now. Things that have nothing to do with Callum. I don't think it's wise for you to act on your . . . urges while you're so unsettled."

Okay, now she'd crossed a line.

"Look, lady, the last thing you need to worry about is me acting on any urges with that pinhead. But thanks for the warning. I'm well aware that you would disapprove of me making moves on your angel."

She didn't even flinch. "It's not that I disapprove—"

I slashed a hand through the air to stop her. "Save it."

I got up and left the room before she could say anything else. As I stormed up the stairs, my mind raced.

On one level I understood and agreed with Kira's warning. The last thing I needed right then was a man in my life. Especially a man who was the poster boy for everything I hated.

On the other hand, I was pissed. How dare she imply I

wasn't good enough for her son? Sure, she hadn't said that, but I knew her whole line about avoiding complications was bullshit. She didn't want a person like me influencing her saint of a son. God forbid I get my claws in him.

Not that he wanted my claws in him. Dammit! Why was I so upset about that? Sure, my female parts were very aware of his male parts. But it wasn't like I hadn't been attracted to guys before and resisted it.

How long had it been since I'd had sex anyway? Having reached my room, I sat down with a piece of paper to figure it out. Let's see, add that, and carry the four. Holy Shit! I hadn't had sex in twenty years.

No wonder Callum was looking good. After twenty years of sexual drought, just about any man would have appealed to me.

I sat back in my chair with a sigh of relief. Now that I knew I wasn't really attracted to him, I could relax. As long as I remembered that it wasn't him, but my raging libido, I could handle it. As for Momma Murdoch, she could take a long walk off a short pier for all I cared. Like I'd want to join her goody two-shoes family—all that closeness and bonding and shit. Poor Sydney didn't know what she was getting herself into tying herself down to these people. An eternity filled with nagging and everyone always knowing her business. No thank you. Not for this chick.

A knock sounded at the door. Hannah, who I'd learned basically ran Kira's household, stuck her head in after I responded.

"Raven, Alaric is downstairs waiting for you with the cases of Lifeblood."

"Thanks, Hannah," I said.

She nodded and left. After she closed the door, I slumped in my seat. The food in my stomach churned at the thought of synthetic blood. I'd gotten used to the bagged stuff, or at least I could tolerate it. It was actual blood from a person. But the idea of depending on fake blood unsettled me. I knew it wasn't only the idea of it being fake, though. My conscience battled with my logic. I knew I had to drink the stuff if I wanted to win my father's seal of approval. However, the fact I had to turn my back on everything I believed to win that approval troubled me. But what choice did I have?

I drug myself out of the chair and trudged downstairs only to stop short at the bottom of the steps. Standing in the foyer windows was an all-American surfer boy in board shorts and a T-shirt. His hair seemed impossibly blond in the sunlight from the windows as he watched me slowly descend the last step.

"Raven?" he said, walking toward me, his flip-flops scuffling on the marble tiles. He was adorable. I wanted to ruffle his hair.

"Yeah. You're Alaric?" I asked, a little confused. When I'd heard that Alaric was Logan's lab assistant, I pictured a geeky guy with glasses and a white coat. But this Alaric had broad shoulders and a killer grin. He looked like he belonged on a beach instead of in a lab.

"That's me. Logan sent me over with the Lifeblood." His tone sounded brusque, like he resented playing delivery boy.

"Okay. Well, thanks," I said.

He stood there for a moment just looking at me. His expression wasn't giving anything away. After a moment I was starting to feel uncomfortable. What was his problem?

"Do I need to sign for it or something?" I asked.

He grimaced. "You're not what I expected."

I frowned. "What do you mean by that?"

"You don't look like a conniving bitch."

That stopped me in my tracks. "Excuse me?"

"Are you or aren't you the one who tried to destroy Lifeblood?"

I raised my chin at his challenge. "Yeah, that's me. You got a problem?"

"Yeah, I got a big problem. I didn't spend three years of my life helping to create Lifeblood to hand it over to the person who tried to stop its creation."

I leaned forward, ready to smack this asshole back to kingdom come if necessary. Who the hell did he think he was anyway?

"Look, dude, underneath this pink twinset and sensible

khaki pants, I am still a bitch. I suggest you back off."

Before he could respond, another voice spoke.

"That's enough," Kira said from behind me. Her voice, while quiet, oozed authority.

Alaric took a step back and grimaced. "Sorry, Kira."

I turned to look at her. She stood at doorway of the dining room, her hands on her hips and a massive frown on her face.

"Hey, Kira," I said, resolved not to apologize when I had been defending myself.

"Alaric, you have no right to attack her. Logan agreed to give her the Lifeblood."

"But—" he protested.

"Hush," she said. "I wasn't finished. It's time we put the past behind us and move on. Raven is here to learn. We don't want to teach her that we are unable to forgive."

I raised my eyebrows and smiled at him. He looked like he wanted to speak but knew better than to contradict the older vampire.

"And you," she said, focusing her laser gaze on me, "need to learn some restraint. You can't go around threatening everyone who says something you don't like."

I didn't say anything. What was the point?

"Now, Alaric, please bring the cases into the kitchen."

He nodded and went to grab the two large cases from the floor next to the front door. The contents of the boxes clanged together as he walked. I followed them to the kitchen, curious to see what was in the crates.

Alaric deposited the boxes of Lifeblood on the large center island in the kitchen with a thud. He opened one and stepped back.

I peeked into the box. My eyes widened when I saw that two dozen glass bottles rested inside. A cloud of gas from the dry ice lifted from the box and hovered around us. Alaric waved it away and reached in for a bottle.

"The dry ice is just to keep it cold for transport. You can just store the bottles in the fridge from now on," he explained, handing Kira the bottle.

I reached in and picked up another bottle, which prompted Alaric to glare at me. Tough noogies, I thought, holding the frosty glass up to the light. The container was shaped like an old-fashioned Coke bottle. Only, the contents were deep red instead of bubbly brown.

"So you drink it cold?"

"Actually, we designed it to be consumed warm. You just pop it in the microwave for thirty seconds."

I stared at him with wide eyes. "Microwave the blood?"

Gross, I thought. I knew a lot of vamps heated bagged blood, and it made me want to barf. Real blood should be warmed the natural way—by the human body.

"It's not real blood, dear," Kira said.

"Yeah, but it still seems odd," I replied, shaking the bottle. The liquid inside had a viscous quality. "It's thick."

"Yeah, that's because of the cold. It thins when it's heated."

"Hmm. Can I open it?" I asked.

"Yeah," he said, his tone still unfriendly.

Twisting the top caused a loud popping sound. I looked at Alaric in confusion.

"That's just the seal popping. It's airtight to preserve it until it's opened."

I nodded and placed the metal top on the counter. Lifting the bottle to my nose, I took a tentative sniff. Hmm. It sure smelled like blood. My mouth started watering immediately. My fangs even started to descend. I hadn't had any bagged blood yet this morning.

"Why don't we heat it up so you can try it?" Kira asked.

They both stared at me expectantly as I argued with myself. My appetite said go for it. My brain resisted though, apprehensive about trying something so foreign. I knew that one sip probably wouldn't harm me, but that same sip would wash away years of resistance to progress.

Finally, Kira grew impatient and made the decision for me. Taking the bottle from me, she placed it in the microwave and set the timer for half a minute.

I watched the glass spin on the turntable as if it moved in

slow motion, the timer counting down the seconds until I became a hypocrite.

The ding of the microwave made me jump. It was time. I knew they wouldn't let me out of this room until I tried it.

Kira removed the bottle and poured it into a glass. She handed it to me with a smile.

"If it makes you feel any better, I've tried it myself, and it's delicious."

She obviously thought I was worried about the taste. I didn't bother correcting her. I'm sure she'd dismiss my misgivings as silly.

I took the glass from her and looked at it. I swirled the liquid around. I sniffed it again.

"Raven, it's not wine. You don't have to test the bouquet."

I narrowed my eyes at Alaric's sarcasm. I wish he'd just leave. But I knew he'd never miss this. I was glad Callum wasn't there too. He'd have teased me even worse than Alaric.

Finally, I made myself lift the glass, which tapped against my fangs. Closing my eyes, I took a sip. The warm fluid slid smoothly across my tongue, making my taste buds come alive.

My eyes shot open in surprise. It tasted exactly like blood fresh from the source. I couldn't believe something synthetic could taste so authentic. It sure as hell beat bagged blood, too.

I looked at Alaric and Kira, who stared at me expectantly. The room was dead silent as they waited for my reaction. The only one I gave them was lifting the glass again. Only this time instead of a sip, I gulped down the rest of the liquid.

Kira laughed when I finally took a breath and slammed the glass down on the counter.

"Alaric, I do believe she likes it," she said.

I licked my lips. "Can I have another glass?"

Alaric joined Kira's laughter. "You'd better slow down You only have two cases."

"I can't believe it," I said, sticking my finger in the glass and licking the residue off with my tongue.

"Thanks," Alaric said, his tone much friendlier than it had been a few minutes ago. He was obviously proud of his part in creating Lifeblood.

"Alaric and Logan subjected Callum and I to taste tests for months. By the end, we couldn't tell the Lifeblood from the real blood."

I nodded. "It's fantastic."

"So you think you can handle giving up human donors if you have this instead?" Kira asked.

"Let's just say I can handle it for the rest of my confinement," I said.

Alaric and Kira looked at each other nervously.

"But Raven, you can't seriously think you'll be allowed to feed off humans ever again."

"Why not?" I asked.

"Once Lifeblood is released to the general vamp population, the council intends to make it totally illegal to feed directly from humans. In cases of emergency, bagged blood will be okay. However, Lifeblood will be the main source of sustenance for all vampires."

I paused. All along I thought the "no human meal" rule was part of my punishment. This was the first I'd heard about the council outlawing feeding, period.

"You're joking," I said, my voice serious.

"No. It's already in the works," Alaric said.

As it stood now, feeding from humans was allowed only in cases of emergency. Since I didn't follow the Brethren rules, I ignored that law. But most other vamps didn't. Soon, almost every vampire in existence would depend on fake blood for survival. It was an abomination.

"That's bullshit," I said, my voice rising. "The council can't completely outlaw feeding from humans. It's unnatural."

"On the contrary, they can and will," Alaric said. "Our kind has no moral right to feed from humans. And with Lifeblood, with bagged blood as a backup, there is no excuse to continue to treat humans like cattle."

"It figures you'd say that," I shot back. "It must really irk you that you were once nothing but a fragile human."

His jaw clenched. "The fact I was turned against my will has nothing to do with this. We don't need to rely on humans anymore. There's no reason to."

"Whatever," I said with a wave of the hand.

"Raven, are you more mad that times are changing or that your father is the one changing them?" Kira asked.

I flinched.

"Why can't you see that holding on to the past is dangerous?" she continued. "Our entire population is at risk whenever one of us feeds from a human. It's common sense that anything that reduces our risk of discovery is a positive step."

"I still say it's unnatural. We have fangs for a reason. Oh wait, I know. The council can outlaw fangs next."

"Don't be silly," Kira said.

"Am I being silly? This path is a slippery slope. Today it's fake blood; tomorrow it's everyone has to have their fangs removed; next it will be we all have to stake ourselves after ninety years so we have a human lifespan instead of being immortal."

"That will never happen," Alaric said with a snort.

"Won't it? Kira, you're what—seven hundred, give or take?" She nodded. "Back then did you ever imagine you would be able to go in the sun?"

"First of all, I was mortal until my late-husband turned me. So going into the sun was normal for me until I was changed. Second, I also didn't imagine people could fly through the sky in steel tubes. It's called progress, Raven. Welcome to the twenty-first century."

"If you hate all of this so much, why don't you just quit? No one's making you do this," Alaric said, his voice hard.

"Because I don't have a choice!" I said, my voice shaking.

Kira smiled sadly and shook her head. "You always have a choice, Raven. And you need to take a long hard look at the choices you've made and where they've lead you. You're not a victim here."

Funny, I sure as hell felt like one. But maybe she was right. I was tired of constantly fighting for something. Maybe it was time I just accepted that I had no control over the council, my father, or anyone else. Maybe it was time I thought about what I wanted out of life. And figure out if there was a way I could find happiness in this brave new vampire world.

"If you'll excuse me, I think I need some time alone," I said.

They both looked surprised. I couldn't blame them. They expected more arguments from me, but frankly I felt weighed down, unable to continue the good fight one more second.

Finally, Kira nodded. "We can continue this discussion later."

I didn't bother acknowledging either of them as I walked out. I just wanted to go to my room and get in bed. Hiding wouldn't solve my problems, but it sure beat trying to figure out my future right now.

I was almost at the stairs when the front door opened, revealing Callum. The sunlight outlined his large form like a halo. When he saw me, his smile faded.

"Hey," he said, looking uncomfortable.

I lifted a hand in a poor facsimile of a wave and continued my path to the stairs.

"Raven?"

I stopped and looked over my shoulder with one eyebrow raised.

"What's wrong?" he asked, frowning.

"Callum," I said, "I think the better question would be: 'What *isn't* wrong?'"

I didn't wait for him to answer as I turned and trudged up the stairs. He didn't respond, but I could feel his gaze on me the entire way up.

CHAPTER THIRTEEN

The next few days I brooded and moped until I couldn't stand my own company anymore.

It got so bad I actually started looking forward to my shifts at the blood bank. It got me out of the house and kept me busy. Nancy had me working the check-in desk, thus a lot of my nights were spent working with people and organizing paperwork. I never thought I'd enjoy either of those activities, but it beat wallowing in self pity.

At Kira's, things were quiet most days. Callum was busy with some big deal at work, and Kira gave me my space.

One morning, Hannah stuck her head in the kitchen while I was busy chugging my morning dose of Lifeblood.

"Raven, Sydney's on the phone for you."

I frowned and wiped my mouth with the back of my hand. I'd heard the phone ring but didn't give it a second thought since no one called me. However, I quickly remembered why Syd might be calling. Sighing, I trudged to grab the cordless phone from the wall unit next to the fridge.

"Hello?"

She didn't even bother with a greeting. "I am so excited!"

I pulled the phone away from my ear for a second to avoid

the high-pitched squeal that followed.

"You are?"

"Yes!" she enthused. "Oh, no. You didn't forget about our shopping trip today, did you?"

Unfortunately, I hadn't. Syd had called two nights earlier to set up our girls'-day-slash-dress-shopping extravaganza. While part of me longed to get out of the house, I didn't relish the idea of spending the day with an excited bride.

"Nope." I said.

"Oh, good, because I'll be there in five minutes!"

"Great," I said and hung up.

After finishing off the rest of the Lifeblood, I grabbed a bagel for the road. On second thought, I grabbed another bagel and put it in my bag. I figured it'd give me something to munch on if the shopping made me nauseous.

Before I even could make it to the foyer, I heard Sydney's car honk from the driveway.

Five minutes, my ass.

"Raven?" Callum said from the balcony above.

Stopping with my hand on the doorknob, I turned around. "Yeah?"

"Where are you going?"

"I have that thing with Syd, remember?"

"Oh, right. Hold on a second." He trotted down the stairs while I waited impatiently by the door. Syd honked her horn again.

"I really gotta go," I said through a mouthful of bagel.

He reached the bottom of the stairs. As he walked toward me he reached into his back pocket and pulled out his billfold.

"I thought maybe you could use some cash since the council froze your assets," he said, extending a pile of money my direction. I stopped chewing and swallowed hard.

"Excuse me?"

"You know, in case you wanted to buy yourself something," he said with a smile.

Here was the thing. Callum and I had barely spoken three words to each other since our argument the other night. I couldn't believe his first real effort in reopening communication was to offer me money.

"Callum, I imagine you think you're being magnanimous right now. But honestly, it comes off as patronizing. Do you really believe I am so stupid I wouldn't have some money the council couldn't get to? Who do you think paid for the makeover from hell?"

He stood frozen with the money held midair for a moment. Clearing his throat, he slowly withdrew his hand and stuck it in his pocket.

"I'm sorry if I offended you. I just thought—"

"Look, I appreciate the sentiment, okay? But this girl takes care of herself."

I opened the door and walked away. At Syd's car, I glanced back at the house. He stood on the porch with his arms crossed, watching me. I waved and got in, glad to be getting away from his censorious glares.

"What's got Callum so pissed?" Syd asked as I slammed my door.

"I wouldn't take his money," I said.

She waved at Callum and put the car in gear.

"Don't mind him. Murdoch men seem to forget that modern women take care of themselves. They can't help it. It's the rescue instinct."

I gave her a get-real look. "I doubt that was his motive."

She laughed as she hit the gas. "Denial ain't just a river in Egypt."

"What?"

She glanced at me out of the corner of her eye with a smile.

"Oh, come on. It's so obvious you two are hot for each other."

"Why does everyone keep saying that?" I demanded after closing my gaping mouth.

"I've seen you guys together. It reminds me a lot of Logan and me at first. We were interested in each other but didn't want to admit it. So we fought all the time."

"Sydney, I agreed to help you find a wedding dress. But if

you say one more word about Callum today, you're on your own."

She laughed and said, "Fair enough. You're not ready. But feel free to come to me when you want to discuss the man who shall not be mentioned."

"Don't hold your breath," I said, slouching down in my seat.

"I'm immortal now. I can hold it as long as it takes. Now," she said, perking up in her seat, "who's ready to shop?"

I groaned. "I guess I am."

"Ah, come on. How about a little enthusiasm?"

"If you want enthusiasm, you ask Jorge to shop with you. If you want wry commentary and a bad attitude, you ask Raven Coracino."

She slipped a CD in the stereo, and the thumping bass of an upbeat hip-hop song filled the car. She started bobbing her head and said, "Trust me, you're going to have fun today if it kills me."

For some reason, watching her sing along to the song with her auburn hair blowing in the breeze of her rolled-down window, I believed Syd's threat. And it had been so long since I relaxed and let myself have fun that I almost started looking forward to the day.

But I promised myself that no matter what happened, I wasn't going to even let myself think about that guy.

#

I hid behind the stall door, holding it shut with both hands.

"Come on, Raven, you have to come out," Syd demanded.

I glanced over my shoulder at the mirror one more time and tried not to laugh.

"Hell, no!"

"If I could walk around looking like a crazy chicken, you can handle this."

"Huh-uh."

"I'll buy you a mocha with extra whipped cream if you come out."

Okay, now she was playing dirty. I didn't know how she had even talked me into putting the monstrosity on my body. One minute we were laughing over some of the most hideous dresses ever to see the light of day, and the next thing I knew she'd talked me into trying some of them on with her. I decided right then and there that Sydney Worth was trouble.

"All right, fine, but there better not be any photographic equipment within a three-block radius."

She giggled. "Just come out already."

I slowly opened the door and poked my head out, making sure no one was around. The dressing rooms were off a large room with raised platforms and mirrors. The wall divided the area from the rest of the store. When I didn't see any of the overeager employees rushing around or other brides-to-be, I stepped out.

Syd's eyes widened, and then she started laughing so hard she doubled over and slapped her knee. I looked down at myself and couldn't blame her.

"Where are your sheep?" she said, her eyes glistening with mirth.

I wasn't sure why any woman would choose a Little Bo Peep theme for her wedding. The hideous thing weighed a ton and was covered with yards and yards of white lace ruffles and pink satin. Something told me that Syd's reaction, though, was due to the bonnet and crook that completed the ensemble.

"That's funny coming from a woman who looks like an escapee from an aviary," I said, chuckling.

Syd fluffed the large white plumes that sprung from the bodice of her dress. "I kind of like them. I feel like a show girl."

We stood next to each other in front of the mirrored wall and laughed helplessly. It didn't take long for a nosy salesperson to come back to see what all the noise was about. Unfortunately, she arrived at the same time I was making a particularly colorful comment about carrying a blow-up sheep as my bouquet.

Hands on hips, the blue-haired lady, whose name tag read "Doris," gasped with outrage.

"Do you mind? This is a respectable establishment," she said, glaring at us.

"Lady, the fact you carry dresses like these says otherwise," I said, trying to fight a new round of laughter.

"I'm going to have to ask you to leave and never come back to this store," Doris said, raising her chin indignantly.

Ten minutes later, back in our own clothes, we spilled out the front door of the store nearly hysterical with laughter.

"That's a first," Syd said as she gasped for breath. "I've never known anyone to get banned from a bridal shop before."

Wiping tears from my cheeks, I said, "It's too bad. I think you would have looked fabulous in the Carmen Miranda dress."

We walked down the sidewalk, ignoring the stares of passersby. With unspoken agreement, we headed straight for the Starbucks three doors down.

Syd ordered an iced coffee and then told the barista she'd pay for my order too. I balked, but she insisted she owed me for being such a good sport. She was right, so I ordered the biggest mocha on the menu with extra whipped cream.

We took our drinks to a small table in the corner. I sighed and took a long sip of the chocolaty goodness. Heaven.

Across from me, Syd sipped on her drink with a thoughtful smile on her face.

"That was fun," she said, leaning back in her chair.

"Yeah, it was," I said, realizing just then how much I had enjoyed her company. Plus, she had a wicked sense of humor.

"Syd?" I said.

"What?"

"Why are you being so nice to me?"

She hesitated, seeming taken aback by my candor.

"Why wouldn't I be?"

I snorted. "Do I really need to bring up the fact that our first meeting involved chloroform?"

Chuckling, she set down her cup and looked at me.

"Honestly?" she asked.

When I nodded, she continued. "Okay, do you remember the day Logan and I came over to announce our engagement?"

Cringing, I recalled the scene I'd made.

"Unfortunately, yes," I said.

"Well, I'll admit you weren't my favorite person then. I mean, you'd kidnapped me with the intent of ruining everything the man I love had worked for."

Uncomfortable, I took another sip of my drink, waiting for her to get to the point.

"So that day, Logan was angry—rightfully so, I might add. And I was upset. But later, I . . . well, I saw you crying," she said, looking sheepish.

My stomach dropped out from under me. Until she mentioned it, I'd completely forgotten about her seeing me cry my eyes out. Immediately, I felt defensive.

"What does that have to do with anything?" I demanded.

She sighed and put her hand on mine as if to calm me.

"Raven, look, until I saw you so upset, I was convinced you had no heart. When I walked in on you, I was shocked. For the first time, I realized how lonely you must feel. And being no stranger to loneliness myself, I couldn't help but feel for you."

"What do you know about being lonely? Everyone loves you."

"As much as I love Logan and his family, this is all so new to me. I don't know any other vampires, and I don't have any close girlfriends I can confide in. So, yeah, I know about being lonely."

"I hadn't thought of that. It must be tough to get used to all this."

She chuckled. "It's not so bad. But sometimes, it would be nice to have someone who understands this life to talk to. And when I saw you so upset, I thought just maybe you could kind of understand."

"So you've forgiven me for the kidnapping and all?" I asked, hopefully.

"Let's just say I think you've learned your lesson. But if you do ever get a wild hair and decide to wreak havoc, I'll hunt you down myself." The last was said with a smile, so I wasn't offended.

"Deal," I said, holding my hand out.

She shook it back. "Deal."

Weird, I thought. Imagine something as embarrassing as her catching me in my weakest moment forging some kind of bond between us. And I did feel something growing between us. Friendship? Maybe.

Syd sighed, changing the subject. "I guess we need to regroup. Trying on ugly dresses is fun, but I really do need to get serious about my search."

I thought for a moment. "You know, there's a boutique run by a friend of mine, Miranda. She's made a bunch of my clothes. And she carries some wedding dresses."

Syd looked unsure. "No offense, Raven, but I've see some of your old clothes. I don't think leather and latex is my style."

I laughed. "It's not like that. I promise. Let's finish our drinks and stop by. I'll call Miranda and let her know we're coming so she can have some dresses ready for you."

Syd shrugged. "Well her stuff can't be any worse than what we just witnessed in that other store."

I smiled and dialed my phone. "Trust me."

#

The bell above the door to Divine, Miranda's boutique, jingled as we entered. To mortal shoppers, it was an upscale store catering to the discriminating fashionista. To vampires, it was a place to get the inside scoop on the latest gossip as well as chic ensembles.

Miranda and I went way back. Her mother was on the council, so we'd grown up in the same circles. While I was considered the black sheep of my family, Miranda was the apple of her parents' eyes. We'd come to terms with our differing philosophies long ago and remained good friends. My suggestion to Syd that we stop by was partially selfish—I needed to talk to Miranda.

Syd looked nervous as we walked in, but when she saw the interior of the store, she seemed to relax. Classical music and soft lighting added to the comfortable atmosphere.

It didn't take long for Miranda to appear from behind a red silk curtain toward the rear of the store. She smiled and picked up her pace when she saw me. She looked gorgeous as usual.

Her wavy blond hair flirted with her shoulders, and her green eyes sparkled with humor. She wore a classic Diane von Furstenberg wrap dress in kelly green.

She didn't say anything, just walked up and hugged me. I returned the embrace, closing my eyes for moment. It had been a few months since we'd seen each other. Too long.

"Raven," she said, a smile in her voice. She pulled back and eyed my clothes with a discerning glance. "What's up with the clothes?"

I smiled at her typical candor. The tight baby-blue sweater and camel suede skirt I wore must have come as quite a surprise.

"I'll explain it later," I said. "This is Sydney."

The women exchanged warm greetings, sizing each other up a bit as females tend to do.

"Raven said you're looking for a wedding dress," Miranda said.

"Yes, I'm afraid I haven't had much luck so far though," Syd replied.

"Hmm. I'm thinking simple. White silk, strapless, A-line skirt. You're an eight?"

"Wow, yes, you're good," Syd said.

"I have a couple of options that might work. If you ladies want to make yourselves comfortable, I'll bring them out. I'll just be a minute," Miranda said.

While she went into the back, Syd and I made our way to the sitting area at the rear of the store. A chaise lounge and two antique chairs covered in the same red silk as the curtain to the back room beckoned us.

Within a couple of seconds, a girl with beautiful mocha skin came from the back bearing two flutes of sparkling champagne.

We thanked her, but she merely nodded and left again.

Syd raised an eyebrow at me as she took her first sip. "Mmm. Now this is more like it."

"I told you," I said, sampling my own bubbly. Leave it to Miranda to serve premium champagne. It was part of her philosophy. If you treated the customer like a queen, she'd be more willing to spend money like one.

"I'm surprised I haven't heard of this place before," Syd observed, looking around.

"Miranda has a pretty loyal following. But now that you're a vamp, you'll probably hear about her."

"Why's that?" Syd asked.

"Miranda has famous shopping parties here at night for her vamp clientele. Very exclusive. She's also the best source of gossip around."

Syd nodded as Miranda came out carrying an armload of dresses.

"I found several that might work," she said, pausing before us. "Syd, if you'll follow me to the dressing room we'll get you started."

Syd took her champagne and obediently followed Miranda through an archway off the sitting area. After a few moments, Miranda reappeared. Walking over to the girl who'd brought us the wine, she whispered something to her. The girl immediately nodded and went back to the room with Sydney. Miranda poured herself a glass of champagne and sat next to me on the chaise.

"Carmen's going to help Sydney for a few minutes. Plenty of time for you to catch me up on this mess you've gotten yourself into."

I didn't protest. I knew she'd wear me down eventually. I took another sip of wine and immediately launched into a recap of the last two weeks.

"Callum Murdoch, huh? Hot."

"Miranda," I said impatiently, "I think you missed the point of my story."

"Stop it. You and I both know it's about time you gave the straight life a chance."

I grimaced but knew it was useless to argue with her.

"As for me missing the point, you're not fooling me for a minute. Callum has you nervous. I can tell by the way you paused every time you said his name. Plus I've seen the man. He'd make a nun reconsider her vows."

"He's not that hot," I said, lying through my teeth.

She sent me a look.

"Okay, so he's hot. But I can't stand him."

She continued to stare at me.

"I can't," I said, knowing I was protesting too much. I squirmed in my seat. What was it about old friends that didn't let you get away with self-deception?

"All I can tell you is people are placing bets about how long you'll last."

My jaw dropped. "They are?"

"Yep, and so far it's not looking like anyone believes you'll actually make it the full three months."

"Did you bet?"

She looked down, focusing on an invisible piece of lint on her pristine skirt.

"Miranda!" I said.

She looked up guiltily. "What? Raven, I know you. You've probably already contacted your minions to get you out of there."

Now it was my turn to look away.

"See? I knew it!"

"Can you blame me? They have me working at a fucking blood bank. And they're making me go into the sun and drink fake blood," I said, hoping she'd take my side.

"So? It's not like you can get skin cancer. And I'm excited about Lifeblood. So much more convenient than bagged. How is it?"

"It's actually not bad," I admitted grudgingly. "But that's not the point."

"What's your point then? You fucked up. It's time to pay the piper. I'm frankly surprised your father didn't try this sooner."

"Gee thanks, traitor," I said.

"I'm just being honest. You know I love you, but this was going to happen sooner or later. And it could have been worse."

"How?" I asked.

"Your father could have decided to be in charge of your

rehabilitation."

Yikes, I hadn't thought of that. While Callum got on my nerves, I actually enjoyed our verbal sparring. My father would have done nothing but criticize and nag me until I was ready to rip my ears off.

"See, you've got to look on the bright side," she said, sounding too chipper for my taste.

I didn't have time to respond as a vision in white floated into the room.

"Speaking of bright sides," Miranda said, standing to lead Sydney onto the raised platform in front of the chairs. "Sydney, you're radiant."

Thankful for the change in subject, I rose and walked to where they stood.

I had to admit, the dress was pretty fabulous. Strapless with artfully arranged folds along the bodice, the matte satin dress hugged Syd's petite frame. The skirt flared slightly, falling in a cascade to the floor. The overall effect was both quietly elegant and stunning at the same time.

Syd stared at herself in the mirror for a long time, a dazed look on her face.

"Oh my God," she whispered.

"Is that a good thing?" I asked.

She looked at me. "Yes. I love it."

"You should. It looks amazing on you," I said.

"You wouldn't need many alterations in this one, just some tweaking of the hem," Miranda said, circling Syd. "Do you want to try on the others?"

Syd broke from her trance for a moment. "This is it."

Miranda smiled knowingly., "I thought so. Would you like to try on a veil to see the full effect? I have the perfect pair of strappy heels for it too."

Syd nodded eagerly. While Miranda went to gather accessories, I stepped in front of Syd.

"So?"

"Raven, I can't believe it. I'm standing here in the dress I'll be married in." Her eyes glistened with tears, and I panicked, sensing a bonding moment coming.

"It's just so overwhelming, you know?" she said, delicately wiping her eyes.

"I'm sure it is," I said, awkwardly patting her arm.

"You know I was engaged once before, right?"

"No, I didn't," I said, surprised.

"Yeah, my parents picked him out for me. A week before the wedding, I called it off. He wanted me to give up my career goals to stay home and play hostess for his law partners."

"Wow, I had no idea."

"Anyway, with Logan it's different. He knows me and understands how important my work is. And there's not a doubt in my mind I'm making the right decision."

"That's good."

"I'm sorry if this sounds sappy, but when I saw myself in this dress, I was blown away. Buying it means I'm one step closer to marrying the man I'll spend eternity with."

"Uh-huh," I said, not sure how to respond. She was talking about things totally out of my depth. I looked around, hoping Miranda would hurry up.

Syd drug her gaze away from her reflection and looked at me.

"Raven, thank you for this." She grabbed one of my hands. "I can't tell you how much your help has meant to me."

I looked at her for a moment, seeing the sincerity in her eyes. I felt like an ass for making fun of her excitement earlier. This obviously meant a lot to her, and I was kind of proud I'd helped her.

"You're welcome," I said, meaning it.

"Can I ask you something?" she said.

"Sure," I said, feeling kind of warm and gushy.

"Will you be my bridesmaid?" she said hesitantly but with a smile.

I was taken aback.

"Syd, are you sure that's the best idea? Logan hates me. I kidnapped you. I'm here doing time to pay off my debts to your future family. Are you sensing a pattern?"

Syd waved a hand. "I know all that. But I'd like to think we're friends. I know you try to hide it, but you're a warm, funny person. I enjoy spending time with you. And if you don't say yes, then I won't have anyone on my side for the wedding."

I started to crack. Her eyes pleaded with me to say yes. And by the goddess, I wanted to say yes. I liked Sydney, and no one had ever asked me to be a part of something so important to them. I felt flattered. But I worried about the family's reaction. Kira would probably tell Syd I wasn't good enough. Logan would throw a fit. Callum would . . . well, I wasn't sure how he'd react, but I wasn't optimistic.

"Syd, I'm flattered and touched that you want me to be a part of your wedding—"

"Don't say 'but,'" Syd interrupted. "Listen, I know people might not like it, but it's my wedding and my decision. I want you to be my maid of honor. And if anyone has a problem with that, you send them to me."

I admired her spunk, and the idea of her telling them all off intrigued me.

"Oh, what the hell. Sure. I'll do it."

She squealed and leaned forward to hug me. I laughed and hugged her back.

"What did I miss?" Miranda said as she walked back in carrying shoes, a veil, and a jewelry box.

Syd pulled back from the hug and looked at Miranda.

"Raven is going to be my maid of honor." Her excitement was contagious. I stood there smiling like an idiot. Miranda's eyes widened briefly, but she recovered and laughed.

"I hope you're ready for some fireworks," she said.

"I'm counting on it," Syd said with a smirk. "Now, while I try on these things, why don't you see what you have in the way of a bridesmaid dress for my maid of honor?"

Miranda called Carmen back over to help Syd while she pulled me into the store to look at dresses.

"Do you think this is a good idea?" she whispered as she flipped through racks of dresses.

She held up a pink shift dress and shook her head.

"It's what she wants. Plus, I think it would be kind of fun."

"Okay, if you're prepared then I say go for it."

She turned and raised her voice to talk to Syd, "Sydney, what are we going for with this dress?"

Syd looked over her shoulder as she adjusted the veil. "Oh, I don't care. Let Raven decide. The wedding is black tie though, so it needs to be formal."

"Are you sure you want me to choose?" I said.

"Yep, just chose something you love."

I looked uneasily at Miranda. She stared back with a twinkle in her eye.

"I've got just the thing. I'll bring it to the dressing room."

While she wandered off, I headed back to the seating area to see how Syd was doing.

A white tulle veil floated around her head like mist. She now wore chandelier earrings and strappy white heels. The effect was breathtaking.

"Wow, Syd. You're going to knock Logan's socks off," I said.

She fiddled with the veil, making it lay just right on her bare shoulders.

"Miranda is a genius. And I love the beading on the headpiece. I feel like a princess."

"You look like one."

She smiled and thanked me. I excused myself to the changing room, where I waited for Miranda to arrive. It didn't take long. She handed over an armful of dresses.

"Here you go. We'll wait for you in the sitting room."

A few minutes later I pulled the side zipper closed and stared at myself. It was perfect. Opening the fitting room door, I swept my way into the sitting room.

Syd and Miranda both turned to stare.

"I love it!" Syd exclaimed.

"That's the one," Miranda said at the same time.

"You don't think it's too bold for a wedding?" I asked and held my breath.

"Absolutely not. You have to buy that dress," Syd said.

Made of deep ruby velvet, the gown had a corseted top with satin ribbon crisscrossing the bodice and the same ribbon creating the straps on my shoulders. The skirt was fitted and fell to the floor. This was a dress I would have chosen premakeover, except classier.

I'd worried it was too much for a wedding, with its medieval dominatrix theme, but apparently Syd had no problems with it.

"I thought you'd choose that one," Miranda said with a knowing smile. "It's one I made myself."

The next few minutes were a flurry of activity while we chose jewelry and shoes for my dress. Then Syd and I changed back into our clothes while Miranda wrapped everything up.

"Syd, the alterations on your dress should be done by next week," Miranda said. "I'm having a vamp shopping night next Wednesday. Why don't you come? You can get your dress as well as have a chance to meet some new people."

"That sounds like fun. Raven, will you come too?" Syd asked.

Frowning, I said, "Actually, I have to work at the blood bank that night."

"Oh, that's too bad," Syd said. "Well, I'll be here, Miranda."

Jealousy reared its ugly head. Maybe it was immature, but I felt left out.

"Great. And maybe we can all get together soon when Raven's not working," Miranda said. "This has been so much fun."

"Definitely. Miranda, thank you so much for all your help. I hope you'll come to the wedding too."

"I'd love to."

My jealousy faded as I realized I'd now have another ally at the wedding.

Soon, our packages were wrapped and we were heading out the door. Miranda gave me a big hug, whispering in my ear to be smart and call her if I needed anything.

I walked out into the crisp fall air feeling renewed. Maybe things weren't so bad after all. I had one great friendship and another promising one. Maybe with their help I really could make it through what was left of my time. I still hadn't heard from my minions, anyway.

When we reached the house, Sydney wrapped me in a tight hug.

"Thank you for everything. I couldn't have found my perfect dress without you."

I pulled back and smiled at her.

"It was fun."

"Okay, you better get inside. Callum's looking at us from the living room windows with a massive scowl on his face," she said.

I sighed and looked back over my shoulder. Sure enough, he was watching us. Syd waved at him.

"Have fun dealing with that," she laughed as she made her way to the car. "I'll call you later."

I waved at her and turned to go inside. However, I was surprised the prospect of arguing with Callum didn't get me down. For the first time in weeks, I actually felt happy. And no one, not Callum or even my father, could ruin my good mood.

CHAPTER FOURTEEN

A month into my rehabilitation, things were going pretty well. The Murdochs had taken the news about me being Sydney's maid of honor pretty well in public. Syd had confided in me that Logan had flown through the roof at first, but she quickly straightened him out. Kira was cautious but made no protest. Callum didn't have much to say.

In fact, Callum had not been around much. He was busy with the Lifeblood roll out and was working long hours. That suited me just fine. Sydney kept me busy with wedding plans when I wasn't working at the blood bank. And Miranda, Syd, and I had even met a couple of times for girls' nights. So, I didn't even miss him—much.

I got up early one morning, a Friday, to watch the sunrise. It had kind of become a habit for me. It was amazing to be able to do that after so many years of waking at sunset. The brilliant reds, pinks, and yellows reminded me of paintings I had seen throughout the years. But no painting could really do the experience justice.

I threw on some jeans and a long-sleeved T-shirt, intending on grabbing a cup of coffee to take outside to the garden with me. The house was quiet, and I felt a sense of peace. I cherished these times when I wasn't being chaperoned, and I could just be alone with my thoughts.

Rustling sounds emanated from the kitchen, stopping me in my tracks. I hoped whomever it was wouldn't ruin my private time.

Callum was busy loading a filter into the coffee pot when I entered the room. I considered turning back, but his head jerked around almost before I entered the room. Damned vampire hearing.

When he saw it was me, he smiled.

"You're up early," he said, going back to making his coffee.

"Yeah," I replied, not wanting him to know why I was up. "So are you."

"Work," he said, scooping grounds into the machine. "You gonna have some of this?"

I nodded, so he added more coffee and water.

He pressed the start button and turned around, crossing his arms. The room was silent except for the soft gurgling of the coffee machine. I inhaled the scent of French roast and tried to think of something to talk about. On the rare occasions we saw each other, things were strained, and I hated it.

"How's the roll out going?"

He shrugged and lifted a hand to rub his neck. "Fine. Production has started. We plan on shipping out the first batches next month."

"Cool," I said, playing with a hand towel on the counter.

"How are things with you?" he said. I could tell he was just being polite.

"Okay, I guess."

He nodded and checked the pot to see if it was ready. After taking a couple of mugs down from the cabinet, he poured two cups from the pot, emptying it.

He extended a steaming mug toward me across the island. I nodded my thanks and took it from him.

Taking a sip, I thought about how stupid this was. Callum and I had not had a real conversation since the night we went to dinner.

"Listen, I was wondering if maybe sometime this weekend, if you had time, we could have lunch or something." His eyebrows shot up. "You know, to discuss my progress and stuff," I said quickly.

The eyebrows lowered, and he took a gulp of coffee.

"Actually, I planned on working all weekend. However, Mother has been keeping me updated on you. She says you're doing fine. I talked to your father yesterday and relayed the news."

"Oh," I said, unable to think of a more interesting response. "Okay, then."

He began gathering his things and seemed to dismiss me from his mind. To make myself useful, I went to the coffee machine, now through its cycle, intending to make another pot since everyone else would be up soon. I'd never made coffee before, but I figured if mortals could do it, then so could I.

Lost in thought as Callum drained the rest of his coffee, I went to the sink and emptied the grounds down the drain. With a flick of the switch, I started the disposal while I tried to think of something to say to Callum to ease this tension between us. My thoughts were interrupted by a loud clanging sound followed by a buzz.

Callum rushed to the sink as I looked down to see what was happening.

"What did you do?" he asked, flipping the switch off.

"Nothing," I said, which elicited a skeptical frown from him. "I just poured the coffee grounds down there."

Callum started to stick his hand down the drain but paused.

"Whatever you do, don't touch that switch," he said, nodding to the disposal button.

When I nodded, he proceeded to fish around in the disposal for a second. He stopped and looked at me with shock. Closing his eyes, he shook his head.

"Tell me you didn't put the filter down there, too," he said as he pulled out his hand. A clump of shredded paper speckled with black grit dripped from his fingers.

"Oops," I said.

"Raven, normal people throw the filter and grounds in the trash can."

"Excuse me," I said, feeling defensive. "I've never made coffee before."

He ignored me and pulled more soggy mess from the drain, adding it to the pile next to the sink. Callum tried the switch. The low whirring sound that emitted from the sink wasn't a good sign. With a sigh, he turned the switch back off.

Grabbing a hand towel from the counter, he looked at me.

"It's broken. I'd call a plumber, but I have to get out of here. It'll have to wait until Hannah gets up."

"I'll take care of it," I said, wanting to make up for my mistake.

His skeptical look made my hackles rise. "Callum, believe it or not, I am capable of making a phone call."

"Fine. I think the plumber's number is in the drawer by the phone." He looked at his watch. "Okay, I really have to go. Try not to break anything else."

With that he grabbed his briefcase and headed out the door, my one-fingered wave unnoticed in his haste.

I looked out the window over the sink and sighed. Dawn had come and gone without me noticing. Grimacing, I scooped up the pile of coffee and filter to put in the trash. I was embarrassed I couldn't even make coffee without screwing something up. The worst part was I'd been trying to be nice to Callum and ended up annoying him instead. The day was off to a freaking fabulous start. Idly, I wondered what else could go wrong.

Bad idea.

#

Nancy's open-mouthed stare made me pause on my way into the blood bank.

"What happened to your hair?" she asked.

I wanted to turn around and go home. However, Raven Coracino didn't hide from her problems.

"I have no idea," I said, trying to fluff the strands with my fingers.

"Oh dear."

I turned to look in the mirror over the console table in the waiting area.

Yikes! It was worse than I remembered. For some reason, my hair looked like I had combed it with a piece of bacon. It hung limply around my face like wet noodles.

"It looks a little . . . . ..wilted," Nancy said, reaching out to touch it. When she surreptitiously wiped her hand on her pants, I felt the sting of tears.

"I don't know what I did wrong. I followed the hairdresser's instructions like I always do."

"It almost looks like . . . never mind," she said.

"What?"

"I hate to ask this, but did you use shampoo instead of conditioner?"

Now that she mentioned it, I did wonder why it took so long for the "shampoo" to rinse out this morning. The tension between Callum and I, combined with the embarrassment about the disposal, must have distracted me enough to grab the wrong bottle in the shower.

"Oh. My. God." I covered my face with my hands, trying to ward off the tears of frustration that threatened to overwhelm me. I was such an idiot I couldn't even wash my hair correctly.

"There, there, dear. It's not too bad."

"Yes, it is!" I wailed.

"Okay, you're right. It is pretty bad. But there's nothing you can do about it. Now go put on your apron."

I trudged my way to the volunteers' room. Already the waiting room was filling up. Usually the afternoon shifts were pretty slow, but a pileup on the Beltline yesterday had Good Samaritans coming out of the woodwork to donate blood. Freaking Samaritans.

I put my purse in my locker and grabbed the pink apron. If I was lucky, Nancy would let me hand out cookies instead of checking people in. People liked getting cookies. It meant they were done. People waiting to give blood were impatient and antsy. They snapped at the volunteers and demanded to know how much longer it would be. Customer service wasn't my forte even on good days. Today was not a good day.

Nancy was waiting for me at the desk, tapping her foot.

"Raven, you're on check-in duty. I've got to handle the examinations."

"But what about the cookies?" I asked a little desperately.

"It's too busy to waste manpower on that. We'll just put them on the table and let people grab their own."

My shoulders slumped as I took the seat behind the desk. Before I could even work up a good pout, the door opened and three people walked in. Five women in business suits already waited in chairs.

"How long is this going to take?" demanded a fortyish man in a pinstripe suit when he reached the desk.

"There are five people ahead of you in line, and the chairs are full."

"Can you move me ahead in line? I have a meeting in an hour."

"Sorry, it's first come, first served. You'll have to wait like everyone else."

He grabbed the clipboard I offered him after snapping his name at me and stalked to a chair. He was one of the more pleasant visitors I dealt with that afternoon.

By six o'clock, I'd been yelled at by both customers and Nancy, gotten three paper cuts, and spilled a soda all over my apron. The last part kind of made up for some of my aggravation, but on the whole I was not a happy vampire when I left. Hannah picked me up out front.

"How was your day?" she asked warily as I slammed the door.

My look must have explained everything because she turned up the radio and drove off without another word. Soon we reached Kira's house. The plumber's van was already in the driveway.

I ran inside, hoping he hadn't been there long. I'd instructed Kira and Hannah that no one was allowed to handle the disposal issue but me. It was silly, I know, but I needed to prove to everyone that I could fix my mistakes.

As I ran, Kira called out that she and Hannah were heading out for the night and wouldn't be home until late. I acknowledged the information with a wave and hurried on.

He was waiting in the kitchen, drinking a soda.

"I'm so sorry I'm late," I said, throwing my purse on the counter.

"Lady, it's your dime. You want to pay time and a half for me to sit around, it's no skin off my nose."

Wearing a blue chambray shirt embroidered with the name "Hank," he made no move to get up.

"Time and a half?" I asked.

He pointed to the gold wristwatch on his meaty wrist. "You wanted me to come at six. That's an after-hours job. After-hours jobs pay time and a half."

"Fine, whatever. Can you fix it?"

"Depends. I haven't looked yet."

"How long have you been here?"

"About thirty minutes, I'd say."

I rubbed my forehead in a vain effort to ease the ache that had begun forming there.

"Hank, do you think you could take a break from your break and look at the disposal?" I asked through gritted teeth.

"Geez, lady, no need to be rude." He slowly raised himself from the stool with a grunt. After he lumbered over to the sink, he flipped on the water.

"The faucet works," he reported helpfully.

"Yes, I know. I called you about a disposal problem, remember?"

"Yeah, yeah, I know. It never hurts to do a complete diagnostic though."

I rolled my eyes and took a seat on the stool, figuring this was going to be a long process.

Finally, he flipped the switch for the disposal. Nothing had changed since this morning.

"Yep, your disposal's broke, all right."

Thanks, Mr. Obvious.

"Can you fix it?"

"Depends. I need to get under the sink and open 'er up."

"Great."

He grabbed a wrench from his tool bag, and ducked under the sink. I looked away quickly to avoid the view of his butt crack. Within seconds the kitchen was filled with loud clanking sounds. I didn't know much about plumbing, but something didn't give me much faith in Hank's skills.

The phone rang. Thankful for the distraction, I picked it up on the second ring.

When I heard the voice on the other end, I almost hung up.

"Raven? Why are you answering Kira's phone?" my father asked. His voice grated on my nerves, which were already raw from the continued banging by Hank.

"Well, hello, Father. It's nice to talk to you, too," I said.

"I'm calling to talk to Callum," he said, ignoring my sarcasm.

"He's not here." I watched Hank wiggle from beneath the sink and wipe his grimy hands on the butt of his jeans. At least the crack was covered.

"Don't tell me they've left you alone," my father said.

"No, Kira and Hannah are here someplace. Don't worry though. They've hidden all the valuables where I can't find them."

He sighed. "I'd hoped that a third of the way into your time there you'd have learned to curb that tongue of yours."

"You know what? I'm gonna let you go now. Buh-bye."

"Wait. I want to talk to you about something," he said before I could hang up.

"What?"

"Callum has been updating me regularly on your progress. He says you're doing well," he said.

A flush of pleasure started in my middle at his words. Even Hank's renewed clatter didn't bother me this time.

"However, I am sure he's whitewashing things so I won't worry. Don't think you can fake your way through this."

And there went the warm glow.

Taking a deep, calming breath, I tried to tamp down the

urge to yell.

"Tell me something," I said. "If you're so convinced I am going to fail at this, why did you send me here to begin with?"

"It's not your place to question my reasoning. It's your job to do what you're told. And right now I'm telling you that you might have Callum fooled, but you can't fool me. Are you sleeping with him yet?"

My mouth dropped open in shock as my heart plummeted in my chest. I might have done some questionable things in my life. But I had never used sex to get my way. Ever.

"You know what?" I asked my father. "You seem to have made up your mind about me already. So, you'll understand why I am about to hang up on you."

I slammed the phone down so hard that the wall cradle cracked.

"Uh, miss?" Hank's voice cut through the red haze of anger welling up in me. "You're gonna need a brand new disposal unit here."

I'm not exactly sure what happened next. One minute I was pissed at my father and frustrated by the day from hell. And the next minute, the plumber looked like dinner.

He stood next to the sink waiting for my response. I said nothing, just began stalking him. At first he just looked at me curiously, as if politely waiting to see what I had in mind. As I neared, his eyes widened.

"Miss? Are you all right?" he asked. "Look, lady, I'm married, so there's no use in giving me that come-hither stare."

My predatory drive was in full force as I rounded the center island. Before he could say another word, I reached into his mind. It didn't take much force to calm his fears and make him biddable.

I reached out and placed my hands on his shoulders. Inhaling, I caught the scent of sweat and grease. But underneath all that was the hypnotic scent of real blood. The ambrosia I had been denied for weeks.

Stress lowers a vampire's immunity, much like it did in humans, but the effects were exaggerated. Thus, even though I had gulped down a quick bottle of Lifeblood in the car thanks to Hannah, I was ravenous.

My fangs descended as I went in for a taste. I wasn't thinking about the consequences of my actions. However, there really was no threat to the human. Because of my connection to his thoughts, I would know immediately when I had taken too much. But right then I didn't really care. I needed blood, and I needed this act of rebellion even more.

My fangs grazed his neck once, causing his mass to shudder. Opening my mouth wide, I prepared to feast.

Before I could break the skin, though, something grabbed me from behind and tossed me like a rag doll across the room. My body slammed into the refrigerator. Unhurt but dazed, I shook my head to clear it.

Callum stood in front of the plumber like an avenging angel. I started to rise, but the rage in his eyes held me in check. He turned to the plumber and looked into his eyes. After a moment, Hank calmly went to the counter, packed up his bag, and walked out without a word.

There goes dinner, I thought wryly.

But I knew how lucky I was Callum had interceded. The ramifications of such an act would have spelled disaster for my future.

Callum turned back to me, and suddenly I wasn't so grateful he was the one who caught me. His clenched jaw and fists told the tale. I had screwed up royally.

From my position on the floor, I held up a hand.

"Callum, listen, before you—"

"Don't." His voice was eerily calm, more ice than fire.

He wrenched me up by my arms and turned me toward the door. Without a word, he pulled me through the house, up the stairs and straight into a bedroom that must have been his. I didn't bother to fight him. The reality of what I had done was sinking in fast, and my mind was working overtime to figure out what the hell was coming.

He pushed me onto the edge of the bed.

"Don't move," he commanded.

Sitting still, I watched him begin to pace in front of me. His every movement screamed of leashed fury. When he spoke, his voice vibrated despite its quiet tone.

"I brought you up here because I am going to give you one chance to explain yourself. If you fail to give me a pretty damned good reason for what you just did, I will march downstairs and call your father to come get you. Understood?"

He stopped in front of me, demanding an excuse I didn't have. What could I say? That I'd had a bad day? I leaned back on my hands and stared up at him defiantly.

"We both know there's no excuse. Go ahead and make the call."

CHAPTER FIFTEEN

Callum dropped his head for a moment as if praying for patience. Rubbing his eyes, he took a deep breath.

"Why are you so fucking stubborn? Do you want to be exiled? Is that it? Or is it that you are so screwed up that anytime things start going well you have to sabotage yourself?"

"Don't you psychoanalyze me," I said, sitting forward, menace in my voice.

"Someone should! I just don't get it. Things were going so well."

"How would you know? You haven't been around!"

"Mother gives me updates."

I snorted.

"Wait. Did you bite that man to get back at me for something?" His incredulity was evident.

"No."

Closing my eyes, I took a deep breath.

"I don't know!"

Suddenly, I felt tired. Fighting with Callum was exhausting.

"It's been a shitty day, okay?" I said finally.

He sat down next to me, not too close but near enough that I smelled his Callumness, a mixture of woodsy cologne and hot male.

"Tell me what happened?" he asked, sounding genuinely interested.

"Look, it doesn't matter," I said, starting to stand. He grabbed my arm and pulled me back down.

"Stop. Talk to me."

Heaving a sigh, I relented.

"The day had been crap before I got home, but I guess it was the conversation with my father, on top of everything else, that pushed me over the edge," I explained.

"What did he say?"

"He implied that I'd been using sex to manipulate you into giving him good reports."

"What?" Callum's outraged voice bounced off the walls. "What made him think that?"

I wondered briefly if part of his shock was at the idea that someone would think he'd actually sleep with me. Knowing it was an overreaction, I shook those thoughts away as soon as they reared up.

"I don't know, Callum. I guess he figured that's the only way you'd say something complimentary about me."

He frowned. "It doesn't matter why he said it. We both know it's not true. You really have been doing well. Until today. I don't get why you let him push your buttons like that."

"I don't know why either. I tell myself to blow him off, but he always seems to bring out the worst in me."

"Why is that?"

I looked down at my hands, not sure if I wanted to get into that right then. Looking up at Callum, I saw something close to empathy in his eyes. On second thought, maybe it would be nice to get it off my chest.

"What do you know about my mother?"

He blinked at my change in topic.

"Nothing. I wondered why she wasn't in the picture, but I'd never heard anything. Why?"

I stood to give myself some space from his distracting nearness.

"From what I've been told, she was pretty wild. My father turned her when she was still quite young by mortal standards—about sixteen years old. She had been a farm girl. Her father grew grains that he sold at the market in the village. Apparently, Orpheus was smitten from the moment he first saw her.

"The story goes that they fell in love, and he turned her so they could be together forever. He thought she was his soul mate. But after the change, she became unpredictable, drunk on her new powers."

Callum nodded. "So when your father turned her, she gained not only immortality, but a rise in social class. I can see how that might cause someone born into poverty to get a little carried away."

Nodding absently, I continued.

"Father hoped that after I was born she would calm down. Settle into being a mother. Apparently, though, she became even more reckless. One night she walked into a tavern full of mortals. She grabbed a patron and fed on him in front of everyone, claiming she was a goddess," I said, pausing as frustration and sadness filled me.

My mother was a stranger to me for all intents and purposes, but the story of what happened was too horrible to remain unaffected.

"Somehow they subdued her. After chaining her in the town's square, they waited for the sun to kill her."

Callum let out a deep breath. "Shit."

"Of course, it didn't kill her," I said, imaging the terror she had to have experienced. "It must have been agony for her, though, as the effects of the sun allergy took over, covered in rashes and all of her tissues swelling."

Suppressed a shudder, I soldiered on, wanting to get this over with.

"When they discovered the sun hadn't killed her, they decided to stake her. Since she was already weak, she couldn't fight them off. For good measure, they burned her body at midnight in the square."

"That's horrible," Callum said, sounding shocked. "Where was your father through all this?"

"He was off conducting some business with the heads of some of the other families. I had been left with my wet nurse while mother went out."

"Wow." He grew quiet, as if thinking about the implications of my story.

The first prickles of tears began, but I ruthlessly fought them. There was no sense crying for a woman I didn't remember.

"Anyway, my father was worried I would take after her, so he was very strict with me. But the more he pushed me, the more I rebelled. Once he joined the Brethren, he got worse. He became irrational in his demands. It got so bad I left, refusing to attach myself to the sect at all."

"So your decision to fight the advances we've made is a result of his pressure," he concluded.

I shook my head. "Callum, you don't understand. He's fanatical about his beliefs. He sees no grey areas at all. I think when my mother died he decided the only way to protect our kind was to pretend we weren't different. To blend. It's not just that he pressured me—I honestly believe his ideas are harmful.

"Do you know that until I was out on my own, I was never allowed to hunt or go outside by myself? He had vagrants brought to the villa for me to feed from, and he paid them off with large sums of cash. He neglected to teach me about taking care of my needs. I think part of that, too, was to keep me dependent on him."

"I had no idea it was like that for you," he said. "I guess this explains your mistrust of mortals, though."

Nodding, I tried to explain. "When I was young, I blamed them for taking my mother from me. As I grew, though, I realized she had to have been mentally ill. However, my father's increasing efforts to be more like them ruined any chance of me seeing them in a positive light."

He stood and said, "You're a strong woman, Gabriella Coracino."

The corner of my mouth twitched. "No, I'm not, Callum. I'm screwed up. Any fool can see that."

"Anyone raised under those circumstances would have reacted the same way," he said with a frown. "Or else they would have become trembling little pawns."

"Sometimes, I think it would have been easier to become the perfect little vamp princess he wanted. At least then maybe he'd love me."

I bit my tongue, angry I'd said it out loud. I waited for Callum to tell me I was being silly and to stop with the self-pity. Instead, he put his hands on my shoulders and looked me straight in the eye.

"You know what?" he said. "Screw him."

Blinking, I wondered if I misheard him.

"What?"

"You heard me. Screw him," he repeated. "If he can't see that you're a smart, strong woman, then that's his problem. The best thing you can do is succeed at this challenge he's given you. Then you can move on and never speak to him again."

Smiling, I felt all warm and mushy at his defense of me.

"However," he said, crossing his arms in front of his chest. "No more biting the help, okay?"

I grimaced at the reminder. "Look, I'm sorry about that. I shouldn't have tried to take my frustration out on the plumber."

"No, you shouldn't have. Frankly, I'm surprised, despite what you just told me about your old man, that one bad phone call can make you relapse like that."

"It wasn't just the phone call. The blood bank sucked worse than usual, and I broke the disposal, and then there was this morning."

His eyebrows knit together. "This morning?"

I shifted uncomfortably, not wanting to admit how much our tense conversation had upset me.

"What about this morning, Gabby?" he asked, not letting me avoid his gaze.

I sighed. "It's not a big deal, okay? I just felt like you brushed me off."

He hesitated and then laughed. "I find it hard to believe anyone could brush you off without hearing about it."

When I didn't laugh with him, he frowned.

"Is this about the coffee episode?"

Shaking my head, I said, "No, before that. It was like you didn't even want to be in the same room as me."

He blew out a breath. "Okay, I know I was short with you. I could say it's stress from work, but that's not the whole truth."

I waited expectantly while he seemed to gather his thoughts.

"Truth is, I thought that some space might help both of us. Things were pretty tense that night after we went to dinner. I didn't want to tempt either of us into doing something we might both regret."

My jaw dropped. Did he just say he'd regret sleeping with me?

"You are so fucking full of yourself!" I said.

His eyes widened, surprised by my sudden attack.

"What? What'd I do?" He asked, taken aback.

"I'll have you know that no man sleeps with me and regrets it. You'd be lucky to get me into bed!" I said, my arms flying around, heralding my Italian ancestry.

"You're right," he said quietly, stopping me in my tracks.

"What?" Now it was my turn to be confused.

"I didn't mean to imply I would regret sleeping with you, you silly woman. I meant that if we slept together there might be consequences we don't want to deal with."

"Oh," I said, feeling foolish.

"Yeah."

"Like what?" I asked, moving a step closer to him.

"Like if your father found out, he might call the whole thing off and send you to Norway."

"But he already thinks we're sleeping together, remember?" I said.

"True." He moved a little closer. "But I wouldn't want you thinking you don't have to follow through with your training because we . . . were intimate."

"Yeah, right. Like you'd let me slack off," I said, brushing his concerns off with a wave of my hand. "What else?"

His voice lowered slightly as he moved toward me.

"If my family found out, they'd feel the need to be in our business."

"So we wouldn't tell them," I said.

His eyes flicked to my mouth and stayed there. My lips—and various other parts—went on red alert. The conversation was turning me on. Oh, yeah, that was definitely lust I was feeling.

My mind tried to intervene. She tried to remind me this was the man I once swore was the complete opposite of everything I wanted. But my hormones shut her up before she could get much further.

I didn't know if it was the fact he listened to me whine about my father and then took my side. I didn't know if it was the fact he seemed to genuinely want me to succeed. I didn't know if it was his tight ass or his very kissable lips. All I knew was that I had to have him right then—or sooner if possible.

Callum's thoughts seemed to have followed the direction of my own. His palm had begun a lazy path up my bare arm, which was exposed by a pink tank top.

"So what you're saying is there really is no reason we can't do this?" he said, his voice almost a whisper.

"None that I can think of," I replied, my heart beating heavily in my chest.

I swear my nipples stood up to wave at him.

"Let's say I did this," he said, reaching up to cup my right breast. I bit back a moan as the heat of his hand seared through the thin fabric of my top.

"Would you have any objections?"

His breath was coming faster now, even as he tried to maintain his nonchalant façade.

"I wouldn't mind it one bit," I said, playing along.

"And, if I did this?" I asked.

His eyes flared as I took hold of his package.

"Is that all right with you?" I queried innocently.

He swallowed hard. "Uh-huh."

Chuckling, I continued to caress him. His other hand came up, giving him two handfuls of breast.

"Gabby?" His voice was thick, along with his member.

"Yes, Callum," I said, looking him straight in the eye.

"I'm going to fuck you now."

Oh goody!

Before I could say it aloud, though, he swooped in and claimed my lips.

The next few seconds were a blur, lost in a tangle of lips and tongues and fangs. I wanted to swallow him whole. Consume him.

This time it wasn't my sexual drought making me ravenous. It was all Callum—his expert tongue, his heady scent, his roving, possessive hands.

I grasped the back of his head, taking a handful of hair as I angled for leverage. He grabbed a handful of my own hair and thrust his tongue deeper.

We fell on the bed into a heap of tangled limbs. The frame creaked in protest, but we didn't care. We were too busy fighting with buttons and zippers. I finally gave up on his second button and ripped the shirt open, revealing his smooth, muscled chest. Crisp golden hairs winked at me in the light, inviting me to play. I started by laving his nipple with my tongue. He groaned and squeezed my ass, urging me on.

His other nipple received the same treatment. Before I could explore further, though, he flipped me over. Our eyes met, burning into each other. He pushed up my shirt and yanked down my sheer bra. Soon he was making me groan too.

I felt like a cat, wanting to climb all over him while purring in delight. My hands roamed his body, exploring every contour.

He moved on me restlessly, as if wanting to touch all of me at once. And oh, how I wanted him to. His hand reached up under my short skirt as he kissed me again. He didn't bother teasing me.

Instead, he ripped off my panties and threw them over his shoulder. Shoving the skirt up over my hips, he pulled away from my lips to survey the territory he'd uncovered.

I prayed he would go exploring with his mouth there too. The goddess must have been listening because in an instant he did. His warm, wet tongue made me writhe even as I pressed myself into his mouth. His fingers thrust into me and I cried out.

I was crazy with the wanting. Begging aloud for mercy. Then, mercifully, I shot out of my skin before plunging back into my body.

When I recovered some of my wits, Callum was staring at me with pure male satisfaction. Smiling, I pulled him to my mouth and kissed him hard, tasting my own essence.

It was my turn to flip him over, not bothering to rearrange my clothing. His khaki pants were tented and radiating heat. Making quick work of the zipper, I released his cock. A bead of moisture glistened on the tip. Using my hand, I spread it around as I tested its girth.

With my tongue, I traced the rigid lines of his shaft. He jumped a bit when I nipped him with my fangs, but settled down when I followed it with a tongue swirl.

After torturing him for a few moments, I took him into my mouth. He grabbed my torso, urging me to swing my body around. Soon, his mouth was once again bringing me back to climax. I worked faster, trying to get him there too.

Time stopped for an instant as we both hovered on the edge. Finally, we tumbled over together, moaning into each other.

I've heard mortals need time to recuperate after le petite mort. And don't get me started on the whole condom choreography they have to endure. Poor things.

All vamps had to worry about was getting pregnant, but since females only had three fertile times a year, it was pretty easy to plan around. Plus, males could tell when we were in heat, so to speak. So there was no awkward discussion needed. In other words, we were cleared for takeoff.

He had me on my back before the aftershocks started. I grabbed his face and brought it to me as he plunged. His mouth muffled my excitement as I finally felt him hard and strong inside of me.

Callum reared back to increase the tempo. He smiled, his fangs flashing and sweat trickling down his temple. The image was so endearing and erotic I almost came right then.

I wrapped my legs tighter around his hips, wanting to absorb him into me. He lowered himself onto my chest, even as he added a little swirling motion to his thrusts.

Nuzzling my face into his neck, I inhaled the combination of aroused male and blood. His mouth found my neck too. We writhed together, delaying the moment.

Finally I couldn't stand it anymore. We both bit at the same moment.

The world went black with pain for a second. Then bright white light burst on the inside of my eyelids. His blood was chocolate and whiskey and sex combined. The taste mixed with the ecstasy of pleasure-pain as he fed, and the feel of his cock slamming into me was almost too much. I was drowning in the pleasure, sure I was going to die right then. But I couldn't stop. The connection was so complete it felt as if I lived within his skin.

Another explosion, this one rocking me to my core, thrust me to a whole other metaphysical plane. I swear I saw the face of the goddess smiling at me before I slammed back down to earth.

Callum's harsh breath in my ear was the first sound I heard. He swallowed hard and kissed me on my cheek. My mind was a kaleidoscope of thoughts, never really settling on anything coherent. I felt rejuvenated. Brand new.

Neither of us moved for a long time until my arm, which was trapped between us, fell asleep. I shifted slightly, trying to get feeling back in the offending limb. Callum didn't move. He must have fallen asleep, I decided.

"Callum?" I whispered.

"Mrhm."

"Callum."

I wiggled a little bit.

"Yes."

"My arm's asleep."

He lifted slightly, looking at me with half-closed eyes. I freed my arm and shook it.

"Your pillow talk leaves a lot to be desired," he said, grinning.

I chuckled.

"Hmm," I said, wrapping both arms, despite the pins and needles, around his neck. "How about: Oh, Callum, I finally feel like a woman?"

He laughed. "Better. But you forgot to mention my manly proportions."

He shifted his hips to poke the aforementioned proportions against me.

"Well, they are definitely manly, and . . . er . . . quite proportionate."

He nipped at my lips as punishment for my impertinence.

"I guess I should move, but you make a great pillow," he said with a sigh.

"That's okay, you make a decent blanket," I said.

While I was enjoying the banter, it felt like we were both avoiding the fact we'd just had wild monkey sex and what it meant. Not that I felt like going into overanalyzation mode when I had a very sexy man on top of me, but it was there, hovering on the fringes.

"Uh-oh. What's the frown about?" he said.

"Nothing."

"Liar."

"Okay, you're right. I was starting to think. Maybe you should distract me."

He groaned and rolled off me. "Woman, you can't be ready again."

I smiled. He was so full of it. Being a vamp meant he could do it all night long, and we both knew it.

"So do you want to start talking or should I?" I asked innocently.

He rolled back onto me so fast he almost knocked the breath out of me.

"You wanna be on top this time?"

No more talking was required as I saddled up and prepared to ride my stallion into the sunrise.

CHAPTER SIXTEEN

A tickling sensation on my nose woke me up. Without opening my eyes, I scratched it. A few seconds passed. Another tickle. This time I swatted at it. I must have overshot my aim because my hand smacked something that wasn't my face.

"Ow!"

I opened my eyes to see Callum rubbing his own nose.

"Oops."

"Remind me to duck next time I try to wake you," he said.

I stretched like a cat, enjoying the delicious lethargy of postcoital bliss. While I rubbed against the warm male body next to mine, my mind focused on Callum's words.

Did he mean what he said? Would there be a next time?

He kissed my forehead and sighed as his hand groped for my breast. He sure wasn't acting like a man with regrets. I decided to play it casual and see where the morning took us.

"Listen, as much as I'd like to go for round number five, I think you'd better get back to your room before everyone wakes up," he said into my hair.

I sighed, not wanting to move. Callum's warm body was the perfect antidote to the chilly autumn morning. But he was right. We'd agreed to keep things under wraps. Goddess knew I didn't need Kira shooting me death looks over my morning coffee.

"What time is it?" I mumbled from my place in the crook of his neck.

"It's just after six."

I groaned again for good measure. We had finally passed out around four a.m., wrapped around each other.

"Okay, I guess I'll get up," I groaned.

As I started to rise, though, he pulled me back down. His lips found mine, but I protested, not wanting to scare him off with my funky morning breath. He laughed at me and proceeded to give me a morning kiss I'd not soon forget.

"Now, go before I decide to forget my mother is three doors down the hall."

Reluctantly, I pulled away. Before I could make it far, though, I felt a smack on my ass.

"Hey, what was that for?" I said with mock indignation.

He grinned, looking boyish with his disheveled hair and sheet-creased face.

"Just thought I'd help you wake up a little more," he said.

I shook my head at him and reached for my clothes, which had eventually landed on the floor during our second round the night before.

Memories of the night flooded my mind, making me smile as I struggled to clothe myself with dignity. Not an easy feat with a sexy man watching my every move from his perch on the bed. He lay there with his arms behind his head, looking like a sultan among the rumpled sheets and pillows.

"You look pretty pleased with yourself," I said, pulling my tank top over my head.

"I was just thinking I was right," he said, with a wicked gleam in his eyes.

"I'm almost afraid to ask. What were you right about?" I said, standing with my hands on my hips.

For some reason I couldn't stop smiling.

"About you being a screamer."

I picked up a discarded pillow from the floor and threw it. Bulls-eye! He pulled the pillow from his face with a ferocious frown.

"Gabby, do you need another spanking?" he said, slowly rising and coming toward me.

I squealed, something I never did, and ran. He caught me just before I reached the door. He swung me around, laughing, and swooped in for another kiss. I've never laughed and kissed before, and I decided I'd have to do it more often.

When he finished, he pulled back slightly.

"I had fun," he whispered, his mouth so close it tickled my sensitive lips.

Little Callum was hard against my hip. I realized then that he was naked, while I was fully clothed. For some reason, it turned me on all over again.

"Me too," I said.

I took advantage of the angle and took a peek south—enjoying the manly landscape.

"Good. Now get going. If my mother sees you she'll know what's up."

"'Cause I'm wearing the same clothes from last night?" I asked.

"That and the fact your tank top is on inside out."

I glanced down to confirm, and sure enough the damned thing was on wrong. My cheeks warmed as I realized I had been so busy staring at Callum earlier that I couldn't even dress myself.

"Don't worry. I like it, especially since you forgot to put on your bra, too," he said.

Heaving an exasperated sigh at my absentmindedness, I stalked over and snatched the bra off the picture frame it was hanging from.

Callum was chuckling as I walked past him. He grabbed my arm.

His hand came out from behind his back with a scrap of black lace hanging from his index finger.

"Your panties too."

I tried to grab them, but he was too quick.

"I think I'll keep these, if you don't mind," he said. "They'll be my hostage. If you ever want to see them again, you have to come again tonight."

Swooping past him, I opened the door. I glanced over my shoulder to where he stood waiting for my response. Just before I closed the door, I gave it to him.

"Trust me, Callum. We'll both be coming tonight."

#

Three hours later, I padded down the stairs feeling great. After I'd gone back to my room, my bed beckoned me. The nap and a shower afterward made me feel like a new woman.

Of course, the ten orgasms I'd had the night before hadn't hurt either.

The scents of coffee and bacon enticed me into the dining room. I swung open the louvered doors and stopped dead in my tracks. Callum, Kira, and Hannah all stopped what they were doing to look up at me.

Until that moment, I hadn't really thought about how difficult it might be to maintain my cool in front of others about sleeping with Callum. I mean, a woman didn't have multiple rounds of mind-blowing sex with a man one night and then casually eat breakfast with his mother the next morning. At least, I'd never done it.

"Raven? Are you all right, dear?" Kira said, looking concerned.

Great, so much for playing it cool, I thought, realizing I'd been standing there for several seconds with my mouth hanging open. My eyes shot to Callum, who grinned and winked at me from behind his coffee mug.

"I'm fine, I just hadn't realized I'd slept in so much later than everyone else," I said lamely, motioning to the nearly empty plates in front of them.

Continuing into the room, I took a seat across from Callum. That was my first mistake. Now I'd have to look at him the whole meal and try to pretend I hadn't seen him naked as recently as three hours earlier.

Avoiding his gaze, I reached for the coffee pot and filled the mug next to my plate to near brimming. Hannah hovered around the table making sure everyone had plenty to eat. When she touched my arm, I jumped—spilling coffee all over my plate.

"Shit!" I yelled, jumping up to avoid the hot liquid.

"Oh my, you're jumpy today," Hannah said, tsking at the coffee stains on the white table cloth.

Swiping at the beads of coffee on my jeans with a napkin, I fought to keep my cool.

"Sorry, I just didn't sleep well."

Callum cleared his throat. I looked up at him, which was my second mistake.

The bastard was laughing at me. Luckily, I didn't think anyone else noticed since they were too busy cleaning up the mess. He quickly covered his mouth with his napkin when I narrowed my eyes at him.

Even as I grew more frustrated, I couldn't help the smile that threatened to expose itself. He was too damned cute sitting there. His white T-shirt with the Murdoch Biotech logo on the pocket stretched across his broad shoulders quite nicely—the same shoulders I'd clawed in ecstasy hours earlier.

His eyes held mine, and it was obvious he was thinking about last night too. The spell was broken as Hannah bumped into me as she cleared away the coffee-splattered dishes.

"I'll just get you another plate, Raven," she said, and went back to the kitchen.

Her interruption was a relief. Our secret wouldn't remain one for long if we kept staring at each other like two dogs in heat. I shook myself as Kira retook her seat at the head of the table.

"Kira, I'm sorry."

She waved my apology away. "No harm done. Lack of sleep tends to mess with one's coordination."

I nodded and retook my seat, avoiding Callum's gaze as much as possible.

"Hannah told me the disposal was still broken. I do hope you weren't so worried about that you couldn't sleep."

I had been taking my first, much-needed sip of coffee as she asked. Barely managing not to choke, I managed to swallow slowly, formulating my response. Finally, I decided to lie through my teeth, hoping Callum would play along.

"I was just so disappointed he couldn't fix it. He said the entire unit needed to be replaced."

"Well, dear, I'm sure we can wait a couple of days until he can come back with the replacement. How long did he say it would be?"

My mind raced. How was I going to explain to Kira that the plumber wouldn't be back ever since he probably didn't even remember being there after Callum cleared his mind. My eyes shot to Callum for help.

"Mother, I got here just as the plumber was telling her about his fees. They were outrageous. I think we should get a second opinion."

"If you think that's best, dear," she said, looking completely oblivious to the fact we were both lying through our teeth. "I'm sure we can find someone more reasonable."

Hannah came back in carrying the new plate and utensils for me. I murmured my thanks as she placed them in front of me.

"Hannah, do you have the number of any other plumbers?" Kira asked her household manager. "Callum said the one yesterday was trying to charge too much."

Hannah's eyebrows knitted. "That's impossible. I've used Hank for some time. He's always been quite fair."

Callum and I shared an uneasy look, wondering if we'd been caught.

"Perhaps with you. But maybe he sensed Raven was not knowledgeable about such things and tried to make some extra money," Callum said.

Hannah looked unconvinced. "I highly doubt it, but if you think we need someone else to come out then we can. If you want, I can talk to them so we're sure to get a fair deal," she offered.

I should have felt relieved that we'd gotten away with covering up Hank's brush with becoming my meal, but my pride stung. I didn't want Hannah or Kira thinking I couldn't handle something as simple as negotiating a fair price with a mortal serviceman.

Callum must have known what I was thinking because he shook his head slightly, telling me to keep my mouth shut. Finally, my common sense beat my pride into submission.

Breakfast continued as we all chatted about our plans for the day. Kira had just asked me what I was going to do when the doorbell rang.

Hannah left the room to answer the door. I was telling Kira about my plans to relax, but didn't get very far before Hannah came back with Miranda in tow.

"Raven, you have a visitor," Hannah said unnecessarily.

I jumped out of my seat to give my friend a hug.

"Miranda! What a great surprise," I said.

"Sorry to drop in like this, but I was in the neighborhood," she said, hugging me back.

"No problem at all," I replied.

Remembering the other people in the room, I turned to introduce Miranda.

"I'm sorry. Miranda, this is Kira Murdoch," I said, leading her to Kira.

The women shook hands. "Miranda, so nice to see you again. How is your mother?" Kira asked.

"She's doing well, thank you for asking. I'll tell her you asked about her."

I was surprised by the fact they'd already met, but I wasn't sure why. Miranda was well-known in Brethren circles. I was the one who was the outcast.

Callum stood and came around the table. "Miranda, it's been a couple of years. Good to see you."

As they shook hands and exchanged pleasantries, I had a brief spurt of insecurity. Miranda and Callum would have made a great couple. Standing next to each other, they looked like the Ken and Barbie of the vampire world.

Recalling Miranda's comments about Callum being hot didn't help matters.

"So, I'm sure you guys will excuse us," I said, totally

interrupting Miranda as she shared a story about a mutual friend with him. "We've got lots to catch up on."

I pretty much jerked her away from Callum in my haste to separate them. Miranda only had to time to wave at Kira and Callum as I pulled her out of the room.

"That was rude," she said, tugging at my hand.

I didn't say anything as I lead her to my room, wanting to get as much space between her and Callum as possible.

"What's your problem?" she demanded as I closed the door behind us.

"Nothing. Just needed to get out of there."

"Something's up. I can tell," she said. "Spill it."

I strolled over to the chair in the corner of the room and plopped down.

"What? Nothing's wrong," I said, attempting to look casual.

Her eyes narrowed. "You've had sex!"

"What?" I yelped as I sprang from the chair. "What gave you that idea?"

"Raven, I've known you for two hundred years. Don't even try to play dumb with me. Plus, you've got that glowy thing going for you."

"Glowy thing?" I asked.

"You know, it's like this aura of satisfaction people give off after they've just had really good sex."

I went into the bathroom to check myself in the mirror. Nope, still the same, I decided. Miranda came up behind me.

"You're crazy," I said. "I don't look glowy."

"Ah, but the fact you checked to begin with verifies my hunch," she said, sounding all superior like she'd caught me, which, of course, she had.

"Crap, okay. If I tell you, it's in the vault of secrecy, okay? I swear to the goddess if you leak what I'm about to tell you, you're going down."

"Ooh, threats. It must be really good. Okay, I promise," she said, sounding excited.

I turned from the mirror to lean against the counter. Taking a deep breath, I debated how much to tell her.

"Yes, I had sex."

She waited. When I said nothing else, she groaned.

"That's it? That's all you're going to tell me?"

"Yep," I said and went back into the bedroom.

She followed me like a bloodhound following a scent.

"You're a tease, you know that? Well, actually I guess you're not, seeing as how you did the deed with someone recently," she said.

I could see the wheels spinning in her head. It wouldn't take her long to drag all the details out of me, but I didn't want to just spill it all like some gossipy teenager. I was still getting used to the idea that Callum and I had gotten freaky.

"Wait! It was Callum wasn't it?"

So much for drawing the mystery out.

"Yes," I admitted since there really wasn't any point in denying it.

She squealed and clapped her hands.

"I knew it! He kept looking at you when I was talking to him. Then you were acting all weird. I mean weird for you, that is."

"Thanks."

I sat on the bed, figuring it might take her a few minutes to get the squeals out of her system. Her comment about Callum looking at me gave me a nice little thrill though.

"Why don't you sound more giddy?" she asked, frowning. "Don't tell me it was bad. Oh God, that's the worst."

Sighing, I fell back on the bed. "No, it was amazing."

"Well then, what's the problem?" she asked, sitting next to me.

"He's so not my type."

"And that's a problem because? Seriously, Raven, Callum's the first decent vamp you've been with since I've known you. Besides, who cares? It's not like you're interested in a relationship with him."

Her laughter grated on my nerves. Not sure why since she was right. First of all, my father would have a field day if he found out I was dating his idea of the perfect Brethren citizen.

Second, I could hardly stand Callum most days. Except in bed. And when he made me laugh. But other than that there was nothing. Oh, and he was kind of smart and a total babe. But that was all.

"You're right," I said, sitting up. "I should just go with the flow and enjoy the ride while it lasts, right?"

"Right," she said, looking a little concerned. "Are you sure you're not interested in more than sex from him?"

My laughter sounded harsh to my own ears.

"Don't be silly. He's just a convenient source of pleasure for the time being."

"Okay, if you say so," she said, looking unconvinced. "But you know, he is considered kind of a catch."

"Well this chick isn't trying to reel him in, okay? Just drop it."

"Fine," she said.

"Fine."

We sat in silence for a few moments, mine brooding and hers more thoughtful.

"If you don't want to talk about Callum, then I guess I should tell you why I came over."

I perked up, happy for the change in subject.

She reached into her purse and pulled out a piece of paper.

"This note was delivered to my shop last night."

Curious, I took the note from her and read it.

Mistress R,
All is ready. Call to put plan "Raven's Wing" into action.
Freddie

My heart dropped. I'd forgotten all about my email to the minions. I should feel ecstatic that I could get out of here now. Instead, I felt conflicted. "Raven?"

I looked up distractedly. "Yeah."

"What are you going to do?"

"I don't know," I said, meaning it.

"If you want my opinion, and even if you don't, I think

calling that number would be a huge mistake."

"Why's that?" I asked, more curious about her reasoning than anything.

"Two things. First of all, from what I can see, things here aren't so bad. You seem to be getting along with the Murdochs. And if you don't mind me saying, you seem more centered now than I've seen you in decades."

Pondering what she said, I decided she was right in some respects. The only thing I disagreed with was the part about me being centered, whatever that meant. If it meant I was calmer, she was wrong. After my night with Callum, I felt totally unsettled. I couldn't put my finger on what it was exactly. I didn't regret sleeping with Callum, but I felt like maybe the experience was more than I bargained for in some way.

"What's the second thing?" I asked, not wanting to analyze my feelings about last night anymore.

"Your father expects you to screw up."

The last thing I needed right then was to think about my father. I was so sick of thinking about his reaction to every move I made.

"I told you I don't know what I am going to do. I need to think about it some more."

Her eyebrows knitted into a frown. "But you'll think about what I said?"

I sighed. "Yeah, I'll think about it."

"Good. Because I meant what I said. This three-month crash course may turn out to be a good thing for you."

"What do you mean?"

"It's just I've seen you struggle for so many years against your father. It's almost like you've forgotten to live your own life. It's time you forget about him and do what makes you happy. Use the rest of your time here to figure out what you want to do."

"You've been watching daytime TV again haven't you?"

She laughed. "Nah, I just want you to be happy for a change."

I smiled. It felt so good to have Miranda in my corner.

"You're a good friend, you know that?" I said.

She reached over and hugged me.

"So are you, when you're not trying to act all tough. Now, we have to stop this, or I'm going to get all sentimental."

I chuckled, feeling kind of misty myself.

"You know what? I think I'll stick it out here for a while longer," I said. "I can always keep the number handy in case things head south."

Miranda just smiled as I got up to hide the note in a black beaded purse in the back of my closet.

"Hey, I've been thinking. We should plan a shower for Sydney," Miranda said as I came back to the bed.

"A shower?"

"Yeah, you know, silly games, finger foods, presents. As the bridesmaid, it's one of your duties. But since we both know you have no idea what you're doing, I thought I could help out," she said.

I groaned. "Do I have to?"

"Raven, Sydney doesn't have many friends in the vampire community yet, and from what I can tell, she didn't have many in her old life except Jorge and Geraldine. I think it would be nice."

"Who would we invite?"

She tapped her finger on her lip for a moment as she thought.

"Well, let's see. Besides you and me, we could invite Jorge and Geraldine, Kira and Hannah. Oh, and she hit it off with some of the ladies at the midnight shopping event she came to at my store. We could invite them too."

"That doesn't sound too bad," I said. I figured for Sydney's sake I could put up with a couple of hours of girlie chitchat.

"Where would we have it?" I asked.

"Do you think Kira would let us do it here?"

"I guess I could ask. I know she loves Syd. She'd probably like to help out."

"Okay, you ask her, and then we'll figure out the details. She'll probably want to invite some of her friends, too," she said. "I think we could throw it together in couple of weeks, don't you?"

"I have no idea, but if you think that's enough time then that's what I'll tell Kira. Wait, do I need to plan a bachelorette thingie too?" I asked.

"Good point. Why don't we plan on doing that the same night? We can have the shower and then go out on the town."

"That might work. Do you think we need to invite everyone to that too? I'm not sure Syd would be comfortable getting crazy with her future mother-in-law there."

"Hmmm," Miranda said, mulling it over. "I think it would be fun to keep the group small. So we'll wait for everyone else to go, and then Syd, Jorge, Geraldine, you, and me can go do the bachelorette portion of the evening."

"You know what might be fun?" I said, warming up to the idea. "We should keep the second half of the night a secret from Syd. We can just kidnap her after the shower."

"Great idea!" she said. "We can rent a limo and have it come pick the five of us up."

"Cool. Now . . ."

We spent the next hour planning. By the time she left, I was excited. Having something fun to focus on besides my own problems was nice. Plus, I liked Syd and wanted to do something cool for her. I knew what it was like to feel alone. So I figured putting up with polite small talk and oohing and aahing over China patterns was a small price to pay to help the bride enjoy herself.

Later I was sitting at the desk writing down a list of things to do for the shower. The task was taking all my concentration, so I didn't hear the door open. Suddenly, a pair of hands landed over my eyes. I shrieked and lashed out, ready to defend myself against my attacker.

Whipping around, I saw Callum laughing at me.

"Jumpy today, aren't we?"

"Callum! You scared the shit out of me. What do you mean sneaking up on me like that?"

"I knocked on the door, opened it, and walked over to you.

You're a vampire, Gabby. You should have heard me before I even got to the door."

My cheeks heated. I felt like an idiot because he was right.

"Sorry, I guess I was distracted."

"What were you doing?" he asked, trying to look around me.

"Nothing."

Snatching the paper from the desk, I hid it behind my back. For some reason I was embarrassed to tell him what I was doing.

"What are you hiding?" he asked, his expression playful but curious.

"Callum, it's nothing."

His eyes narrowed as he frowned. "Gabby, show me the paper."

"No."

"Don't make me take it from you," he said. The warning echoed with his sharp tone.

"Mind your own business," I said, backing away from him.

His expression turned serious, but he tried and failed to sound like he was teasing. "You're planning something bad aren't you? Or, wait, is it from another man?"

That stopped me in my tracks. Was that jealousy I saw on his face?

"It's not from another man, idiot."

He looked unconvinced. "Then it's something bad. What are you planning, Gabby?"

"Callum, drop it. I promise I'm not doing anything wrong."

I felt a brief twinge of guilt when I remembered the note Miranda had delivered earlier.

Before I could react, he lunged at me and grabbed the paper.

"Hey!" I said, trying to snatch it back.

He turned his back to me, warding me off with one muscled arm.

"Flowers, invitations, cake, limo, naughty veil? What the hell is this?" he asked, still keeping me at arm's length.

"I'm planning a wedding shower for Sydney, okay?" I said, my voice high and my cheeks in flames.

He turned around, a stunned look on his face.

"Why didn't you just tell me that to begin with?"

"Because I'm embarrassed, okay?"

"Why would you be embarrassed? I think it's great you're throwing Syd a shower." He was smiling at me now, and it made me nervous.

"Actually, it's more than great," he said. "You're a good friend, Gabby. This is going to mean a lot to Syd."

"Look, don't think this means I've gone soft or anything," I said, crossing my arms. "It was Miranda's idea."

"Don't forget who you're talking to here. I saw through your tough exterior from day one, remember?"

"Don't go telling everyone, okay? I have a rep to protect."

He moved toward me with a sexy look in his eyes. I held up a hand as I backed away.

"I'm pissed at you. Don't even think about trying any moves."

He kept coming.

"You didn't mind my moves last night," he said, taking my hand.

I shook him off. "Hey, I thought we were keeping this under wraps."

He took my hand again and kissed it before I could pull away.

"Mother and Hannah left right after Miranda. Won't be back for hours," he said. Pulling me toward him, he began nuzzling my neck.

I was weakening. My body wanted to melt into his. But my pride was still stinging.

"You think you can just walk in here and seduce me?"

"Yep," he said, cupping my breast and grazing my neck with his fangs.

Pride be damned. What kind of idiot would I be to turn down amazing sex over a stupid to-do list?

CHAPTER SEVENTEEN

The day of the shower arrived in no time. Much to my relief, Kira had been thrilled to help out. Between the shower and the bachelorette plans, my time at the blood bank, and my nights with Callum, life was busy. It was also fun.

Callum had proved to be an imaginative and fun lover. The only problem was keeping myself in check when we were in public. It didn't help that he was always sending me clandestine looks and finding excuses to touch me. But it was a small price to pay for our nights together.

Kira seemed clueless about the shenanigans going on under her roof, which was lucky since we spent a lot of time together running errands and preparing for the shower. She wasn't so bad to hang out with as long as she wasn't extolling the virtues of the Brethren Sect.

The event began at seven in the evening and would go until nine. Because we'd decided on a romance theme for the shower, the house was filled with red roses and scented candles. An exclusive vampire catering service stood ready to pass out hors d'oeuvres and drinks, including Lifeblood.

When Syd arrived and saw everything, her eyes went all misty.

"Raven, I can't tell you how much this means to me. It's perfect," she said, giving me a hug.

She went on to say hello to Kira and Miranda, who were setting up the favors. As I watched them hug and laugh, a warm feeling spread through my insides. It amazed me that something I did was making someone so happy. It was a novel feeling. I found myself actually looking forward to the shower—silly games, small talk, and all.

By eight o'clock, however, I was having second thoughts. Kira and Miranda had each invited a few vamp ladies from their social circle. I didn't really know any of them.

But they knew me.

News of my punishment had spread through the gossip mill like wildfire. Miranda had warned me about it before the shower, but I'd shrugged it off, thinking everyone would be so focused on Syd it wouldn't matter. I couldn't have been more wrong.

It started the minute the guests began to arrive. Lydia Abernathy and Helen Mariades, two ladies from Kira's book group, were effusive in their compliments to Syd. However, when I approached them to thank them for coming, they literally turned their backs on me. I was left standing there with a rapidly receding smile and my hand extended.

Knowing most vampires were big supporters of my father's agenda, I shook the incident off.

Miranda had seen what happened, though.

"Ignore them," she advised, taking my arm and leading me back into the fray.

She stayed by my side as everyone else arrived, making sure to introduce me. I appreciated her support, but it couldn't hide the chilly reception I got from most of the attendees.

After everyone arrived we played the requisite bridal shower game—with a twist. Unfortunately, trying to get a group of women who averaged at least three hundred years in age excited about pin the fangs on the groom was tough.

Sydney didn't seem to care, though. When we brought out the cardboard cutout of Logan wearing a tux, she giggled. Even though some of the other ladies weren't enthusiastic, Jorge, Geraldine, Miranda, and I played it up. Jorge won, but I think he cheated so he could win the spa gift certificate prize.

After Jorge stopped jumping up and down, I went to the center of the room and tapped a fork on my flute of Lifeblood.

"Ladies, if I can have your attention," I said, pausing to give everyone a chance to finish their conversations. "It's time for Sydney to open her presents."

Everyone seemed excited as they took their seats. Miranda lead Syd to the seat of honor in the circle of chairs. Sydney had no idea that the guests had been instructed to buy gifts related to the romance theme. Miranda and I figured that two vampires didn't really need the traditional china and crystal, so we thought we'd stock Syd up on naughty lingerie and other naughty gifts.

Sitting opposite from Syd, I prepared to record each item as she opened it. Plus I wanted a good view of her reactions to her presents.

The first gift was from Miriam Duchamp, a former courtesan from Paris. She was one of Kira's friends, and while she had not snubbed me like the others, she'd been a bit of a snob when we were introduced.

As Syd pulled the crimson satin sheets from the gift bag, a brief flicker of shock passed over her features. Quickly schooling her expression, Syd graciously thanked Miriam.

Biting back a smile, I wrote down the information for Syd to use for thank you notes. Miriam caught my eye and winked. I smiled back, instantly forgiving her earlier coldness. Anyone who'd give a bride satin sheets couldn't be too bad.

Jorge's gift was second. When she opened the box, she blushed clear to her hairline. She cleared her throat and quickly closed the box. But since everyone was in on the joke, they demanded she show what she'd received.

Her face flaming, she stole a glance at Kira.

"Well, it appears to be an assortment of . . . items one might use in the bedroom," she said.

Jorge had surpassed subtle, giving Syd a sex-toy gift pack

from Naughty Notions, a local sex shop.

"Sydney, there's no need to be shy. I might be your future mother-in-law, but I know a vibrator when I see one," Kira said, causing the room to burst into laughter.

Soon, Syd relaxed and enjoyed showing off her naughty gifts. The variety was mind-boggling: books on Kama Sutra and Tantric sex; a naughty board game; a gift basket filled with flavored massage oils, edible underwear, and handcuffs; several pieces of lingerie in every color and style imaginable; and his-and-hers blindfolds.

Everyone was having a great time, even the older ladies. Some of them even started debating the merits of cherry-flavored massage oil versus mint. For the record, mint won because it "added a nice tingling sensation," according to Miriam.

Kira was the only one who whose gift didn't go with the theme.

"I thought since you missed Logan's first four centuries, you might like to have some of the memorabilia I've collected over the years," she said as Syd unwrapped the gift.

The box contained a large photo album, which Kira explained held photos of Logan's life, including anecdotes from times before cameras were invented.

Syd jumped up and hugged her soon-to-be mother in law. There wasn't a dry eye in the place by the time they were done.

As touched as I was by the scene, part of me felt jealous that Kira welcomed Sydney so easily into her family. I knew if Callum and I were dating, she wouldn't be so thrilled. Not that we were dating, but still. It was the principle of the matter.

I was so lost in my thoughts that Miranda had to remind me that Syd had one more gift to open. Jumping out of my seat, I ran to the foyer and retrieved the box I'd hidden there earlier.

"This is from me," I said, feeling a little sheepish.

Her eyes widened when she saw the huge package I placed on the floor in front of her.

"Uh-oh. After everything else, I'm afraid too see what you came up with," she joked.

Because my gift followed Kira's sentimental one, I was glad I had decided to forgo the naughty gifts everyone else had favored.

Syd tore at the paper, revealing a plain cardboard box. Opening the flaps, she dug through mounds of tissue. My nerves started to get the best of me as I worried whether she'd like it. Giving gifts was a new thing for me, and I'd agonized for days about what to buy her.

She pulled out the brown leather overnight bag and shot me a confused look.

"Open it," I said, smiling.

As she unzipped it, the room was quiet as everyone waited in anticipation.

She dug around in the bag and withdrew a bottle of champagne, a mix CD I'd made of romantic music, and an envelope. She opened it and gasped.

"Oh, Raven, you shouldn't have!" she exclaimed. "She's booked us for a week at the Inn on Biltmore Estate in Asheville!"

All eyes swiveled to me in shock. I guess everyone was surprised I could come up with a decent gift.

"You said you didn't have honeymoon plans yet, so I figured this might take some of the pressure off you," I said with a shrug. "I also booked you guys for a couple's massage at the spa."

The inn was located on the grounds of the historic Biltmore Estate, a famous home once owned by the Vanderbilt family. The property was nestled into the Blue Ridge Mountains, a popular spot for romantic getaways.

Syd moved so fast I barely saw her, almost knocking me down as she hugged me.

"Thank you so much!" she whispered as she squeezed me tight.

"It's no big deal," I said, hugging her back.

She sniffed, and I knew the tears were coming.

"Hey, don't go crying all over me. This shirt is new," I said, trying to lighten things up before I began crying too.

She pulled away but remained at my side as she chatted with the other guests about the gift. I felt embarrassed to be the focus of so much attention, so I quickly signaled for the waiter to bring in the cake.

As everyone dug into the chocolate confection, Kira approached me.

"Raven, you did a wonderful job pulling this together for Sydney. I know it means a lot to her," she said, smiling at me.

"You and Hannah did a lot of the work," I said, brushing off her compliment.

"You did most of it. And that gift! It was so thoughtful of you to think of that for them. I have to admit I was skeptical about you being a bridesmaid at first. But I was wrong," she said. "In fact, I'm starting to think I was wrong about a lot of things where you're concerned."

My mouth dropped open in shock.

"Kira, I don't know what to say."

"You don't have to say anything. Your actions have shown me everything I need to know."

She patted me on the arm and went to get some cake. I stood there grinning stupidly for a few minutes before Miranda came to see what was going on.

"What was all that about?" she asked.

I shook my head to clear it. "She complimented me on the shower," I said, not ready to discuss the rest of what Kira had said.

"Well, you deserve it. I know Sydney had a great time."

"If you think this was great, just wait until we start the bachelorette portion of the evening."

Miranda laughed. "It's a good thing Callum and Alaric agreed to do the bachelor party tonight too. I have a feeling it's going to be a long night."

"Callum agreed to confiscate Logan's cell phone so he can't check in," I said. "Knowing him, he'd blow the surprise."

"Oh, come on. He's not that bad," she said.

I shot her a skeptical look.

"Anyway," she said, "where are we going? I can't believe you wouldn't let me help with the bachelorette plans too."

"You'll just have to wait and find out with everyone else."

"Are you this much of a tease with Callum, too?" she asked.

Quickly glancing around to be sure no one heard her, I elbowed her in the arm.

"Hush! No one is supposed to know about that, remember? Besides, we both know when it comes to teases you hold the title."

She huffed in indignation. "I do not!"

"Oh, yeah? Who's the born-again virgin?"

She crossed her arm and scowled at me. "I am not, and you know it."

"You might as well be. It's been what? A century and a half since you slept with that pirate guy. What was his name again?"

"Captain Nick Slade was not a pirate. He was a privateer. And our affair was three centuries ago, give or take."

"Sure. A privateer who slept with you and then shipped out without saying good-bye," I said, rolling my eyes. "Didn't he also abscond with several pieces of your jewelry?"

"It's not nice to tease me about that, you know. I was heartbroken for a decade," she said. "Besides, there have been other men since him."

"Name one," I challenged.

She thought for a moment. "Vladimir from Kiev."

"That's right. Wasn't he the gambler who had to skip town to avoid his creditors?"

"Yes, but he was very romantic when he wasn't drunk."

"Who else?"

"Pierre DuMonde, the count from Paris."

"You mean the one who claimed the French Revolution left his noble family impoverished. Didn't he borrow money from you and then disappear?"

"Yes," she admitted. "Now you see why I swore off men. Since I had terrible taste, why bother?"

"You make a good point," I said.

Since I'd been with my fair share of assholes, I could relate to her sentiment. With Callum, though, I had the perfect setup.

No strings and no expectations. Although, I had warned him that if he came home reeking of cheap stripper perfume, there'd be hell to pay. But who could blame me for that? While this thing between us lasted, he was going to be a one-woman vampire—or else.

The guests had finished their cake and were starting to gather their things. For a few minutes the room was a flurry of hugs and chatter.

"Raven, I just wanted to thank you for putting together such a lovely shower," one of the earlier snubbers said.

Her friend nodded eagerly. "It's the best shower we've been to in decades."

Shocked that they went out of their way to compliment me, I smiled graciously.

"Thank you so much for coming. We'll see you both at the wedding?"

"Yes, we're looking forward to it. Sydney will make a lovely bride, and that Logan is quite a catch."

I thanked them again and showed them to the door. The rest of the guests had similar nice things to say as they left. As Kira finished seeing everyone off, I walked back into the sitting room.

Dropping onto a nearby chair, I felt proud of myself. This was the first time I'd done something unselfish in a long time. Glancing at Syd, who was chatting with Jorge and Miranda, I was happy she'd enjoyed herself.

I also felt as if I'd passed some kind of test. As if I proved to everyone I was more than a troublemaker.

Kira came in after everyone left.

"Well, that was fun," she said, walking over to Syd. "However, it's time for this old woman to turn in."

We all chuckled. Callum's mom looked younger than most of us.

"Thank you so much, Kira. I had a wonderful time," Syd said, giving the woman a hug.

"Raven did most of the work. Thank her."

Her praise shouldn't have meant as much as it did. But I

wasn't going to analyze it. The night was young, and there was still more fun to be had. I wasn't going to let my brain stand in the way of enjoying myself.

Kira said goodnight to everyone and left, winking at me on her way out. She was in on the bachelorette plan, so her exit was prearranged.

"Raven, thank you so much for everything," Syd said, coming to my side. "This was so much fun."

"Looks like you got enough stuff to open your own sex shop," I said, surveying her gifts.

She laughed. "Yeah, I think Logan will be quite pleased with the haul. I wish we could try some of the stuff out tonight, but he'll probably be too drunk after the bachelor outing."

I caught my cohorts' eyes, letting them know it was time to let the cat out of the bag. They came over and stood behind me.

"Actually, you'll probably be pretty drunk yourself," I said causally.

"What?" she asked, looking at each of us curiously.

"Girlfriend, we're going out!" Jorge announced.

"Sydney Worth, it's time for your bachelorette party!" Miranda said, holding up the bag of surprises I'd assembled before the shower.

Syd's mouth dropped open. "You guys didn't have to do this!"

"Oh, yes we did! You can't get married until you've been embarrassed in public," Geraldine said.

"Yay!" Syd said, obviously getting into the spirit.

I grabbed the first item out of the bag. The black T-shirt had "Bride" written on the front in red rhinestones.

"Oh my God, I love it," Syd said, giggling as she took it from me. She slipped it on right over her black wrap dress.

Next, I pulled out a length of black tulle. Syd laughed when she saw it was no normal veil.

"Miranda made this especially for tonight," I said, placing it on Sydney's head. The black material fell just below her shoulders. Little penis charms and condoms were attached with red satin ribbons.

Syd ran to the mirror in the foyer and laughed at her reflection. "I look like the slutty bride of Dracula!"

"If the shoe fits, girl," Jorge said, winking at her.

"But wait, that's not all," I said, digging into the bag again. "I also got a little something for the rest of us to wear."

Out came four black feather boas and one red one.

As I passed them out, I said, "The black ones are for us and the red one is for Syd."

"I've always wanted a black boa!" Jorge said as he flipped the end of his over his shoulder with a flourish.

The doorbell rang, signaling the arrival of the limo.

Miranda went to get the door as I explained the plan for the evening.

"Everyone listen up. Our first stop is the Black Widow for a few cocktails," I said, referring to a local vamp bar. "Then it's off to the Karaoke Krypt."

"Raven, I hate to be a wet blanket," said Geraldine. "But is it okay for us to go to vampire bars?"

I waved away her concern. "You'll be fine. These are Brethren establishments, so they're pretty mortal friendly. Okay, everyone ready?"

As we made our way outside to the stretch Hummer limo, Syd pulled me aside.

"Raven, thank you. This means so much to me," she said.

"You may not be thanking me in the morning."

"Hey, I'm a vampire. We don't get hangovers," Syd said with a laugh.

"I wasn't talking about the liquor."

"Oh?" she asked, looking nervous. "You're not going to get me in trouble with Logan are you?"

"Nah. But I do plan on embarrassing the shit out of you. Be prepared. You will be singing karaoke before the night's over."

I pulled a camera out of my bag.

"There will be photographic evidence."

She laughed. "Hey, wait. There isn't a chance we'll run into the guys, is there?"

Shaking my head, I said, "Nope. Callum assured me they

were hitting a vamp club in Chapel Hill."

"Good. I'd hate for Logan to hear me doing karaoke. He might call off the wedding."

We both laughed and loaded into the monster limo. The interior had neon lights running along the ceiling and behind the two long leather benches that spanned the length of the vehicle. Our driver, Lance, was a vampire who specialized in vampire events. Thus, he had cold bagged blood chilling in ice buckets along with bottles of champagne and beer.

"Okay, people," he said before he closed the window connecting the driver's area from the back. "Who's ready to have fun?"

"We are!" we all shouted in unison.

He laughed and hit a switch, closing the window. Within seconds, the Hummer was on the move with ABBA's "Dancing Queen" blasting from the speakers.

Watching everyone sing along, I couldn't help but smile. For the first time in a long time, I felt like I belonged.

Jorge leaned over and put his arm around me as he handed me a recently opened bottle of champagne. "Drink up," he shouted.

I chugged down some bubbly goodness, avoiding the errant feathers of my boa.

They all sang into their champagne glasses. No one was on key, of course, but no one seemed to care.

What the hell, I decided, belting out the next line with gusto.

And the weird thing was, after four hundred years, I felt like I finally was having the time of my life.

CHAPTER EIGHTEEN

At four a.m., the limo pulled smoothly back into Kira's driveway. Geraldine was passed out in one of the seats with Jorge's snoring face on her shoulder. Poor mortals couldn't keep up with us vamps when it came to liquor consumption.

Lucky for them, we were strong enough to carry them out of the last bar to the limo. They'd done pretty well, though, each lasting long enough to make asses out of themselves during a duet of "Islands in the Stream." Jorge did a mean impression of Dolly Parton.

To be fair, Miranda, Sydney, and I were dragging as well. The night had been a total blast, though, with lots of laughter, booze, and horrible renditions of Top 40 songs. After several drinks, they finally convinced me to do my worst on stage.

Let's just say, I will never be able to hear "Like a Virgin" again without cringing.

The Hummer rolled to a stop. Syd, who was sprawled out next to me with her veil askew, perked up.

"Am I home?" she slurred.

"Sorry, this is me," I said, gathering my boa and purse. "Miranda's going to make sure you get home okay."

I looked at Miranda for confirmation. She nodded slowly.

Laughing, I took in her smeared mascara and wild hair.

"Syd, just a word of advice," I said. "You might want to drink some Lifeblood before you hit the sack. You won't have a hangover, but dehydration is almost as bad."

"Oh, that's a good idea," she said, hiccupping.

"I hope you had fun," I said.

"It was a blast. I need to get married more often."

I laughed and gave her and Miranda quick hugs before stepping out, careful not to wake the sleeping beauties.

Miranda rolled down the window and poked her head out.

"Raven, I'll make sure the mortals get home, too."

"Thanks," I said. "By the way, I'm excited Syd asked you to be in the wedding."

She smiled sleepily. "Me too. I hope she remembers it in the morning."

"She will," I said with a chuckle. "Call me tomorrow?"

She waved and ducked back inside. I went to the front of the car to take care of the bill with Lance.

"Thanks," I said, handing him his fee plus a large tip. "It was great."

"I'll say. This is the craziest bachelorette I've handled in a long time."

I laughed. "Really?"

"Sure, I've never had anyone flash passing cars from the sunroof before."

"I think Geraldine had a few too many Cosmos," I said, laughing.

He joined in for a moment before sobering.

"Listen," he said, clearing his throat. "You wouldn't want to grab a drink sometime, would you?"

His offer took me off guard. Lance was a good-looking guy. Plus, he'd proved he had a great sense of humor putting up with us all night. Yet, I hesitated. As nice as he was, he paled in comparison to a certain golden-haired sex god.

I was about to politely turn him down when a deep voice stopped me cold.

"Say good night to the man, Gabby."

I swung around, finding Callum standing not five feet away with his arms crossed. He'd obviously heard us pull in.

"Callum! I didn't see you there," I said, feeling flustered. I didn't have anything to feel guilty about, but I couldn't help feeling that way.

"Obviously," he said, staring me down.

I turned to Lance, about to explain that I couldn't go out with him. However, he beat me to the punch.

"Geez, sorry. I didn't know you were married. You weren't wearing a ring, so I figured . . . Anyway, my mistake. Hope you have a good night."

My mouth fell open. He thought Callum was my *husband?*

"No," I started to explain, but stopped myself. What was the use? Even though I wasn't married—yikes—to Callum, he was still the reason I wasn't interested in Lance.

"I mean, yes, sorry about that. Take care of my friends, okay?"

"Sure thing," he said.

I stepped back as he put the Hummer into gear and pulled away. Delaying the inevitable, I watched it all the way down the driveway until I could barely see the taillights in the distance.

The thing is I knew what had just happened looked bad. Callum's frown and crossed arms spoke volumes. I resented feeling defensive when I hadn't done anything wrong, though.

He cleared his throat, managing to make the sound angry. Pasting a big smile on my face, I turned to face the music.

"Hi! How was your night?" I said, trying to sound oblivious to his anger.

"I had a good time, Gabriella," he said, walking toward me.

Uh-oh. Using my full name wasn't a good sign.

"It appears you had a good time too," he said, stopping in front of me. "The question is: how good of a time?"

"Excuse me?" I said, offended by his implication.

"It seems limo boy took quite a shine to you," he said, his voice hard. "And you him."

"Look, you ass, you're jumping to some pretty idiotic conclusions here."

"Am I?"

"Yes, you are. However, I don't feel the need to justify my actions to you."

I started to walk away, high on getting the last word. His hand grabbed the back of my shirt, swinging me around.

"You're not going to deny you were flirting with him?"

I sighed, pulling my arm from his grasp. "Callum, green isn't your color."

His eyebrows lowered. "I'm not jealous."

"Ha, ha, hahaha, I say."

His scowl deepened. "I'm not. I was merely under the impression that our arrangement was exclusive until we decided to end it."

Of course, I thought that, too. It thrilled me a little to hear he agreed. But I couldn't let him off that easily. It was so fun seeing him jealous.

"When did we decide that?" I asked, examining my fingernails.

"Oh? Great, then. As a matter of fact, I have the number of a very flexible stripper in my pants pocket as we speak."

I stopped picking at a cuticle and looked up.

"What?"

He nodded. "Candi is working her way through college by stripping. She wants to be a kindergarten teacher."

My eyes narrowed.

"Show me the number," I demanded, holding my hand out.

His eyes widened. "You don't believe me?"

I snapped my fingers, too angry to speak.

Grinning, he pulled a cocktail napkin out of his pant's pocket and held it up. "You mean this?"

I snatched it away from him before he could react.

Sure enough, written on the crumpled napkin was a phone number. "Candi" was written underneath. The slut actually dotted the i with a freaking heart.

Without hesitation I ripped the napkin into about a thousand tiny little pieces. Callum didn't react—even when I tossed the remains into the air like confetti.

"That was mature," he said, brushing errant napkin bits off his shoulder.

"Fuck maturity."

"Not so easy when the shoe's on the other foot is it?" he asked, crossing his arms with a smug smile.

"This is not the same at all, and you know it! Lance asked me out without any encouragement from me. Candi-with-an-*i* rubbed her tits all over you."

I was whisper-shrieking by then. The thought of some bimbo flirting with him made me want to kick something. "Furthermore, I was about to turn him down when you interrupted. But you," I continued, pacing now. "You come home with a phone number in your pocket!"

"Gabby," he said calmly as I carried on.

"And how dare you act all jealous when what you did was twice as bad!"

"Gabby!"

"What?" I yelled, not caring if woke up the entire neighborhood.

"Candi gave the number to Logan, not me. He passed it to me as a joke. I forgot it was in my pocket until just now."

"Oh," I said, feeling stupid but still suspicious.

"Furthermore, she was not a stripper, but a cocktail waitress at Bella Lugosi's. We didn't even go to a strip club."

His lips started twitching as I stood there feeling like a total ass. So I hit him on the arm.

"I hate you."

"No, you don't," he said, smiling.

I couldn't resist smiling back, relieved I didn't have to go kill Candi. Plus, he looked kind of adorable standing there.

"So, I guess we're both kind of idiots, huh?" I said.

He ran a hand through his hair.

"You make me crazy, you know that?"

"Yeah, I do," I said, grinning like a loon.

"So," he said, slipping his hands in his pockets and rocking back on his heels. "Wanna go get naked?"

"Damn straight!"

#

Life was busy for the next few weeks. In addition to volunteering three times a week at the blood bank, I also was helping Sydney make final preparations for the wedding.

Logan and Callum had decided to use the wedding as the official launch of Lifeblood. It would be served at the reception along with the traditional wedding fare. Therefore, Callum was busy finalizing the plans for Lifeblood's debut along with the big roll out, which would happen the week after the wedding.

Despite our busy schedules, we managed to spend almost every night together. After our silly argument the night of the bachelorette party, things seemed to fall into a comfortable routine. After everyone had gone to bed, one of us would sneak into the other's room. We'd give the mattress a thorough work out, and then we'd talk about our day. Sometimes we talked about our pasts.

We never talked about the future, though.

I'd held firm to my decision to take things one day at a time. So far it had been working, too. The only complaint I had, really, was that each morning Callum would rush off to work and I'd go do my thing, never being alone again until late at night. We'd managed to keep things a secret, being polite but reserved in the company of others. But after a while that seemed to wear on me too.

A week before the wedding, I was just getting off my shift at the blood bank. Usually Hannah or Alaric came to pick me up, but that day I walked outside to find Callum waiting for me. His hair glistened in the late-afternoon sun as he leaned against his car.

"Hey, what are you doing here?" I asked, smiling when I saw him.

He straightened from his slouch and walked to the passenger door, opening it with a flourish.

"You're chariot awaits," he said.

His eyes sparkled with mischief as he helped me into the car. Sliding into the driver's side, he turned the key, making the engine roar to life.

"I thought you had a meeting this afternoon," I said, wondering what was up.

He slid his sunglasses onto his nose.

"I do."

"Oh," I said, disappointed he was going to have to rush back to the office.

"With you," he said, shifting the car into gear and sliding into traffic.

"And just what are we meeting about?" I asked, getting the gist of things.

"I have an extensive oral presentation I'd like to give you."

A flare of lust shot through my body. By goddess, he was sexy. I decided to play along to see how far he'd take this.

"Is that so?" I asked. "I don't believe I have you on my agenda."

"Really? I'm afraid I must insist. The matter is of utmost urgency," he said, slipping his warm palm onto my thigh.

"I suppose I could make an exception. However, I must insist on thorough *dick*-tation."

He sent me a heated look over the rims of his Revos. "That can be arranged. As a matter of fact, I insist."

I laughed then, unable to resist. Callum continually surprised me. When we'd first met, I would have bet cash money the man couldn't screw his way out of a paper bag. However, I was quickly becoming addicted to his body along with his wicked sensual humor.

"So, Mr. CEO, where will this meeting take place?" I asked, knowing that Kira had a bridge game at her house that day.

"I thought we'd go to my place," he said casually.

I hesitated. For some reason, the idea of seeing his home felt significant—like we were taking things to a new level. Plus, while we'd had a couple of quickies during the day before, this was the first time we'd be able to take our time and enjoy ourselves without the cover of darkness.

"Gabby?" he asked, shooting me a concerned look. "Is that all right?"

"What?" I said, shaking myself from my paranoid thoughts.

"Yeah, that's great. I have to admit I've wondered what sort of place you lived in."

His lips quirked. "I've almost forgotten myself. The only time I've been back in the last couple of months was to pick up clothes and mail."

Part of me felt bad that I was the reason his life had been disturbed. Why, I had no idea. He was a big boy, after all.

Still, some feeling niggled at me as I watched him, admiring his strong profile with the bright afternoon sun behind it. He glowed with vitality—a man with a purpose and direction.

Suddenly, I knew what the feeling was—affection. An overwhelming urge to give him a hug came over me.

The car swerved.

"Hey, careful," he said, gently extracting my arms from around his neck with one hand while the other righted the car from its swerve.

"What was that for?" He didn't sound angry so much as confused.

"I have no idea," I said, honestly.

He shot me an amused glance. "You like me." A statement, not a question.

I shrugged. "You're all right, I guess."

His smile turned smug.

Feeling embarrassed about my sudden show of affection and the strange feeling swirling in my belly, I looked out the car window. Callum smoothly turned into a drive between two six-story red brick buildings connected by an ornate wrought-iron gate.

"Wow, you live here?" I asked. "It looks like we're in Paris."

He nodded. "The architects designed the buildings to resemble Second Empire architecture in Paris," he said.

For some reason, I'd imagined Callum living in a modern condo building in the heart of Raleigh's bar scene. Instead, this place was in an older, more historic section of downtown. Although new, the building had character and class. Kind of like the Callum I knew now, instead of the one I'd thought was materialistic and shallow a few months ago.

We parked underground and went up the elevator to the sixth floor. When he opened the door to his corner unit, my mouth dropped open. I'd expected a bachelor pad, but what greeted me looked like something out of *Architectural Digest*.

While the furniture was all done in dark leather, that's where the bachelor stereotype ended. Beautiful hardwood floors gleamed in the light from dozens of large windows. Vintage artwork and sculptures were scattered throughout, lending elegance to the room. The living area opened onto a large kitchen with stainless steel appliances and green marble countertops. The man even had plants—large palms and airy ferns scattered through the rooms.

But the highlight of the condo was a large sitting area situated in one of the round towers I'd noticed from outside the building. Surrounded by double-paned windows, the spot was sun-washed and cheerful. In addition to more comfortable-looking leather chairs, a large telescope stood next to one of the windows.

I wandered over to it and took in the view of downtown Raleigh.

"It was the view that sold me," Callum said, coming up behind me. "But if you think this is good, you need to go upstairs."

I looked at him curiously. Originally, I'd thought the condo was one floor, but looking over his shoulder, I noticed a spiral staircase leading up.

"Go on," he said, urging me toward the stairs.

When I got to the top, I was shocked to find an even better view.

"Oh, it's a cupola," I said. "Callum, this is amazing."

The space was the same size as the sitting area below it, but the panorama was even more spectacular since the room was above the main roof of the building—giving me a 360-degree view.

He came up behind me as I marveled at the gorgeous view. Beyond the modest skyline of the city, I could see the orange, yellow, and red foliage that was a hallmark of autumn in

Raleigh.

"So you like it?" he asked.

Turning, I wrapped my arms around his neck.

"I have to admit I'm shocked. Your mother had to have decorated it for you," I said, teasing him.

"She did not!" he said, shooting me a mock-offended look.

I narrowed my eyes at him.

"Okay, maybe she helped a little. But she didn't make any decisions without my input."

"Well, I like it so far," I said. "But I'm afraid I must reserve judgment until I see the bedroom."

"Don't forget the master bath," he said. "Did I mention I have a Jacuzzi tub?"

"No, you did not. How intriguing," I replied, playing along. "Yes, indeed, we must conduct a thorough exploration there as well. If you think there's time."

All this verbal foreplay was making my blood heat. I wasn't sure if I could make it back downstairs and all the way to the bedroom before ripping his clothes off.

"Did I mention Mother has an event to attend tonight?"

My eyes widened. "So you mean if we tour your house for hours and hours we won't be missed?"

"If by tour my house you meant have sex in every room, then yes, you are correct."

Our eyes held for a moment. I couldn't stand it any longer. The need to have him had been building ever since I'd seen him outside the blood bank. Now that need was smoldering, threatening to consume me.

"Callum?" I said.

"Yes, Gabby?"

"Fuck the tour."

I grabbed his head and crashed my lips into his. He didn't hesitate as he claimed my mouth. Our tongues tangled wildly as we groped at each other. It had only been about ten hours since our last lusty episode, but it didn't seem to matter. I needed my fix and I needed it then.

We spent almost no time on the preliminaries. After a few

moments of feverish kisses, he grabbed my skirt and hiked it up over my hips. As he reached for my panties, I bit back a smile. His head shot up when he encountered nothing but skin.

"You're a naughty, naughty girl," he said, smiling wickedly.

"Punish me," I demanded.

He began to stroke me, slowly at first and then faster as he realized I was already wet and raring to go. As he explored, I worked on his belt and zipper. Finally, I got his rod in my hand, hot and ready. I wanted him to brand me with it.

Before I knew it, he had me bent over the back of an armchair facing the windows. With a thrust of his hips, he was home. We groaned in unison as he slid in easily. Grasping the arms of the chair with my fingers, I gave myself leverage to push back, meeting him thrust for thrust.

He reached under me to grab my breasts, lifting me backward toward him until I was almost standing. With one hand he turned my head, allowing him access to my mouth. As he continued to pound into me, he tangled his tongue with my own. I reached behind me to grasp one of his arms for balance.

We kissed and screwed like there was no tomorrow, which was closer to the truth than I wanted to admit.

Callum twined his fingers with mine. With one hand on the back of the chair, I squeezed his hand with my other one. Suddenly, he withdrew. Spinning me around, he lifted me. My ass balanced against the back of the chair as he plunged in again. My breasts crushed against his chest, and the kissing resumed.

I didn't know which sensation I enjoyed more, the feeling of him rubbing against my clit or the feeling of him inside me. Hell, who was I kidding? I loved it all.

When he pulled back from the kiss, my eyes opened. Our eyes burned into each other as he reached down to rub me with his hand. Reaching for climax with all my being, I closed my eyes.

"Look at me," he commanded. "I want to see your eyes when you come for me."

I obeyed. His green gaze watched me intently. Before I

could think, the orgasm slammed through me. My cries echoed off the walls of the cupola, reverberating through my body along with the waves of pure bliss. Through it all, his gaze held mine.

Helpless to protect myself from the intimacy of the moment, I leaned forward and sank my fangs into his neck. His blood filled my mouth, tasting like wine. At that moment, he shouted his release. Pulling away, I licked the wound one last time. Shuddering, he wrapped his arms around me and we collapsed into each other—a sweaty mass of nerve endings.

Lifting my heavy lids, I peered over his shoulder. The sun was setting over Raleigh, its rays gilding everything in sight. I felt as if my body had been dipped in that golden light, glowing in the aftermath of our lovemaking.

As Callum began stroking my back, I knew things had changed. A subtle shift had occurred the moment he grasped my hand. Kissing his sweat-dampened shoulder, I wondered if he had felt it too.

The playfulness that normally accompanied our lovemaking was missing. Our movements had been almost desperate as opposed to the lazy sensuality of our previous encounters. Desperation over what, I had no clue. Perhaps it was the sense that our time was running out.

Sydney's wedding would be in just a week. My father would be there for both the festivities and to pass judgment on my progress. Since even he couldn't argue that I'd changed, the event would mark the end of my time with Callum.

For the first time, the thought depressed me. I never thought I'd say this, but I'd miss Callum. Not only his body, which was glorious, but also *him*. I'd miss his wicked sense of humor and his quick mind. I'd even miss our verbal sparring, which I enjoyed more than I'd ever admit.

He shifted, bringing me back to the present.

"Wow," he said, kissing my forehead.

"Wow, indeed," I said, shaking off the dark thoughts.

He gently took my chin in his hands, staring into my eyes.

"What's wrong?"

Looking into his green eyes, I suddenly knew I was about to cry. Moving quickly to avoid letting the tears fall, I pulled away.

"Not a thing," I said, my voice overly cheerful. I busied myself with lowering my skirt and readjusting my blouse as I avoided his gaze.

Out of the corner of my eye, I saw him shoot me look.

"Why is it I get the feeling you're lying?" he said as he zipped himself up, leaving his dress shirt untucked.

Walking to him, I put my arms around his neck.

"Callum, nothing's wrong. I promise," I said, hoping he couldn't see the sadness I was trying to conceal.

He caressed my cheek. "Good, because that was amazing."

Despite my confusion over my feelings, I knew one thing. I was going to squeeze every bit of enjoyment I could out of the time we had left together. Starting at that moment.

Smiling, I said, "Yes, it was. Now, how about we check out that Jacuzzi?"

His devilish smile reappeared.

"Excellent idea. I'm feeling quite dirty."

He kept me so busy the rest of the night that my brain didn't have time to process my earlier reaction. But on some level, I was aware we made our way through his condo—christening furniture, kitchen counters, and yes, the Jacuzzi—that a shift had occurred in our relationship.

It didn't feel like just sex anymore. Instead, everything felt significant. It seemed our bodies were trying to communicate something to each other. From deep inside, I felt a yearning to brand his body with my own. I'd never felt so in synch with someone.

Later, as we lay in his bed, Callum held me and stroked my hair. We didn't speak, but we didn't need to.

Even as I basked in the pleasure we were sharing, my mind sensed something big was going on. Something I wasn't ready to face or acknowledge.

CHAPTER NINETEEN

Callum had picked my father up from the airport the day before the rehearsal, but wouldn't give me any details about what was said.

Even though I hadn't seen Orpheus, it was as if the air itself shimmered with his presence. His failure to contact me after he'd arrived was subtle psychological warfare on his part. He wanted me anxious and wondering about his intentions.

Callum had assured me everything was going to be okay, but I didn't believe him. It seemed that either way I was going to lose something. If I failed to pass muster, it was exile city. However, if my father declared my punishment a success, I wasn't going to be much better off. I still had no plan for my future. Still, everything I'd been through these last months had shown me I needed a new direction.

As much as I hated to admit it, this Brethren stuff beat my old life in a lot of ways. If I kept taking Sun Shield, I could finally go hit the beach during the daytime. I'd heard people talking about that for centuries and always wondered what all the fuss was about.

I still wasn't completely comfortable with Lifeblood, but it didn't totally suck. I mean, it sure beat skulking in alleys looking for low-lifes to feed from. Plus, there was always the fear of being seen by a mortal and not being able to erase the human's memory in time. Lifeblood was like fast food—quick and easy. Only Logan had created it so it was almost healthier than feeding directly from humans since the formula had perfectly balanced vitamin and mineral content.

And as much as I'd never thought I'd say this, even mortals weren't so horrible. I'd spent a lot of time with Jorge and Geraldine, plus the blood bank people, and they didn't totally suck. Sure there were a few assholes to deal with, but you had those in the vampire world too. For too long, I'd spent all my time with my minions. It was nice being worshipped and all, but sometimes I missed having someone I could just hang out with.

So, yeah, I had a lot of thinking to do about my future. Included in that was some major soul-searching about my relationship with my father. After talking with Callum, I'd realized how much of my supposed goals had been a way to get back at Orpheus. I sounded like those weak-minded mortals who paid fortunes to shrinks when they just needed to get over it. Move on. Stop living in the past and all that feel-good bullshit.

Unfortunately, the night of the rehearsal was not time to make any major life decisions. I had to be in full maid of honor mode for Syd's sake. In a way, I was kind of looking forward to the whole wedding thing.

Syd was ecstatic about spending the rest of eternity with Logan. I still didn't get her attraction to the guy, but I understood how much it meant to her. Her excitement was contagious. I felt honored to be included in something that meant so much to her.

"You nervous?" Callum asked as he drove to the restaurant for the rehearsal dinner.

We'd just come from a quick run-through of the ceremony at Logan's house. Since the wedding party was small, the officiant, Gwen, had made quick work of the formalities.

"Nope," I said, lying through my teeth. Most of the day I'd managed to avoid thinking about my father. But now I was less than ten minutes from seeing him for the first time since our fateful meeting in his office three months ago.

Callum glanced at me from the corner of his eye, a smile spreading across his features.

"Gabby, it's just me. It's okay to admit it," he said. The light from the dashboard cast a cool glow over his features. I'd much rather stare at him than think about my father. But maybe talking about it with Callum would help release some of the butterflies doing somersaults in my stomach.

"Okay," I said, turning in my seat to face him. "Here's the deal. I've been doing pretty well these last couple of months, right?"

He nodded. "You've done amazingly well."

I let the warmth of his words marinate for a second before continuing.

"So, the thing is, I'm always an idiot when my father is around. It's like something inside me snaps, and I'm suddenly this bundle of angst. Every word he says, every move he makes pisses me off. What if that happens tonight, and I do something really stupid?"

There, I'd said it. It might sound silly, but that's how I felt.

"First of all, that was the old you. You've changed, Gabby. You've still got a mouth on you and are the most stubborn woman I've ever met," he said.

"Thanks for the vote of confidence," I said.

He laughed. "No, what I mean is you're still you but different in some ways. It's like you used to be so defensive all the time. But now you are more relaxed, more confident. I have to think that will come into play tonight with your father, too. You recognize how he antagonizes you, so it will be easier to control your own behavior in reaction to it."

I sighed, feeling more confident. He was right, I was different. I wasn't going to let my father goad me into acting like a child any more.

"And if that doesn't work, come find me, and I'll help you channel your aggression," he said, wiggling his eyebrows at me.

That startled a laugh out of me.

"That's all we need— to get caught in the bathroom stall going at it like teenagers."

"Speaking of which, are you sure you want to spend the night at Sydney's tonight?"

"Well, I don't *want* to, but since Logan will be sleeping at your mother's, I didn't want Syd to spend the night alone. We're gonna do beauty treatments and gossip about boys," I said with a chuckle.

"You know what that means, then, don't you?" he asked.

"Yes, no playtime for little Callum and little Raven," I said with a pout.

"So," he said, "if your father declares you fit to be released back into the world, do you think you'll be leaving after the wedding?"

The words were said casually, but I knew what he was really asking: Was this the end of the road?

I had to choose my words carefully.

"I'm not sure. Do you think there's any particular reason I might want to stick around?"

"I don't know. Is there?" he asked. He kept his eyes on the road, but his stiff posture spoke volumes.

"Callum—" I began, only to be interrupted by the chirp of his cell phone.

He looked frustrated at the interruption but glanced at the caller ID.

"Shit, it's Jorge. Hold that thought, okay?" he said before answering. I nodded but felt relieved. Goddess only knew what kind of trouble my mouth had been about to get me into.

"Yes, we're pulling into the driveway now. See? Yes, hi," Callum said, waving his hand at Jorge who stood in front of the restaurant looking impatient.

Callum hung up the phone.

"He's a little dictator, that guy," he said.

"He's just anxious for everything to go smoothly for Syd and Logan."

Callum pulled in front of the valet stand. However, instead of opening his door he held up a finger to the guy waiting to take the car. Turning his back to the window, he looked at me.

"Listen, I know the next twenty-four hours are going to be pretty crazy. But there's something I want to talk to you about. Do you think we might be able to find some time tomorrow after the reception?"

My heart stuttered in my chest. Did he want to talk about what I thought he wanted to talk about? My mind was processing possibilities at warp speed.

Jorge knocked impatiently on the window. Callum ignored him as he waited for my answer. The lights on the dash illuminated his face. He wasn't playing around this time.

"Um, yeah, I think so," I said lamely.

But what was I supposed to say? Jorge fogging up the window behind Callum didn't help.

Callum smiled. "Good. Just promise me you won't leave until we've talked?"

"Sure," I said, freaking out in my head.

Tell me now!

We stared at each other for a moment in silence as if we were each trying to read the other's mind.

Jorge rapped again, his muffled demands that we "get out now!" coming through the window.

"The dictator calls," Callum said, reaching for his door handle.

#

Our conversation—combined with Jorge's demands that we get inside and act like a proper best man and maid of honor—distracted me so much I forgot all about my father.

That is, until I took ten steps into the restaurant and saw him.

My steps faltered. Callum's warm hand on my back urged me on. "Be cool."

Tossing my hair over my shoulder, I straightened my backbone and continued into the room. Father was talking to another member of the council, yet his eyes shot to me instantly, as if he'd sensed my presence.

He must not have recognized me at first because his gaze

passed over me and then quickly reversed its path. The silvery orbs narrowed for a moment and then widened as he realized who I was.

Thankful for the time to get my wits together, I grabbed a glass of white wine from the tray of a passing waiter. Kira called to Callum. He excused himself with an apologetic smile, no doubt worried about leaving me alone. I shrugged and gulped down the rest of the wine, waiting for the inevitable. It didn't take long.

Standing next to a tall plant in the corner of the room, I surveyed the scene. A friend of the Murdoch family owned the Italian restaurant and had rented the space out to them for the evening. The space was decorated to resemble an Italian villa complete with a large mural of a Tuscan hillside. Warm lighting, rustic stone columns, and large terra cotta pots filled with rosemary bushes completed the scene. The tables were decorated with simple white linens and crimson rose centerpieces, with votive candles adding a warm glow to the room.

Within seconds, my father started his way over. I held my ground, making him come to me. He brushed off the attempts of several vampires to gain his attention, keeping his eyes on me.

Finally, he stood before me. I still didn't move, waiting for him to make the first salvo in what I expected to be a heated exchange.

"Gabriella," he said, taking in my new appearance. "I almost didn't recognize you."

Looking down at the simple burgundy wrap dress and black heels I wore, I guessed it wasn't a surprise he was thrown off by my new look. His words didn't sound like a compliment, but not an insult either, so I was unsure how to respond.

"Hello, Father," I said, sidestepping a conversation about my appearance.

"Callum informed me that you were to be the maid of honor in the wedding tomorrow," he said. "I must admit I was surprised to hear that."

"Not as surprised as me," I muttered under my breath. Then louder, "Sydney and I hit it off, I guess."

"Hmm," he said, sounding suspicious. "I also heard something about the shower. It was quite a hit, apparently."

"It was a nice time," I said slowly, trying to figure out where he was going with this.

He took a glass of red wine from a passing waiter and regarded me calmly.

"Kira also pulled me aside to tell me how impressed she's been with your behavior," he said. "I have to admit, Gabriella, I'm surprised by the support you're getting from these people."

His words made a warmth spread through my midsection. People were supporting me?

"Wasn't Callum telling you about my progress all along?"

He grimaced. "Yes, young Callum kept me abreast of the goings-on."

"Yet you refused to believe him," I said.

"Gabriella, it is one thing to get a telephone report. It is another to walk in and see you looking so different and to hear vampires I hold in high esteem raving about you."

"So, what are you saying?" I asked, afraid to let myself be optimistic.

He sighed. "While I am going to withhold my final judgment until I can witness your behavior for myself, I am prepared to say you appear to have made progress."

It was the closest thing to a compliment I'd ever received from my father.

"Thank you," I said. "I'm relieved you are keeping an open mind."

"However," he said, "I am curious about what caused this miraculous transformation."

My eyebrows knit together in confusion. "What do you mean?"

"Gabriella, you have to admit it's rather convenient that after several decades of me trying to get you to change your behavior with little success, you suddenly change your stripes in three months? As I said, convenient."

The nerve of the man!

"Excuse me? Wasn't it you who put together this little test for me? Didn't you hold exile over my head, hoping I would choose to go through this three-month punishment and learn how to be a good vampire?"

"Lower your voice," he commanded. "Yes, indeed, I had hoped this experience would result in changes in your behavior. However, I was not at all optimistic it would work. My main goal was to have you make recompense with the Murdoch family for your crimes. I fully expected that you would still need exile at the end of the exercise."

My blood boiled. I'd been right all along. He wanted me to fail. Yet, even as I yearned to tell him off, I remembered Callum's advice earlier about keeping my cool. Besides, my father was wrong. I had changed. I took a deep breath to calm myself before responding.

"Whatever your expectations were does not matter now. The fact is I am different. Ask any of these people, and they'll tell you that," I said, motioning around the room. "If you chose to believe I am such a talented actress that for three months I could fool everyone, then that's your problem."

I turned and walked away without a glance back. Pride swelled inside me as I calmly made my way into the dining room. For the first time ever, I'd told my father off without yelling or causing a scene.

I could feel his gaze on me as I walked away, but I didn't let myself falter or look back.

Sydney was standing with Logan, Miranda, and Alaric as I approached.

"Raven," Miranda said. "Are you okay?"

Obviously they had all watched our conversation with interest.

"I'm great," I said. "When do we eat?"

Four sets of eyes looked at me in shock, as if surprised by my nonchalance.

"Uh," Syd said. She looked at Logan, who shrugged.

"We actually need to take our seats now," he said, nodding

in Jorge's direction. He stood at the front of the room frantically waving his hands at us. Geraldine stood beside him, shaking her head.

"We'd better move it before he pulls something," I said, following everyone to the long table reserved for the wedding party at the front of the room. Gwen, the officiant, was seated on one side of me, Miranda on the other. Callum, after finishing his conversation with a member of the council, sat at the far end of the table between Alaric and Kira.

Waiters scurried around ushering the rest of the guests to their seats. The guests at our table were busy chatting as the salad course was brought from the kitchen.

"Okay, spill it," Miranda whispered to me as she placed her napkin in her lap.

"What?" I asked, purposefully obtuse.

"Raven, come on. You can't tell me your conversation with your father went well."

"Actually, it did," I said, taking a sip of my wine.

Miranda stared at me with disbelief as I turned to Gwen.

"So, how long have you been a witch?" I asked her, trying to make conversation. Up until then she'd mainly kept to herself, and talking to her gave me an excuse to avoid answering Miranda's questions. My friend gave up on me and turned to talk to Sydney.

Gwen chuckled. "You're a piece of work, girlie."

Taken aback, I stared at her.

"Me? What makes you say that?"

"To answer your question, I've been a witch since birth. The craft has been handed down through the generations in my family from one woman to the next."

I frowned at her. "But what made you say I'm a piece of work?"

"Oh, that," she said with a wave of her beringed hand. "You can't be in this business without getting a feel for people."

I couldn't help but ask, "What feel do I give off?"

She narrowed her eyes as if weighing the pros and cons of sharing her thoughts.

"You wear a mask to hide your insecurity," she said with a shrug.

"What? No I don't," I said, picking up my wine for another sip. "That's ridiculous."

"Let me ask you something then? Have you told your boyfriend over there you're in love with him?"

My mouth reacted to her statement first, spewing wine all over myself. Ignoring the mess, I stared at Gwen with my mouth hanging open. Miranda gasped, grabbed a napkin, and furiously dabbed at my dress.

"Raven, what did you do?" Miranda asked, sounding distraught.

I ignored her and watched Gwen's wrinkled face crack into a wide smile. Behind me Miranda ordered the waiter to bring her something for the stain. Sydney said something to her, but I didn't catch it as I sat frozen.

"You're crazy," I said finally.

"Yes, I'm definitely crazy." The old woman laughed. "But I'm never wrong about these things."

"I don't have a boyfriend."

My heart was pounding double-time as I tried to protest. The witch just laughed again.

"Whatever."

As casually as she pleased, she reached into the bread basket as if she hadn't just rocked my world at its foundation.

"Garlic bread, yummy," the witch said, dismissing me.

Something hit my chest. Looking down, I realized Miranda had just thrown salt on me.

"What the hell?" I said, dusting off my boobs.

"It's salt. You have to rub the stain with salt and lemon juice," she said. Her other hand moved toward me with a slice of lemon.

I slapped at her hand just before she squirted me with the wedge.

"Do you mind?" I said, grabbing the napkin from the table.

She looked hurt but resigned herself to instructing me on the proper way to remove wine from wool.

"Miranda, it's fine. Most of the wine landed on my napkin," I said, holding up the wine-soaked material from my lap. "Besides, it's just white wine. It's not going to stain."

"Yes, but alcohol and wool don't mix," she said, deadly serious.

I looked around the room, finally noticing that every eye was focused on us. Great. I'd managed to make a spectacle of myself after all. And just my luck, my father was at the table nearest ours, scowling at the scene.

"I think I'll take care of this in the bathroom," I said quietly to my friend.

"I'll come with you," she offered, grabbing the lemon wedge again.

"No, I can handle it," I said, rising with as much dignity as I could muster under the watchful gaze of the entire restaurant.

Miranda sank slowly in her seat as she finally saw the attention we'd been getting. I walked behind the table, catching sympathetic looks from Kira and Sydney as I passed. Callum caught my eye, his look asking me if I was okay. I nodded quickly and walked with my head held high. Everyone must have lost interest in the drama because conversations started back up before I'd even left the room.

"Stupid witch!" I said as I rubbed at the wet spots with a damp paper towel. "In love with Callum?"

Was I? I admitted I liked him. And even cared about him. But love? Was I capable of love? It seemed love was for unselfish people, ones who put others before themselves. Love was also for people who could trust. And that definitely wasn't me.

Still, when I looked at Callum sometimes, I felt giddy and light-headed. And my heart felt kind of swollen in my chest. Was that love? I'd be damned if I knew.

I stopped my rubbing to check on the progress only to find tiny white particles of paper towel had balled up all over my chest. As I slammed the towel down, tears stung my eyes.

Why was it that whenever I seemed to be making progress I always found a way to screw it up? I knew I was being hard on myself. After all, I wasn't the first person to spill wine on myself. And in my defense, Gwen's announcement was pretty freaking shocking. But why did it have to happen tonight? I'd done so well handling my father only to make a scene in front of the entire restaurant.

With a dry towel, I swiped at the dress, trying to dislodge the paper particles. I prayed to the goddess. If she would help me get through this with my dignity intact, I would never cuss again. She must have known I was lying, though, because the little balls clung like they'd been glued on.

"Fuck!" I said, giving up on the towels altogether and trying to pick each piece off individually with my fingers. It was possible I was overreacting about the dress. But I was convinced that if I could handle that situation, everything would be okay.

The door to the bathroom opened, and Kira walked in.

"Raven, is everything all right?" she said, coming to stand next to me.

"No," I wailed.

"Oh, dear, no tears. It's not that bad," she said, examining the dress.

"The paper towel crapped all over me!"

Stifling a smile at my histrionics, she calmly reached into her purse and pulled out a lint roller.

"This should take care of that in a jiff," she said, handing it to me.

Damned if she wasn't right. A couple of swipes of the adhesive roller, and the paper lint disappeared.

With a sniff, I handed the roller back to her. "Thanks," I said sullenly.

"Chin up, dear. It was just a little spill."

I leaned against the counter with a sigh. "It's not just that."

She smiled and patted my hand. "I know, dear. But you mustn't let him see you upset."

"You're right," I said. "Callum doesn't need to see me freak."

"Callum? I meant your father," she said, her brow creasing

into a frown.

"Oh! Yes, of course." Was there no end to my ability to make an ass out of myself?

She crossed her arms and regarded me levelly.

"However, since you brought him up, I would like to speak with you about my son."

Oh, shit.

CHAPTER TWENTY

"Oh yeah?" I said, trying to sound casual. "What about Callum?"

Her look spoke volumes. "Raven, let's not play games. I've known about your affair with my son for weeks."

I cringed. There was no talking myself out of this one.

"How did you find out?" I asked.

"Please. I'm sure you both thought you were being covert with your sneaking around. But dear, I'm a 700-year-old vampire. I don't miss much. Besides, all the noise was enough to wake the dead."

"Uh."

I wanted to die right then and there—too bad I was immortal.

She held up a hand. "Don't worry. I know I expressed concern over this possibility at one time. However, over the last several weeks I have begun to suspect I might have been wrong."

My mouth gaped open. "You're not mad?"

"Of course not. You're both centuries past the age of consent."

"Wow, Kira, I don't know what to say."

"Just tell me that you're not going to break his heart," she said.

"I highly doubt that's possible," I said, laughing. "Kira, look, since we're being frank here, I should tell you Callum and I are just having fun. You don't have to worry about me becoming a member of the family or anything."

She shook her head and smiled at me. "You young ones are so blind."

I frowned. What the hell did that mean?

"Just remember this: you've proven to all of us that despite your rebellious tendencies, you're a worthy person. Perhaps you need to prove that to yourself next."

She was speaking in riddles or something because I had no idea what she was trying to tell me.

"Okay," I said, not knowing what else to say.

She patted my hand again.

"I'm glad we had this talk," she said with a wink.

"Uh, yeah, me too."

I felt relieved that it was finally out in the open but confused as hell about what that meant.

"Now, shall we rejoin the dinner?" she said, opening the bathroom door for me.

I nodded and followed her out. Together we walked back into the dining room. Callum caught my eye. As he watched us walk arm-in-arm toward him, his eyes widened. I touched his shoulder as I passed him, letting him know everything was okay.

I resumed my seat, letting Miranda and Syd know everything was fine. And it was.

Everyone else was so busy eating and chatting they'd barely noticed my return, which was a relief after the scene I'd caused when I left. Adding to my relief was the fact Kira hadn't scratched my eyes out. Her philosophical attitude about the whole thing surprised me. But I wasn't about to question my good fortune.

I ignored the crazy witch, Gwen, for the rest of the dinner, instead discussing plans for the next day with Miranda and Syd. Soon dessert was finished, and guests were offered their choice of champagne or Lifeblood served in tall crystal flutes.

The sound of silverware tapping on glass filled the room. Everyone turned their eyes to Callum, who stood.

"I'd like to propose a toast to Sydney and Logan. Logan is my brother, as you all know, and I couldn't be more proud to say that than I am on this occasion. He also chose a wonderful woman with whom to spend eternity. I know Mother would agree when I say we're thrilled to welcome Sydney into our family," he said.

Turning to look at the couple, he raised his glass. "May the centuries bring you much happiness."

All the guests joined in the toast with appreciative murmurs. I tapped my flute of Lifeblood to Miranda's and took a sip, thinking he did a great job toasting the couple.

As soon as the room fell silent, I felt a kick on my ankle.

"Ow," I said, shooting a look at Miranda.

"Toast," she said from the corner of her mouth.

"Yes, Callum did a great job," I said, wondering why she'd kicked me.

"No, idiot, you need to give a toast."

I froze. "What?"

"Maid of honor always gives a toast at rehearsal," she said under her breath.

No one had warned me about that little tradition. I looked around and saw Callum and Alaric looking at me expectantly. Callum motioned to his glass and then at me, a clear signal it was definitely my turn.

Shit.

Standing slowly, I felt all eyes settle on me. My mind, the ungrateful organ, was totally blank as I scrambled to think of something profound to say. Coming up with nothing, I decided to just wing it.

"Hi, I'm Raven," I said inanely, sounding like I was about to give testimony at an Alcoholics Anonymous meeting.

The room was so silent, I could hear my heart pounding in my ears. I saw my father sitting there looking like he was waiting for me to screw this up. People had started to shift in their seats as I stood there staring dumbly at him.

When he glanced at his watch, something shifted inside me. I realized that even though my father might think I was a waste of time, I wasn't. I had friends in that room. I glanced over at the worried faces of the people I'd come to care about over the last few months. My father's judgment didn't matter.

Gathering my thoughts, I attempted to regain control over the toast.

"Oops, sorry, folks. Lost my train of thought for a second. Anyhoo. We're here for Sydney and Logan's special day," I said, smiling at the couple. "For those of you who don't know, I'm the maid of honor. I was surprised when Sydney asked me because let's face it, we all know I don't have the best track record."

A couple of uncomfortable laughs came from the audience. Callum winked at me from the end of the table.

"Despite that," I continued, smiling back at Callum, "Sydney took the time to get to know me. I have to say I am proud to call her my friend. Logan, you're a lucky man."

Sydney beamed at me and took Logan's hand. The look he gave her was so full of love I got a little choked up.

"In fact, Sydney is lucky too. Not only because she found her soul mate in Logan, but also because she is about to become a member of the Murdoch family. I have never seen a group of people who care so much about each other."

I looked at Callum, who was looking back at me with a mixture of amusement and approval in his eyes.

"So let's raise our glasses to this wonderful couple as we prepare to share a celebration of their commitment and love for each other. To Logan and Sydney!"

The entire room stood, shouting their approval and toasting each other. After clinking my glass with Miranda's and even Gwen's, my gaze met Callum's again. He silently raised his glass to me, a sparkle in his eyes.

It was silly, but I really meant everything I said. They say weddings bring out the worst in people. But I felt like this one was bringing out my best, helping me to focus on things that really mattered. Things I had been missing my whole life—like friendship, family, and, yes, even love.

#

The next day dawned with bright blue skies and sunshine—a good sign for the day of a wedding. The house was hopping with activity as I made my way downstairs to find coffee.

Sydney was in the kitchen drinking a glass of Lifeblood.

"I'm getting married today!" she said by way of greeting.

I grinned at my friend, my excitement for her overriding my normal morning grouchiness.

"I know!"

She rattled off her to-do list as I filled a large mug with coffee. Sitting on a barstool at the counter, I listened to her talk about hairdressers, makeup artists, and the million other details we had to take care of.

"Raven, what time did Miranda say she was coming over?" Syd asked suddenly. I had sort of tuned her out, so the question surprised me.

"I think she'll be here by eight. She's bringing our dresses with her," I said, anticipating the eager bride's next question.

"Great, that gives us time to shower. Once she arrives I need you to help me with a special project."

"Oh?" I said, curious.

"I have a gift for Logan I need you to take to him at Kira's house. Miranda can keep me company while you run it over."

I frowned. "Is there a reason I need to be the one to take it? Not that I mind," I said.

Her eyes sparkled with mischief. "Well, I just figured that since you had to be here with me last night that you'd jump at the excuse to go see Callum. Just make it quick. The makeup and hair people get here at two."

My jaw dropped. "Sydney!"

"What? Are you gonna deny you two have been having a passionate affair for the last several weeks?"

"Jesus, does everyone know?"

She nodded. "Pretty much."

"Why didn't you say anything before now?"

"We all figured you two had your reasons for not being out in the open," she said with a shrug.

"Wait, you guys discussed this?"

"Well, Logan and I did. I got the impression Kira knew too."

"Yeah, she does," I said sullenly.

"Raven, seriously, it's not a big deal. I think it's great you two are together."

"We're not together," I said quickly.

"What?" she asked, frowning.

"Well, we're together," I said, clarifying. "But we're not *together* together."

"Hmm," she said. "Well, if you don't want to see Callum, I'll just send Jorge over right now."

"No!" I all but shouted. "I mean, I don't mind."

Her smiled was smug, but I ignored it, preferring to pretend I wasn't acting like a lovesick school girl.

An hour and a half later I pulled up in front of Kira's house. Miranda had let me borrow her car for my errand when she found out that Syd was playing matchmaker.

"Make it a quicky," she said as I walked out the door. "We've got a wedding to put on."

Sitting in front of Kira's house, I felt nervous. The night before at the rehearsal I'd realized a few things. First, I could stand up to my father without making a fool of myself. Second, wine plus wool equals smelly. Third, I cared about Callum.

I wasn't really ready to use the L word, but not saying the word didn't mean I didn't feel something close to it. It was all really confusing because I'd never been in love before.

We hadn't really had a chance to talk after the rehearsal other than a quick good-bye as we went our separate ways. Syd was right, I really did miss him. The idea of seeing him a few moments made me happy. Surely that was a sign of something.

With all these thoughts swirling in my head, I worried that I might say something to give my feelings away when I saw him. He'd said he wanted to talk after the wedding, but I had no guarantee he felt the same way.

"Suck it up," I said, getting out of the car.

I had a mission to accomplish for Syd. In my hand was a small wrapped box, which Syd had confided held an antique pocket watch for her groom. My goal was to deliver the gift, not probe Callum for hints about his feelings.

Since I basically lived at Kira's house, I didn't bother knocking on the door. Letting myself in, I was amazed at the difference between Syd's house and Kira's that morning. Where Syd's was loud and hectic as people hustled about trying to make the place ready for the wedding, Kira's house was silent as a tomb.

"Hello?" I called, my voice echoing.

"We're back here." Kira's voice came from the direction of the dining room.

"Hey, guys," I said, walking into the room.

Kira, Logan and Callum looked up from their breakfast to greet me.

"Raven, how's Syd doing?" Logan asked.

He held a cup of coffee in one hand and the morning paper in the other. For a man about to commit himself to a woman for eternity, he looked pretty relaxed.

"She's great. Very excited," I said, nodding at Kira and Callum. The latter held my gaze for a second longer than necessary. Looking away, I cleared my throat.

"Care to join us for some breakfast?" Kira asked politely. "Hannah made enough food for an army."

The woman in question bustled in. "I can't help it. I cook when I'm nervous."

Callum chuckled. "Hannah, what are you nervous about? Logan's the one about to pick up a ball and chain."

"You know very well you boys are like my own sons," she said with a hand on her hip. "I can't help it if I get a little emotional that one of you is about to fly the coop."

"Hannah, I haven't lived with Mother for more than a century," Logan said, smiling with affection at the woman.

"Still, it's not every day a man takes a wife, Logan."

"Mother's not emotional, though," Callum pointed out.

Kira set down her coffee cup before responding. "That's because I know my boy is marrying the woman he's meant to be with. I only wish your father was here," she said with a regretful sigh.

Hannah swiped at her eyes with a tea towel. "Angus would have been proud of you, Logan."

Logan nodded as if too moved to speak. I shifted uncomfortably, feeling like an intruder.

"Now," Kira said, obviously having recovered from her maudlin thoughts. "Callum, just think, next time it will be you."

Callum slid me a covert gaze from behind his coffee cup. I wanted to run from the room. I was painfully aware that everyone in the room knew that Callum and I had been sleeping together.

Callum cleared his throat and said, "Mother, let's focus on the now. Logan's not even married yet."

"Well, darling, you can't blame me for wanting both of my sons to be married and happy."

Callum shot Logan a pleading look. I stood stock still, too shocked by the conversation to react.

Logan cleared his throat. "Raven, what brings you by this morning?"

Thankful for the change in subject, I shook myself. "Oh, right. Syd wanted me to bring this to you," I said, placing the carefully wrapped box in front of him.

Logan beamed. "If you'll excuse me, I'll open this in private," he said, standing. "Raven, don't leave yet. I need you to take something back to my beautiful bride."

I nodded, stepping out of the way to let him pass.

"Ah, true love. It's so touching, isn't it, Raven?" Kira said.

My teeth clenched. This woman was unbelievable. I almost missed the time when she warned me to stay away from her son.

"Yeah, it's great. Callum, can I talk to you for a moment?" I said, not caring if she thought me rude.

He hesitated, looking from me to his mother.

"Sure," he said slowly, rising from his seat.

"Yes, you two run along," Kira said, smiling.

Callum grabbed my arm and pulled me with him into Kira's office.

"Do you have any idea what that was all about?" he demanded after closing the door with a thud.

Flinching, I weighed my options. Should I tell him that his entire family knew about us? I wasn't sure. After all, such a revelation might require we have a—shudder—relationship talk. Part of me wanted to get things out in the open, but I also wasn't sure what I wanted. Sure, I knew I cared about him, but was I ready to ask him for a relationship? The thought gave me the shakes. What if he laughed in my face?

I went with option B instead.

"I think she's just excited about the wedding," I said, examining a fascinating letter opener on the desk.

"Gabby?" he said.

"Hmm," I replied, picking up a roll of tape.

"I think my mother knows about us," he said, sounding scandalized.

My head shot up. "You do?"

He nodded solemnly. "I'm so sorry."

Frowning, I wondered what he meant.

"That's okay?" I meant it as a statement, but it came out sounding like a question.

"Really? I know you wanted to keep our . . . situation a secret."

Our situation? *What the hell did that mean?*

"It's not a big deal," I said slowly.

"No," he said, picking up a pen and twirling it with his fingers. "I guess it isn't. I mean, with you leaving soon and all."

He looked up at me.

"Right?" he said.

So help me, goddess, I didn't know if he sounded hopeful or disappointed.

"Callum, I—"

Two loud knocks sounded from the door, interrupting me. Logan stuck his head in.

"Sorry, don't mean to interrupt," he said.

"No, that's okay," I said quickly.

He'd saved me as far as I was concerned. Before I could continue my conversation with Callum, I needed to get away from him and figure out what the heck was going on.

"Okay," he said slowly, glancing at his brother. Callum stood with his arms crossed, looking like he definitely minded the interruption.

"Here's the gift for Sydney," Logan said, ignoring Callum. "Please tell her I love the watch, and I'll be carrying it tonight. Also, tell her I love her, and I can't wait to see her coming down the aisle."

His words helped me momentarily forget my problems.

"Logan, I just want to say that I know we've had our disagreements, but I am really happy for you."

Smiling, he handed me the box.

"Thanks, Raven. I'm glad you and Syd hit it off. She'll need good friends around her as she continues to adjust to our way of life."

Instead of answering him, I nodded. His assumption that I'd hang around for a while surprised me. On the other hand, I guess it kind of made sense. Everyone would assume that since they thought Callum and I were dating. But it irked me. Not only because I had no idea if Callum wanted me around, but also because everyone took it for granted that I was now committed to living my life like a good Brethren vamp.

"Well, I guess I'd better be getting back. Don't want the bride worrying that her maid of honor ran away," I said, joking.

Callum's head snapped up.

"Dude, chill," I said. "I was joking."

His worried frown faded, and he laughed at himself.

"Sorry, guess the stress of the day's getting to me."

"Okay, I'm off," I said.

"Gabby, one thing before you go," Callum said, glancing significantly at his brother.

Logan shrugged and left the room.

Callum stood in front of me, his expression serious. Leaning against the desk, I set the present down to give the gorgeous guy in front of me all my attention.

"Promise me you won't leave until we've had a chance to talk tonight," he said.

"Okay, but I already promised you that," I said, smiling despite the churning in my gut. "Wanna give me a hint about the topic?"

I'd been trying to keep it light, but his response caused my smile to waver.

"Your future."

My future? Not our future? Oh God, he was going to dump me.

"Oh, all right," I said, feeling foolish. "Listen, I really need to go. I'll see you in a few hours."

He stepped back and said good-bye, his movements stiff and formal. No kiss, no hug, no flirtation.

I walked back through the house with a heavy heart. Mad at myself for having girlish fantasies about Callum and I ending up together. But who was I kidding? He'd been honest with me from the beginning. No strings. It was all my fault, and I was furious with myself.

My thoughts were such a mess I didn't notice the man standing in the middle of the driveway until I bumped into him.

"Oops, sorr—," I began, only to realize who I'd bumped into. "Oh, Father. Sorry, I didn't see you standing there," I said, stepping back.

His face was an emotionless mask. "You need to pay attention to where you're going, Gabriella."

"Look, I said I was sorry."

He waved a hand, dismissing me. "Don't you have somewhere to be right now?"

His dismissal hurt me more than it should have. But I was already feeling down after my conversation with Callum.

"Yes, I do."

I walked away, leaving him standing there. Perhaps it was rude of me, but I couldn't have cared less at that point.

"Gabriella," his commanding voice stopped me in my

tracks.

Turning, I waited for him to speak. He walked to me slowly, and I really didn't like the look in his eyes.

"We have not yet had a chance to formally discuss the outcome of your time here. Last night, I mentioned that I felt your transformation was convenient," he said.

My hands automatically went to my hips. The defensive posture was an unconscious reaction. Somehow, I just knew I wasn't going to enjoy this conversation. Not that I ever enjoyed talking to him.

"It has become clear to me that your changes were come by honestly," he said, shocking the hell out of me.

My mouth gaped open. He'd caught me off guard.

"Really? I mean, you're right, but I'm surprised by this sudden change of heart."

His smile was cold.

"Let's just say some new information has come to light, which explains what has happened."

Frowning, I tried to decode what he was saying. He sounded like the freakin' Sphinx.

"What information?"

"Your affair with Callum," he said.

"Wait a minute. Aren't you the one who accused me of sleeping with him to begin with?"

He nodded. "Yes, however at the time I thought you were manipulating him."

"And now?" I asked despite my better judgment. I knew he was setting me up for something.

"And now, it's clear Callum was using sex to manipulate you."

"*What?*" I yelled.

"Lower your voice. Shouting accomplishes nothing," he said with maddening calm.

"You're a damned liar! Callum wouldn't do that to me!"

My fingers curled into claws. I couldn't believe my own father was spewing this kind of venom at me. He could not have chosen a more hurtful thing to say. The idea that Callum would betray me that way—well, it was too horrible to contemplate.

"Am I?" he asked, cocking a brow. "In New York I offered him a seat on the council if he could rehabilitate you."

My stomach dropped, and my knees felt weak. I didn't want to believe that Callum was capable of such duplicity. But the truth was, I'd suspected from the beginning that Callum had set this up to make himself look good.

What better way to ensure his future than to turn the black sheep into a docile lamb by manipulating her one weakness—her need for affection. If my soul had not been shrieking at that moment, I would almost have felt the need to applaud the man for his cunning.

The night I'd almost bitten the plumber, Callum must have seen his chance at success severely threatened. What better way to get me back in line than to pretend to care about my problems and then soften me up with mind-numbing sex? And I had been so desperate for someone to give a shit about me that I'd fallen for it like a desperate sucker.

Clenching my teeth to keep from screaming, I looked at my father.

"Why?"

His eyebrow perked up. "Why did he do this? Isn't it obvious? Logan is the brain trust of the family. Callum, as the second son, has always yearned for a more important role. Getting on the council is the first step toward big things for him."

I slashed my hand through the air to stop him. "No, I mean why would you tell me this? Aren't you afraid I'll revert back to my old ways?"

He shook his head. "No, it's apparent you've learned a lot here. Whether it was Callum's manipulation or your own will that was responsible is inconsequential," he said. "I told you because I don't want you getting your hopes up that you and Callum have a future. I saw how you looked at him at the rehearsal. You're in love with him."

I flinched, feeling ten times the fool.

The front door opened, and Callum rushed down the stairs.

"Gabby, you forgot Sydney's gift," he said when he reached us.

His smile faded when he saw us squaring off.

"Am I interrupting something?" he said warily.

"No, you're not," I said, barely able to look him in the face.

Grabbing the gift, I turned on my heel without another word and stormed to the car.

"Gabriella? Come back here! I'm not finished," my father commanded as I got into the car.

"Gabby? Are you all right?" Callum called after me, sounding confused.

As I drove off, I looked in the rearview mirror. My father looked like a storm cloud—angry and about to explode—and Callum was obviously questioning him about what had happened.

I knew there would be hell to pay for walking away from them, but right then I didn't care.

What a fucking idiot I'd been! The speedometer climbed higher and higher as I berated myself, swiping angrily at the tears which poured down my cheeks. Paying no attention to where I was headed, I tried to escape reality. Finally, unable to see through the tears fogging my eyes, I pulled over.

The anger and pain built up so much I needed to hit something. Since the steering wheel was handy, I pounded the damn thing until my palms were red and raw—howling and crying at the injustice of life. It helped a little, but I still felt as if my heart was smoldering to ash inside me. Worn out from the emotional outburst, I thumped my head on the wheel, leaving it there as I gulped air.

The old me would have sought revenge for being made a fool. But the new me . . .

Hell, was there a new me? If everything between Callum and I had been based on a lie, were any of the thoughts and feelings I'd had over the last several weeks real?

Lifting my head, I stared out the windshield looking for the answer in the tall pine trees lining the two-lane road.

Despite Callum's treachery, the fact remained that I'd grown up during the last few months. Considering my age, it was amazing how much I'd changed in such a short time.

Taking a deep breath, I admitted to myself that while Callum might be an asshole, no one else was in on his plan. Sydney really was my friend. Kira believed I was a better person. Jorge and Geraldine had accepted me. Miranda always was and always would be my best friend. Even Logan and Alaric had begun treating me with a sort of grudging respect.

I'd learned that there's more to life than paying my father back for my shitty life, most of which wasn't his fault at all. I'd chosen to rebel. I'd chosen to be selfish and myopic.

Perhaps, in some weird way Callum had done me a favor by leading me on. He'd distracted me from my self-pity long enough to learn that the life I'd been leading wasn't really a life at all. I'd been so stuck in the past I had no clue what I really wanted.

Shaking my head, I realized I still didn't know what I wanted. But I knew this—I could never go back to living my life in the dark. It was time for me to put the past where it belonged and move on. I was a little bit wiser and a lot more heartbroken, but better overall.

Slouched in the seat, I decided what I needed right then was a smoke. Yes, a good dose of nicotine to help clear the cobwebs and help me relax. I reached into my purse and pulled out the pack. One left.

Punching the car's lighter, I realized that the lone cigarette was the last from the pack I'd brought with me to Raleigh. Frowning, I tried to remember how long had it been since I'd had one. It had to have been weeks. How odd, I thought.

The lighter clicked, signaling it was ready. I held the metal to the cig's tip, puffing on it until it glowed red. Taking a long pull, I inhaled the smoke.

Immediately, I began gagging and coughing. The damned thing tasted like ass. Quickly opening the window, I threw the blasted thing outside.

Imagine that, I thought, as the last of the coughs subsided.

I'd gone so long without a cigarette that I'd lost my taste for them. It looked like I'd changed more than I thought.

Glancing at the clock, I realized I'd been sitting on the side of the road for half an hour. Sydney would be wondering where I was by now.

It was decision time. Did I go fulfill my promise to my friend, even if I had to swallow my pride and face Callum and my father?

Or did I run?

In the end, there really was no choice. I couldn't disappoint Syd just because I had some personal problems. I would pretend everything was okay while avoiding Callum as much as possible. If I could get through the next few hours, I'd finally be able to get away long enough to make some real decisions about my future.

Throwing the car in gear, I checked the road for cars before pulling out. As I drove, I pulled Miranda's cell phone from the console. It was time to call the minions.

CHAPTER TWENTY-ONE

Throughout the ceremony that evening, I kept stealing glimpses at Callum despite my better judgment. A few times I caught him looking at me, too. Each time, I snapped my eyes back where they belonged, horrified at my behavior.

Before I knew it, Logan grabbed Sydney and kissed her passionately, eliciting cheers from the guests. Laughing, they pulled apart and went down the aisle hand in hand, accompanied by a bagpipe playing a happy tune.

That's when I realized I would have to walk out with Callum. He was already moving toward me. I inched forward, reluctant but not wanting to cause a scene. When we met in the middle, he held out his arm. Ignoring it, I marched forward with a smile pasted on my face, not caring if he kept up or not. Just behind me, he muttered under his breath about stubborn females.

We reached the foyer and continued to the study where we had been told to go for pictures. Sydney and Logan were already there, locked in a toe-curling kiss. I stopped just inside the room, forcing Callum to bump into my back. I jerked forward, my bouquet flying through the air to land with a thump in the corner.

Callum grabbed my arm to keep me from falling.

"Gabby! Are you okay?" he asked, swinging me around.

The newlyweds didn't seem to notice the ruckus.

"Dammit, Callum, watch where you're going," I said, venting my frustration.

He sighed. "I'm sorry. Listen," he said, moving closer, "we need to talk about what happened this afternoon."

Alaric and Miranda strolled into the room, saving me from having to respond. I scooted away from Callum to go stand next to Miranda.

"Whoa, you guys, get a room," Alaric said.

Syd and Logan, who had finally came up for air, looked surprised to see us.

Logan frowned as if annoyed by our presence, but Sydney couldn't have looked happier.

"We're married!" she said, hugging her husband.

We all laughed and went to take turns congratulating the newlyweds. Soon, though, Jorge burst into the room with the photographer.

"Listen up, people," he said, clapping his hands for attention. "We've got fifteen minutes for photos while the guests enjoy cocktails."

True to his word, fifteen minutes later, after barking orders and lining us up in different groupings for the shots, Jorge pushed us out of the study to go mingle with the guests.

I was walking out with Miranda when Callum stopped me.

"We need to talk," Callum said, pulling me back toward the study.

"Callum, we don't have time. They're about to do the first dance," I said desperately.

Miranda grabbed my other arm. She didn't know that Callum was a lying ass since I hadn't told her, but she'd interpreted my pleading look correctly.

"She's right. You two can talk later," she said, playing tug of war—with me as the rope.

"They won't miss us," he insisted, giving an extra strong yank.

"Ouch! Stop it, you guys," I said, wrenching my arms back from both of them.

Turning to face him, I said, "Callum, now is not the time."

His eyes narrowed. "Fine, we'll go do our duties as the wedding party. Meet me in two hours back in the study."

"They'll be cutting the cake then," Miranda said.

I smiled at her, grateful for the help.

"Yeah," I said.

"Gabriella, you meet me in two hours, or I will come find you and drag you away in front of everyone."

I gasped. "You wouldn't dare."

He crossed his arms, looking deadly serious. "Wanna try me?"

I threw my hands in the air, frustrated by his caveman attitude. "Fine."

He looked shocked by my acquiescence, but what he didn't know was that in an hour the minion rescue squad would be picking me up.

"Fine," he said. With that he walked past us on his way to the party.

A large tent had been rented for the reception and set up in Logan's back yard. The path leading to the tent was lined with luminarias—white paper bags with votive candles inside. Overhead, trellises had been set up with twinkling white lights creating a magical quality to the chilly night.

The interior of the tent was a winter wonderland. On either side of the entrance were large pots filled with white tree branches draped with glittering crystal ornaments. Large silver and crystal snowflakes hung from the tent's draped ceiling. The tables were covered in snowy linens with silver and white candle centerpieces.

At one end, an elaborate buffet had been set up surrounding a huge snowflake ice sculpture. On the other end of the tent, a large dance floor was set up in front of a stage, which held the band.

As we watched Logan and Sydney dance, I felt a mixture of happiness for them and pity for myself. Callum stood across the dance floor next to his mother, scowling as he watched the couple. For an asshole, he looked pretty dashing in his kilt. Made of the Murdoch plaid, the kilt was also worn by Logan and Alaric—but it looked best on Callum. My conscience cried foul at the thought, reminding me he was nothing but a manipulator.

The song soon ended, and other couples went to join Mr. and Mrs. Murdoch on the dance floor. Alaric came and claimed Miranda as his partner. She smiled and shrugged at me as she took his hand.

Turning, I went to find someone to talk to. Geraldine was standing near the bar, which was also made of ice.

"Wow." I surveyed the frozen masterpiece with Logan's and Sydney's monogram carved into the front.

"I know, amazing isn't it?" she said. "Need a drink?"

I nodded, and we both turned to order from the bartender.

"You and Jorge did an amazing job," I said, taking a sip of my martini.

"Thanks. I hope Syd and Logan like it."

"How could they not?" I asked, motioning to the magical atmosphere. "It's like a fairy tale."

She chuckled. "You surprise me."

"What do you mean?" I asked.

"Look at you. You're standing there sipping a martini with a mortal, and I haven't heard one complaint from you all night."

Taking another sip, I thought about what she said. "I guess I was kind of a bitch to you, huh?"

Without hesitation, she nodded. "Honey, you were a bitch to everyone."

I flinched, realizing the truth of her words.

"I'm sorry," I said, meaning it.

"Don't apologize. Seeing you try to become a better person is enough. I'm proud of you."

The corner of my mouth lifted, recognizing the irony of what I was about to say.

"You know, I never thought that I'd say this, but you're pretty cool . . . for a mortal."

She laughed. "You're pretty cool too . . . for a bitch."

We were chatting about her and Jorge's plan to expand their business into party planning when I felt a tap on my shoulder.

My smile wilted when I saw my father standing to my left.

"Gabriella, I must speak to you."

Grimacing, I excused myself from Geraldine. I crossed my arms and prepared to give him a piece of my mind. He was still on my shit list for that afternoon.

"Yes?"

He took my arm and led me toward the entrance of the tent.

"In private," he said, heading toward the house.

Not wanting to make a scene, I allowed him to lead me inside the house to the study.

"Father, if you have something to say to me, you could have said it outside."

His jaw clenched. "And risk you throwing a tantrum? I think not."

"Listen, I have had enough of this," I said, placing my hands on my hips. "I am not a child. If you want to talk to me, you'd better show me a little respect."

He snorted and shook his head.

"Fine, we'll play this your way," he said, sounding bored. "Your behavior this afternoon makes me wonder how much you actually have changed."

My mouth gaped open.

"My behavior? Mine?" I said. "You know what? I don't get you. I have spent the last three months working my ass off. And do you tell me you're proud of me? No. You tell me that the man I love has been using sex to manipulate me. How exactly did you expect me to react?"

"Perhaps I could have been a tad more sensitive with my wording, but the fact remains the same. You may think I'm callous, but I honestly thought I was helping you. Just as sending you here was my way of helping you."

I actually sputtered with outrage. "You're insane."

"Let's not forget I still have not given my official verdict about your rehabilitation."

"Is that a threat?"

He shrugged. "It's simply a fact. I have no guarantees you won't revert back to your troublemaking tomorrow or next year or a decade from now."

"You know what? You can go fuck yourself. I am sick and tired of this war between us. If you can't accept me for who I am and love me simply because I am your own flesh and blood, then I want nothing to do with you. As for worrying about me starting my subversive activities again, don't bother. I've realized that all of that was some twisted attempt on my part to earn your love. But you know what? I'm done."

"My love? What do think all of this has been? Why do you think I still bother to try to change you?"

Bitter laughter flew from my mouth before I could stop it.

"If this is the way you love someone, I'd hate to see what you do to your enemies. I am through being the whipping boy because of what happened to mother."

His cheeks flushed angry red, and his eyes practically glowed with anger.

Good. It was time to lay everything on the table.

"You think I don't know that she is what this is all about?" I said. "Please. I don't know if it's guilt on your part or if you truly blame me for what happened to her, but it doesn't matter. You can send me to Norway, or you can lock me up, but it won't bring her back."

Jaw clenched, he looked about ready to slap me.

"You have crossed the line. Get out of my sight." His voice was deadly calm, dripping with ice.

"Fine," I said, turning to the door.

"One more thing," he said quietly. "Watch yourself. One false move and you'll earn yourself a two-hundred-year vacation."

"Whatever," I said, throwing my hair over my shoulder and stalking out.

His warning echoed in my head, but I couldn't have cared less. Soon, I'd be free. My father would probably hunt me down. But he could rot for all I cared at that moment.

"There you are," Callum said, entering the room. "I was looking for you."

My heart stopped beating for a moment. I had really hoped to avoid him until Freddie picked me up.

"Here I am," I said lamely, too shocked at seeing him to think straight.

"Let's go into the study so we can talk," he said, taking my arm.

I started to tell him I couldn't talk when the doorbell rang.

"Hold that thought," Callum said. "I'll just see who that is."

I turned to watch him, and the grandfather clock caught my eye. Quarter after eight.

Holy shit!

Callum was already reaching for the doorknob.

"Callum, wait!"

But it was too late. He had already pulled the door open. From my vantage point, I couldn't see who was on the other side. But I knew.

Running to the door, I heard Callum say, "Can I help you?"

I reached him just in time to see and hear Freddie, say, "I'm here for Mistress Raven."

Callum's head swiveled to me so fast I'm surprised it didn't fly off his neck.

"*Raven*? Do you know this guy?"

Freddie stood on the porch wearing ratty jeans and a Marilyn Manson T-shirt. His hair looked as if it hadn't seen a comb in weeks. At seventeen, he was one of my youngest minions. But he was loyal and available to pick me up.

Casting a sideways glance at Callum, who was frowning, I moved forward, trying to block Freddie from his gaze.

"I told you to wait in the car," I whispered.

"I did. But when you didn't show up, I figured I'd come see if you needed backup with your escape," he said, trying to peek around me.

I gritted my teeth. "Your idea of backup is ringing the freaking door bell?"

He started to talk, but I waved a hand.

"Never mind. Go back to the car, I'll be there in a minute," I said, starting to close the door.

"What if he tries to stop you from escaping?" Freddie said, stepping forward before I could close him out. "You might need my help."

Right, because a scrawny teen like Freddie stood a chance against Callum—a three-hundred-year-old vampire. Idiot.

"Raven? Might I have a word with you?" Callum said from behind me, his voice sounding overly polite.

Looking over my shoulder, I cringed at the leashed anger on his face.

"Callum, I—" I began.

Behind me, I heard Freddie walk in and close the door.

"No explanation needed," Callum said, cutting me off. "It's quite obvious you're running away."

The indignation on his face made me see red. It reminded me that this man was full of shit and could not be trusted. He didn't care about me. He just didn't want me to leave because he might lose his precious seat on the council.

"I'm not running away, Callum," I said, my anger rising. "I'm getting the hell away from you and your lies."

He frowned. "What lies?"

"Don't play dumb with me, asshole," I said loudly. "My father—"

Realizing I had been about to lose it, I sucked it all down and wadded it up into a tiny ball of pain in my gut. A deep breath helped me regain control.

Callum's eyes narrowed. "What about your father?"

"Never mind," I said. "I'm leaving, all right? That's all you need to know."

"Why?" The one word shot out like a bullet.

"Like you don't already know," I said.

"Gabby, don't do this. Don't run away because you're scared. I don't know what set you off, but I think you need to calm down so we can discuss this. You're way too emotional to act rationally right now."

White hot anger exploded in my head at his patronizing

tone.

"Emotional? Emotional!" I sputtered, stalking toward him.

He held his hands up to ward me off. "Okay, maybe emotional was the wrong word. I meant you're upset."

I stopped in my tracks. "You're wrong. I'm not upset. I'm just done, Callum."

"Listen, dude," Freddie interjected, "is this going to take long? My mom only lets me have the car out until ten."

"No, dude," Callum said, looking at me, his eyes suddenly hard. "She just needs to get her purse and then she can scamper off."

The glare I sent him would have turned a lesser man to stone.

"I must have been high to sleep with you!"

"Whoa! You slept with him? Talk about sleeping with the enemy, Mistress Raven," Freddie said, watching the exchange with rapt attention.

"Shut. Up," I said, glaring at my mouthy minion. Callum talked again before I could continue.

"This is rich," he said scraping his fingers through his hair. "You know what I think? I think you knew I was going to tell you I'd fallen in love with you. And you're so scared of trusting anyone you'd rather be alone than face it."

My laughter left a bitter taste in my mouth. I might have been a bitch, but I'd never tell someone I loved them if I didn't mean it.

Funny, until ten hours earlier I hadn't believed Callum capable of such lies.

"Nice try, Romeo. The only person you love is yourself and your ambition. Now, if you'll excuse me, I have to be going."

With a nod to Freddie, I turned on shaky legs to leave. The door was about to close when Callum's voice rang out.

"Fine! Run. Ruin your life. In less than twenty-four hours your father will find you and have you on the first flight to Norway."

Halting in the doorway, I turned.

"I'd rather be locked in an icy prison than have to listen to one more of your lies!"

Slamming the door, I marched down the steps with Freddie hot on my trail.

"Wow, you really told him, huh?"

The weird thing was, I didn't feel triumphant in the least for getting the last word in. In fact, I'd never felt more miserable in my life.

CHAPTER TWENTY-TWO

A motley crew of minions bowed as I entered the living room of the run-down farmhouse. They all looked shocked to see me. I suppose it was the new look. They were used to me wearing black leather, not ball gowns.

"Where is everybody?" I asked.

Freddie cleared his throat behind me as the other people shuffled their feet and avoided my eyes.

"Yeah, about that. Some of the other minions decided they didn't want to wait around for you to get in touch, so they bailed."

"So much for loyalty," I said, shrugging. With seven people left, the six before me and Freddie at my side, that meant about fourteen people were missing.

"Where did they go?" I asked.

"Well, a few decided to form a band, others decided that being your minion—forgive me, Mistress—sucked, and the rest are probably grounded or hanging out at the mall."

Freddie cringed as if waiting for one of my trademark rages, but oddly I couldn't work up to feeling annoyed. I was shocked that I wasn't upset, but figured the stress of the day was distracting me.

"All right, so it's just us," I said, causing the minions to look at each other as if confused by my nonchalant attitude. "Someone update me on what you've been doing."

Janice, a pixy dressed in black from head to toe with the exception of her lily-white face, stepped forward.

"Mistress," she said, bowing.

"No, no. No more bowing," I said.

Janice looked up from her bent-over posture, looking confused. "But, Mistress, you told us if we didn't bow to you, you'd kick us out of the group."

Had I really said that? Why did these kids put up with me?

"Well, I've decided that was a stupid rule. From now on the rule is anyone who bows gets kicked out."

She snapped up so fast she put a hand to her head as if dizzy.

"Yes, Mistress—"

I cut her off again. "And no more of this 'Mistress' crap. Just call me by my first name."

"Yes, R-Raven," Janice said, looking uneasily at the others, who appeared shocked.

"No, not Raven. Call me Gabby." I paused. Callum had been the only one to call me that.

"On second thought, call me Gabriella."

"Ga-Gabriella?" she stammered. "I thought your name was Raven?"

I sighed. "Look, my real name is Gabriella. Raven was kind of a nickname."

"Oh, I see," she said, appearing not to see at all. "Well, per your email, we rented this new lair and got it all set up."

Looking around, I nodded. "Yes, this is a much better location. That old warehouse totally sucked. Too dreary. I like the new digs."

The old farmhouse was on the outskirts of Raleigh, far away from prying eyes. It had a kind of rustic appeal with its faded eyelet curtains and wide-planked pine floors.

"The lady who rented it to us was really nice. Paul and I posed as newlyweds and asked for lots of privacy," Janice said, sending a shy glance at Paul, who was kind of cute if a person liked computer nerds. Obviously, Janice did.

"And you accessed my accounts to pay for it?" I asked.

"Yes, Mis— I mean Gabriella," Paul said, hastily correcting himself. "I hacked into the bank system."

I sent him an approving nod. "Good job. And the furniture came with the place?"

Janice nodded. I glanced around the room, taking in the old, but well-maintained furniture. The place was homey.

"We stocked the kitchen and the bathrooms."

"Great, because I have a feeling I'll be hiding out here for a few days until the heat wears off."

"You think they'll come after you?" Freddie asked, looking excited by the prospect.

"Yes, I do," I said, thinking of how angry my father would be when he found out I'd left.

"I think we should ambush them," Freddie declared. The others cheered, looking like bloodthirsty children.

"Wait a minute," I said, holding my hands up. "Nobody is going to ambush anyone, got it?"

"But why?" Freddie asked, whining like a child.

"We don't do that anymore. We're going to lay low while I figure out a new plan."

Seven sets of eyes looked at me with disappointment. I couldn't help but feel I had let them down.

"What happened to you? You used to get excited about planning ambushes," Freddie said.

"I grew up."

#

Three days later, I had Janice drop me off at Miranda's shop. Not only was I curious about why no one had come after me yet, but the minions were driving me nuts. All the whining and talk about computer games was enough to make any vampiress long for a stake.

Plus, I had a craving for Lifeblood. I'd had the minions stock the fridge with bagged blood. But I'd gotten so used to the synthetic stuff that the plastic taste of the bagged disgusted me. I knew Miranda would have some Lifeblood handy. Luckily, I'd happened to have a bottle Sun Shield in my purse when I left, so I wasn't forced to limited my movements to the night.

Sneaking through the back door, I tiptoed through the storeroom, listening for signs of life. It was early—seven a.m.—but I knew workaholic Miranda would be there getting ready to open for the day. I just needed to be sure she was alone.

The sound of a keyboard clicking came from the front of the store, but no voices. I breathed a sigh of relief and started to walk normally.

"Who's there?" Miranda called. "You came to the wrong place if you're looking for a weak woman to rob."

Laughing, I pulled aside the curtain and entered the main store area. "It's just me."

She was standing next to the desk with her legs braced and her fangs extended. Obviously, she really had thought I was an intruder.

Her posture relaxed instantly when she saw me. "Goddammit, Raven. Give me a heart attack will ya?"

"Jeez, sorry. I didn't mean to scare you," I said, feeling guilty for sneaking up on her.

Her relief turned to anger. "Where the hell have you been?"

Despite her angry tone, she rushed over and wrapped me in a hug. I squeezed her back, happy to be with someone I trusted again. The minions were okay, but I suspected they were planning a mutiny if I didn't give them some dirty work to do.

"I've been hiding out, trying to come up with a plan. I figured you might have some information for me," I said, pulling back from the hug.

"You mean you haven't heard?" she said, her eyes wide.

I hesitated. This couldn't be good.

"Heard what?" I asked warily.

"Girlfriend, you'd better sit down for this."

Preparing myself for the worst, I let her lead me to a pair of chairs in the dressing area. The same area where Sydney had asked me to be in her wedding a couple of months earlier—the day we became friends. I felt a twinge in the area of my chest at the thought. I missed her, and felt bad about leaving without saying good-bye. But it couldn't be helped, I reminded myself.

Focusing on Miranda and her news, I took a deep breath. "Okay, before you tell me, do you have any Lifeblood?"

She nodded and went to grab me a bottle. When she returned, I took a healthy chug. It hit the spot. Feeling better, I nodded, letting her know I was ready for the news.

"So when you left, things got pretty ugly. Callum was really pissed off. I was outside talking to Jorge and Geraldine when he stormed past. We all figured you were the only one who could make him that mad, so we followed," she said, pausing for a breath. I grimaced at the reminder of the fight he and I had had.

"Anyway, so he goes up to your father at the reception."

She paused again.

"And?" I asked impatiently, practically holding my breath.

"And he demanded to know what your father had said to you that afternoon. Callum said that you'd left, but before you did you said something about your father and accused Callum of being a liar."

"He confronted my father?" I asked, dumbfounded.

"Yes, can you believe it? So, your father flips and demands to know why Callum let you leave. They argued for a few minutes about whether your father should chase you down right then, but Callum demanded they let you go."

"What?" I was totally confused.

The last time I'd seen Callum, he'd looked like he was about to go nuclear. Then he turned around and confronted my father? It didn't make sense.

"Yeah, so your father tells him that his impertinence is threatening his seat on the council. And do you know what Callum said?"

I couldn't begin to imagine, but I wished she would stop being dramatic and get to the damned point. Luckily, she didn't wait for me to ask.

"He said, 'You can shove the seat up your ass for all I care!'" Miranda hooted with laughter.

"He did what?" I gasped.

"Yeah, so get this, your father gets all offended. But Callum's not done. He tells your father that he'd better exonerate you of all charges or he is halting the distribution of Lifeblood!"

All the air left my body. I heard her words, but I couldn't believe them. Callum not only gave up his chance at the council, but also threatened my father?

What the hell?

"But why did he do that?" I asked.

The look she gave me clearly told me she thought I was an idiot.

"What?" I asked.

"You're a fool. If it isn't obvious why that man would defend you, then there's no helping you."

"But he used me!" I said, struggling to hang on to reality as I thought I knew it.

"You mean for the council seat he gave up for you?"

"But . . . but . . ."

"Raven, that man loves you. He confronted your father, gave up his future on the council, threatened to cancel the distribution of Lifeblood, and convinced your father to call off the dogs. If those aren't actions of a man in love, I don't know what is."

I slumped back in my seat as the truth hit me like a a zap of lightning. My father had lied to me. I didn't know why, but at that moment it didn't matter.

"Oh no!" I said. "Miranda, he told me he was going to tell me he loved me that night and I laughed at him!"

"You did what?" she shrieked. "How could you?"

"It wasn't my fault! My father told me Callum had used me to get on the council. I had no reason to think he was lying."

"You mean except for the fact that Callum had never lied to you before, and your father is an asshole?"

"Yeah," I said, "except for that. I am an idiot! What am I going to do?"

What, indeed? If Callum hadn't betrayed me, I was back to

square one. What did I want? It was time to make some decisions.

She leaned forward, looking me in the eyes. "The first thing you have to do is admit you're in love with him."

"Uh," I said hesitantly.

Crap. My mind was scrambling, trying to process everything she'd told me while my heart was trying to figure out where it stood. I thought about my time with him—all our fights and sex and laughter.

Then it hit me. Would I have felt so betrayed by his supposed lies if I didn't care so much about him? Would I have run and hidden from the pain if I didn't love him?

There it was. The moment of clarity. Like a shiny beacon, the truth came to me. I loved Callum Murdoch. I loved him so much it hurt.

And instead of trusting that, I'd freaked out at the first hint of trouble and run away. Instead of asking him about my father's lies, I'd attacked. Then, the worst sin of all, I'd laughed in his face when he told me he loved me.

Miranda watched me as I struggled with my emotions. She must have seen the light click on because she smiled.

"Say it," she demanded.

Sighing, I steeled myself. Saying it aloud felt more real.

"I l-love Callum."

Suddenly, I felt nauseous. I'd never said that about anyone before. And to admit it after I'd screwed up so badly really sucked.

"Good, now you're ready for the next step," Miranda said, pausing dramatically. "Groveling."

"Ah, shit, really?" I whined.

"Afraid so, sister. You need to get on your knees and beg that man to take you back."

"Maybe I could just send him a card or something," I said, feeling frantic at the idea of supplicating myself even if it was to the man I loved.

She gave me the idiot look again.

"Groveling, it's the only way."

"But how?"

"You can start by calling him," she said, getting up and walking to the desk. She picked up the phone and waved it in the air. "Now."

"Now?"

"Now."

Crap.

Dragging myself from the chair, I trudged to her. She forced the phone in my hand.

"I'll even dial for you," she said oh so helpfully.

With each ring my heart beat faster. The line clicked, and suddenly Callum's voice was in my ear.

"Hello?"

"Uh."

"Hello?" he said again, sounding annoyed.

I cleared my throat and tried again. "Callum?" My voice sounded like a croak.

"Who is this?" he demanded.

"It's Gabby," I said, cringing.

The line was silent for a second, then a loud click.

I held the phone away from my ear as disappointment washed over me. I'd hoped it would be as simple as a quick "I'm sorry" over the phone. Unfortunately, it didn't appear I was getting off that easily.

"He hung up?" Miranda asked.

I nodded.

"I expected that," she said.

"Thanks for the warning," I said, replacing the receiver in its cradle.

"Sweetie, you didn't think this was going to be easy did you? You screwed up big-time. You've got to swallow your pride and keep trying until he listens."

"I guess," I said, picking the phone back up.

Ten calls later, I threw the phone against the wall.

"That's it! He's not even answering anymore," I said.

"You owe me a new phone," she said, picking at a cuticle. "I need a manicure."

Her calm infuriated me. Here I was trying to beg the love of my life to take me back, and she just sat there thinking about her damned nails.

"To hell with a manicure. I need a new plan."

Her head snapped up. "Oh, no. You've got that look in your eyes."

"He's not going to take my calls, Miranda. I can only assume approaching him in person would not be pleasant either. He'll push me away."

"If that happens, then you just keep trying. Don't let him ignore you."

My eyes narrowed. Don't let him ignore me?

"Miranda, you're a genius," I said, grabbing her in a hug.

"I am?"

"Yep, can I use your cell phone since I broke your other one?"

She gave me a wary look but handed me her cell. Give the girl some credit, she did know me pretty well. And once she found out my new plan, she'd freak. Let her freak, I decided.

If I had to beg Callum for forgiveness, I was going to do it on my own terms.

Freddie answered on the second ring.

"Gather the minions. I've got a job for you."

#

The sound of a metal scraping on the wooden floor echoed down the hall. Smiling, I listened at the door. The minions had returned to the farmhouse with their cargo an hour earlier. Impatient as I was, he needed to calm down before I went in there.

Finally, the room fell silent. He was either worn out, which was unlikely unless he hadn't fed for a while, or he was plotting. I'd have bet money on the latter.

The door creaked on its hinges as I eased it open. The only light in the room came from the small lamp on the bureau across from the bed. But it was fairly easy to spot my quarry lying spread-eagle on top of the cheery yellow-and-white quilt.

Callum looked up when the door opened. The minute he

recognized me, his eyes widened, and muffled shouts came from the gag covering his mouth.

He looked adorable.

"Calm down. I'm not going to hurt you," I said, moving toward the bed. He began thrashing, making the bed frame scratch against the beautiful hardwood floors.

"Now, now. If you ruin those, I'll never get my deposit back."

He stilled and looked at me like I was a lunatic.

Sitting on the edge of the bed, I placed a hand on his knee. He jerked his leg away but didn't get far.

"Callum, I know you're angry. But I figured this was the only way to make you listen to me."

His arms strained against his manacles, making his biceps bulge. Once he forgave me, I'd have to convince him to let me tie him up again. He was too sexy.

Shaking my head, I tried to stay on topic.

"Okay, so you hate me for thinking you were a big fat liar. And I really can't blame you. I'd be pissed too."

He nodded enthusiastically.

"Yes, I thought so. Anyway, here's the deal. My father lied to me and told me you were having sex with me to manipulate me into changing. He promised you a council seat if you succeeded in making me transform."

He snorted and looked away.

"I know it sounds stupid when I say it aloud, but you have to understand. I was feeling pretty insecure about us. For some reason my warped brain figured you manipulating me made more sense than the idea that you had feelings for me, too. And we have never discussed our arrangement being more than sex."

He looked back at me and shook his head. The action wasn't so much a you're-a-fool shake as an I-pity-you shake. I chose to take that as progress.

"I know it's pathetic, but it's not like I had a lot of reason to believe there was a future for us," I said, stroking his leg. He didn't pull away but mumbled something that sounded argumentative.

"Let me finish," I said. "Now, where was I? Oh, yeah, so anyway, when he told me that, I freaked. I know I should have asked you, but I was angry and hurt. Plus, you know me—I tend to act first and ask questions later."

Another snort.

"I'm working on it, okay? So I admit I should have talked to you. And I admit I shouldn't have run off."

I paused, gathering my strength for what I was about to say. It scared me shitless, but I couldn't very well kidnap the man without being totally open and honest, could I?

"All right. So here's the deal. I kind of—" I paused. "Iloveyoucanyouforgiveme?"

He squinted and shook his head as if he didn't quite catch what I'd said.

Groaning, I took a deep breath. "I. Love. You. Can. You. Forgive. Me?"

With a hard shake to his head, he mumbled something.

My heart dropped. Here I'd laid my soul bare, and all I got was a head shake. But then I remembered how I'd laughed at him when he told me he loved me.

Wait a minute, I thought. *He told me he loved me.*

Perhaps, instead of jumping to conclusions again, I should ungag him, I thought.

"Okay, I'm going to remove your gag. But I'm warning you now, if the first words out of your mouth are in any way negative, I'm not going to be happy."

Reaching behind his head, I untied the handkerchief. He worked his jaw for a minute, and I felt a hint of guilt when I saw the red marks by his mouth. I couldn't decide if the intensity in his eyes was a good or bad thing. So I just waited. It didn't take long for him to speak.

"First of all, don't you ever gag me again," he said in a hoarse voice. He cleared his throat before continuing.

"Second, while kidnapping me was probably not the most conventional form of groveling I've ever seen, it's definitely the most original."

Nodding, I held my breath.

"Third, will you please untie me?"

My eyes narrowed. "Why would I do that?"

"Because I'll be damned if I am going to tell you I forgive you and then later have you accuse me of doing so only because I was under duress."

I gasped. "You'd do that?"

"What? Forgive you? I guess you'll have to untie me to see."

I thought about the pros and cons for a moment.

"Do you promise not to escape?"

"Gabriella, untie me now."

"No, Callum, you have to promise you won't leave until we sort this out."

"Woman, does everything have to be an argument with you?" he shouted hoarsely.

Silent, I watched him, waiting for the response I wanted. The silent treatment seemed to work as he sighed.

"Fine, I promise not to escape until I've said my piece."

That didn't sound too promising, but I knew he'd refuse to speak to me anymore unless he was unchained. Reaching into my back pocket, I pulled out the keys. His eyes shot to the jingling keychain.

"I'm going to unlock you," I said, stalling for time.

"Any day now," he said.

"Oh, fine," I said, making quick work of the locks. He almost knocked me to the floor in his haste to get out of the bed. For a moment I thought he was rushing to the door. Instead, he did some stretches and worked the kinks out of his muscles. His back was to me, so I couldn't get a feel for his mood. Something told me it wasn't good.

Finally, he popped his knuckles and turned to me. The look in his eyes made me back away.

"Callum, let's not do anything rash," I said, stopping when the backs of my knees hit the bed.

"Rash? You mean like kidnapping you and tying you up?"

He kept coming until I fell back on the bed. I tried to scramble over the other side, but he grabbed my leg. Hard metal clamped over my ankle before I could get away.

"No!" I yelled, struggling against him as he got one of my hands locked too. In no time he had both my arms and one leg shackled. I kicked so much with my other leg that he'd given up on it. Smart move since I couldn't do much without the use of three of my appendages.

"Dammit, Callum!" I yelled as he calmly got up and dragged a chair over to the bed. "Let me go!"

"So sorry, but it had to be done. Now, do I need to use the gag too?" he asked politely.

"Try it and you'll pull away a bloody stump!"

"I'll take that as a no, then," he said, making himself comfortable.

"It's my turn to talk," he said calmly. "So kindly shut the hell up."

I figured he was angry enough that I should probably keep my mouth shut for once. Clamping my lips closed, I nodded.

"That's better. Since you seem to be so hell bent on hashing this out tonight, I'll start by saying you are the most infuriating woman I have ever met. You don't listen, you're stubborn, and you're generally a pain in my ass."

Not the most auspicious beginning, I thought.

"However, you are also strong, independent, and the most passionate women I've ever met. And I meant what I said. I was going to tell you that I loved you the night of the wedding."

"Were?" I said, forgetting my vow to remain silent. He scowled at me, so I clamped my lips tight.

"During the fight, I was so angry I wasn't really listening to your words. After, however, I remembered that you'd called me a liar. Plus, you'd started to say something about Orpheus but stopped yourself. Knowing how you and your father work, I put two and two together.

"When he and I talked, it became apparent that he had some misguided notion that he was protecting you by telling you those lies."

I opened my mouth to comment, but he waved the handkerchief at me, so I shut up.

"Once I convinced him to not chase you down, I did some

thinking. I figured if you were that upset over my supposed lies that you probably had some feelings for me. However, since I know you, it was clear you needed time to figure things out on your own.

"When you called, I was shocked. I had assumed it would take you a lot longer to figure out you were in love with me and even longer to get up the courage to approach me about it."

"But why did you hang up?" I asked.

He didn't threaten me with a gag again, so he must have been distracted by his explanation.

"I hung up because a phone call wasn't going to cut it. You had some serious making up to do. However, it didn't occur to me you'd go so far as to kidnap me," he said, chuckling. "I should have known better given your history."

"So what are you saying?" I asked.

"I'm saying that I love you, too, you silly woman. I just needed to be sure that when you came to me you were positive this was what you wanted."

A bucketful of relief washed over me. But I still had some questions.

"What do you mean by 'this is what you wanted'?"

"Are you sure you aren't going to change your mind about us?" he asked. For the first time since I'd known him, he looked vulnerable.

"Callum, how can anyone be sure their mind won't change? All I can tell you is that I am positive I love you."

He nodded. "Good, because we're getting married."

My body tried to jerk upright, but the restraints held me down. "*What?*"

He smiled wickedly. "Yep, that's right. And I'm not letting you free until you agree."

"Why can't we just live together?" I said a little desperately.

Married? If I were mortal, I would have had a stroke.

"Nope. You're going to be my wife and we're going to have kids."

"*Kids?*" If I hadn't already been lying down, I would have fainted.

"Four of them," he said, nodding

"Callum, I think you're crazy."

"Sweetheart, I'm crazy about you. I can't imagine spending eternity with anyone else."

"But we fight all the time," I said.

"That just means we get to have make up sex."

"But . . . but married?"

He stood and leaned over me. His mouth covered mine for a kiss that made my hips go up in flames. Once he had me writhing, he pulled away slightly.

"Married," he whispered.

In my dazed state, I smiled. I loved this man with all of me. No one else had ever challenged me as much or made me feel as alive as I did when I was with Callum.

And let's be perfectly honest, no other man was strong enough to put up with my crap. Yes, it might be a match made in hell, but it was the right one for me.

"All right," I said with a sigh. "But if you think I'm wearing white at the wedding, you're going to have a fight on your hands."

He chuckled and kissed me again. Where the last kiss was hot as a flame, this one was as sweet as honey. I poured every bit of myself into it hoping I could show him how much he meant to me.

"Callum," I whispered finally, "I said yes. You can take off the cuffs now."

"I don't think so," he said with a wicked smile as he moved down my body.

I started to protest, but he did something involving his mouth and my nipple that made my eyes cross.

It took about thirty minutes for the pins and needles to begin shooting through my limbs. But did I complain?

Hell, no.

I'd have all eternity to pick fights with Callum.

-The End-

ABOUT THE AUTHOR

Kate Eden comes from a long line of mouthy broads who love to read, so it's probably no surprise she caught the writing bug early. An avid romance fan since her early teens, Kate loves writing–and reading–stories about plucky heroines, sexy heroes, and the weird and wild journey people take on their way to love. She loves good food, cheap booze, and believes laughter is the cure for just about everything.

Connect with me online:
Twitter: @KateEdenAuthor
Facebook: facebook.com/AuthorKateEden
Web site: www.KateEden.com

AN INTERVIEW WITH KATE EDEN

How did you get started writing?

My mom worked for a bookstore when I was a kid, so I grew up reading. I was also born with that lethal combination of having an overactive imagination and being easily bored. Put all that together and the urge to write was pretty much guaranteed. I dabbled at it for years before getting serious, but now that I'm doing it for real, I don't know what took me so long. It's the most fun thing ever.

Your Murdoch Vampires series features a family of vampires who blend into human society. Did you make that choice for a reason?

I really love the idea of putting powerful beings in painfully awkward situations. Every day life is hard enough without also having to hide that you need blood to survive and you're older than America. Having the family blend into human society basically created lots of comedic opportunities. Plus, even though I love books with intense world building, sometimes it's fun not to have to wade through all sorts of arcane rules to get to the main story.

How many books do you have planned for the Murdoch Vampires?

I'm having too much fun with them right now to think about not writing them anymore. In addition to The Hot Scot and Rebel Child, I also have a novel in the works for Raven's friend Miranda that I hope to release by the end of 2013. After that, we'll see. I'll write them as long as readers want them.

Any other series in the works?

I have some erotic novellas in the pipeline that I hope to release, as well. Readers should definitely keep an eye on my web site, Twitter and Facebook pages for news on upcoming releases.

And now the burning question all readers of the Murdoch Vampires have been wondering? Logan or Callum?

You can't make me choose! I love them both. But right now, I'm finding Nick, the hero of Miranda's book pretty irresistible. The beauty of writing these books is I get to make hot men bend to my will every day. It's pretty awesome!

Made in the USA
Lexington, KY
27 February 2017